"MAYHEM SAM"

— A SPLATTER WESTERN —

J.D. GRAVES

DEATH'S HEAD PRESS

Published by Death's Head Press,
an imprint of Dead Sky Publishing, LLC
Miami Beach, Florida
www.deadskypublishing.com

Cover by Luke Spooner

Illustration by Mike Fiorentino, Jr.

Edited by Candace Nola

This book is dedicated to *your* mother,
whoever...wherever...she may be.

"One does not run away—Let me again head for the roads, burdened with vice, the vice that drove roots of suffering into myself, from years of liberty—the vice that rises heavenward, beats me, throws me down, drags me along."

—Arthur Rimbaud, *A Season in Hell*
Self-Published, 1873

"This is the excellent foppery of the world that when we are sick in fortune—often the surfeit of our own behavior—we make guilty of our disasters the sun, the moon, and the stars, as if we were villains by necessity, fools by heavenly compulsion, knaves, thieves, and treacherous by spherical predominance, drunkards, liars, and adulterers by an enforced obedience of planetary influence, and all that we are evil in by a divine thrusting-on."

—William Shakespeare, *King Lear Act 1, Sc. 2*
First Published 1608

"If I owned Hell and Texas, I would rent out Texas and live in Hell."

— Union General Philip Sheridan, Fifth Military District, March 1867

LATE DECEMBER 1867

OUTSIDE BOULDER — BEFORE THE BLAST

FRANK DIDN'T KNOW ABOUT the dynamite. No one knew but Samantha, not even Chance or Claire. She'd run the line two nights before and lit the fuse the moment she saw Frank step into her sun scorched view and whistle loud.

"Mrs. Jakes," He called. His voice was a summer night of crickets. "C'mon out and listen to my offer."

She knew—he knew—she would refuse. That's why he still wore his gun. It's why he didn't bring the baby. They'd all come too far and lost too much to make a simple one-for-one trade. For Samantha, it was no longer about the money.

Frank called again, "Mrs. Jakes!"

Samantha watched the sparking fuse disappear out Aunt Clara's backdoor. She pictured it snaking unseen around the property. If her measurements held true, they only had seven minutes before the gold, and everything went kaboom. Maybe less. For someone as wily as Frank Lovecock, she wondered if he even suspected it was an option. Probably not since after the raid on the Garden Bloom, all he'd done was underestimate her.

When one loses everything, she reasoned, *what's left?*

Samantha moved to Claire's body. The child's sweaty hair still felt warm. If she wasn't in heaven yet, she was well on her way. Samantha pictured white clouds swirling as angels flew between their ancestors. The peasant's dream of eternal reward after suffering through a lifetime.

Why, the very idea.

In the gospel, according to the Good Book, all the forgiveness afforded the human spirit would never let Samantha see such sights. No, what's done is done, it is what it is. Her own death, she hoped, would be quicker than her mama's. For the last three years, she'd hoped and prayed every day she'd see her mama again. After the past year, she was done praying for miracles. After the last nine months, Heaven and Hell didn't hold any appeal...too packed with sinners and saints and she couldn't tell the difference. After the past thirty weeks, she only hoped for a blessed purgatory. They'd done so much wandering on their runaway scrape, what was a little more? But after the past seven days, an infinite black void would be a welcomed relief.

However, she hadn't earned it yet. Frank Lovecock remained upright. "Mrs. Jakes! The boy'll die soon, if'n we don't settle this now!"

Papa's voice between her ears, *when trouble comes Sammie Jane, you can't waste time on fear.*

"What. Fool's. Hollering. Out. Side?" Chance coughed as blood dried beneath him on the floor. Her savior—the outlaw. The man with the beautiful face. Now a dying pile of meat and bones.

"I think you know Chance." She didn't look at him—she couldn't. The need to keep her wits now stronger than ever. Besides, she didn't want the wet constellation pattern—blasted across his chest—to be the last image of the dusty knuckler she took with her out the door.

Claire's forehead met Samantha's lips. Her smell—a flood of familiar history written in generations of blood—swiftly faded.

Chance wheezed. "I'm sorry, Sam."

In the gospel according to the Gentleman's Ettiquete Book, *If you submit to flattery, you must also submit to the imputation of folly and self-conceit.*

"Don't apologize," Samantha said. "You got no reason to be sorry. As far as I'm concerned—you done your part—gave us a chance. We made it here, didn't we...?" She paused as the weight of her next words lifted from her shoulders. "...just nowhere else to go."

Samantha's lips moved next to her younger sister's ear and whispered. For better or worse, the Gray sisters'll keep that last secret between them forever.

Samantha turned—stooped—then stood. She knocked the dust off her wide brim sombrero. The one she bought outside Fort Worth. Before they threw in their lot with that ill-fated cattle drive and all the unnecessary hell it unleashed. The once white hat now bent and misshapen and spotted allover red.

Samantha Jakes Née Gray pulled on her ruined hat. Checked Papa's Navy Colt. Two bullets left. The cylinder snapped closed. Her dusty boots toed the threshold. And Chance wheezed once more, "What are you gonna do about the baby?"

She hesitated in the doorway. No one would've expected this thin silhouette of only nineteen years to collect so many doggone tombstones. Here in Boulder, the fuse may be burning slowly, but Samantha already lit it back in

Texas. Well before she met Captain Jakes and allowed that cruel bastard to steal a kiss and create all of this mayhem.

"What am I gonna do?" She asked and looked over her shoulder, "What a girl's gotta do."

She touched her hat's brim. It dipped once at the outlaw—her savior. Then out she stepped to go kill Frank.

JULY 1867

MORNING IN SHERMANBURG — A TREASURE HUNT

CHANCE'S EMPTY GUTS BUBBLED with dread—not hunger. The bank vault was no bigger than a broom closet and just as full. Frank Lovecock looked disgusted at its bare shelves, then down at the dead Bank President. Smoke leaked from his left eye socket. Blood pooled underneath a shocked expression. Still unable to accept how a pack of pungent heathens wandered in off the street and pulled iron. Frank sank his teeth into his bottom lip—whistled through the gap—a rusty squeal. Chance winced. Corking his ear with a dirty finger. Five weeks ride from New Orleans and Frank's unique prosody—somewhere between the end of days and a lonesome train—still stung every time. Chance's guts rumbled harder. His groin ached too, but he dared not look away.

Frank nodded at Doc Buie, who removed his bowler hat. His movements were deliberate, almost ceremonial. A horseshoe of ginger encircled a bald crown and wreathed his chin. A rust-colored bandana dried his pate. Doc replaced the hat and removed his glasses. Breath fogged the little lenses. He squinted at the faithful, knees bent like true believers at his feet, ready for a fire and brimstone sermon in the church of Lovecock.

Frank's best deacon preached. "This upstart dude gave his life for a few stacks of measly paper. It appears he owned just as many brains as I figured, the way he spoke nonsense to the barrel of a gun. Now I know how smart the rest of you good country folks are without forcing Captain Lovecock here to leak your intelligence across the floorboards." Doc Buie's toothy smile beamed with sparkling cruelty. He pulled the wire frames over his ears and adjusted them to his liking. One gnarled hand replaced the bowler cap, and the other brought up his Colt Dragoon. "Now if you would please be so kind—I'm going to ask a simple question and your cooperation is most appreciated." He checked the big gun's cylinder, then slammed it closed and leveled it at a thin-lipped woman. "And as custom dictates...ladies first."

Somebody's shrew wife averted her eyes. Muzzle pressed against her sweating forehead—thin lips a-trembling. "If you would be so kind, ma'am, please tell me where your cocksucking boss hid the gold. If not—you're welcome to join him in hell."

Her eyes clenched tight, and so did her jaw. Chance watched her from across the room. Her steely hesitation due to one of two things: Either she didn't know and had resigned herself to her fate, or she knew and was at peace with taking it to her grave.

"You got until the count of three," Doc Buie counted, "One...two..."

And right before the fatal third, another four-eyed raw-bones leaned forward and blurted out, "Are you talking about the Jakes' gold?"

Frank's head snapped sideways. He whistled at the Wayne Brothers. Elias, the smaller of the two, dragged the squealer over by the collar. He dropped him at Frank's boots. Frank leaned in close and fogged the thin man's glasses. His voice a plague of locust, "You got something you wanna say?"

"Only what I've heard...same as you."

"Go on boy," Frank hissed. "What've I heard?"

"Well..." the teller said nervously. His voice towards the floor. "Everybody talks about the gold. Rumor has it Captain Jakes stole it off the last transport...after news broke Lee surrendered. They say he kept it here for a time...until the carpetbaggers came. All I know's the Union army nor the Pinkerton's..."

Frank cut him off. "Where'd he moved it to?"

The thin teller pointed, "Mr. Cannon there...the fella you shot...he'd know more about it than any of us. Rumor tells of cahoots."

Frank spoke slowly to the teller as if he were five, "Where. Did. The. Gold. Go?"

"I hear at his house. But the Pinkertons came. Found nothing."

Frank whistled for Ezekiel Wayne. The lumbering brute scooped the man in one arm and tossed him at a nearby desk. A county wall map hung above, and Kid Nobody yanked it down. The dim faced Kid wiped a blood spatter from the paper—mouth breathing slack-jawed, "Point to the house?"

The teller studied a spell before obliging. "Sweet Pine road here outside of town. I don't rightly remember which plantation is his, but I'd know it on sight." The teller's eye shut quick, and his mouth jerked sideways. A desperate attempt to keep the last words from escaping.

Both the teller and Chance realized the terrible mistake.

Frank whistled again. Kid Nobody folded the map. Angel Ojete's knife reflected in the teller's glasses. The scapular he wore around his neck dangled with the weight of a dozen dried human ears.

The Mexican snorted a laugh. "If you lying, this blade'll do more than cut restraints."

With one violent slash, he freed the teller's hands.

"Back to the road, boys." Frank stepped towards the front door.

"What about the bankers?" Angel asked.

Frank turned and eyed him slowly.

"Afraid they'll talk?" Doc Buie laughed, "Need their tongues for the collection?"

Angel touched his necklace of ears. "Think there's room enough, sure."

All eyes went to Frank. His dark mouth twitched. All it took was one head nod and hysteria erupted. Ojete, Kid Nobody, and both Wayne brothers seized a bound captive.

Chance didn't join their perfect butchery. He hung back with a quintet of Irishmen, who guffawed lyrically as their fellow killers moved down the line extracting tongues. One sang *Danny Boy* in a low brogue. *The pipes, the pipes are calling*. Sweat broke under his hat. Next came an urge to purge—he fought it off. Not that he could expel anything, mind you. Their long road from New Orleans was a whirlwind trail of hunger, exhaustion, and dead bodies. For his troubles, Chance grew a saddle sore the size of a large egg. It ached between his legs. Its dull throb a constant.

Frank whistled. It pierced the moans of their writhing victims. The gang looked at their leader. Frank touched the talisman, a short black obelisk dangling around his neck. A strange shadow passed over his eyes. "Keep the woman...she's coming with us."

The big Wayne dropped the stone-faced crone next to the thin teller. Frank squatted and sniffed. "Live around here?"

She remained mute. Frank snatched her grey hair bun. The woman's face whitened. "Yes!"

Frank pointed at the teller. "D'you know the hole this jink's taking us to?"

Again, she nodded.

Frank sneered. His eyes charred with darkness, "You're going to redeem your sullenness from earlier, and if'n you don't, the boys will relieve themselves in your privy and leave you bleeding in a ditch. D'you understand?"

The woman broke completely. Moments earlier, she'd been okay with dying, but now her death included variables. It was clear she never considered such an outcome.

Frank and Doc Buie conferred briefly, then Doc said, "Pretty boy..."

Chance turned around. The Doc cleaned blood from his eyeglasses and said, "You and the Tasmanian shall be our forlorn hope."

Chance didn't understand.

"Means the two of you will be in the vanguard...first out the door." Doc spoke to the rest of the gang: The Wayne brothers with their matching faces yet different heights, Angel Ojete and his necklace of ears, that mouth-breathing psychopath, Kid Nobody, Andrews the Tasmanian, and the five Irishmen. Chance couldn't understand nor remember their names.

"The rest of you file out slowly. Don't draw attention. We ride west." Map clenched in his bloodied fist, "We ain't nowhere near done with this here treasure hunt."

WINTER 1866

SHERMANBURG HERALD — VOL. 11 NO. 150. 1ST
EDITION

HOLD THE SHERMANBERG HERALD between your
hands. Smell the velvet musk of newsprint ink. See five
narrow columns of stacked nineteenth century journal-
ism. Scan left to right, up and down, then back again.
Read good news, bad news, public notices and commercial
advertisements. Find the subjects freely forming together
to make a whole, similar to children at play or Dixieland
Jazz.

In the gospel, according to this newspaper: The unprece-
dented success of Homer Hubert's Superb Bitters is a
most glorious endorsement of their virtues. Purely organic
vegetable. They will invigorate and reinforce the system
against the evil of unwholesome water. Will cure dyspep-
sia, headaches, jaundice, sea sickness and general debility.
Homer Hubert's Superb Bitters will create a healthy ap-
petite and invigorate the organs of digestions and moder-
ately increase the temperature of the body. They contain
no dangerous drug and are a general corroborant of the
system. Ask for them by name at your local druggist.

In the gospel, according to this newspaper: Blood Feather,
the infamous Indian Chief was an accomplished orator.
Colonel Woolford Merkin of the U.S. army was a great
friend of the chief, and being ordered to Kingdom Strait

Bloody Feather addressed him as follows: "Brother, on your journey to this place, be a king yourself. You white folks think your children are blessings. My utmost hope for you is to sire thousands. And above all, wherever you go, may you never find a quart of whiskey above three shillings."

In the gospel, according to the newspaper: WORDS ADDRESSED TO ALL. In the oppressive heat of summer. Folks become more or less predisposed to absorb the poisons aerating from refuse and offal. This is the prevailing causes of the diseases: Diarrhea, Dysentery, Cholera, and last though not least, looseness of the bowels, which is a common symptom of these complaints, and ought in every instance to be checked by a doctor or pastor. If neglected, the bowels welcome that fatal scourge, Cholera. How can we prevent these diseases, and, if suffering, what is the cure? The grand preventative is cleanliness and pure air.

The cure, Bo Johnson's Carminative Syrup, a preparation composed of gums and barks indigenous to South America, where the formula has been adopted as being the most efficacious of all disorders of the bowels. Bo Johnson's Carminative Syrup never fails to relieve and cure every case of diarrhea, dysentery, and cholera. Prepared by Beauregard Johnson, 444 Broadway, N.Y. Sixty cents: small bottle. One dollar: large size.

In the gospel, according to this newspaper: WEDDING NOTICE: Captain Elrod Sinclair Jakes, Shermanberg's very own Confederate hero, who helped defeat the Yankees at the battle of Galveston and served out the war defending the cause in Austin under the direct command of Governor Murrah, has on this past Saturday, announced intentions to wed in holy matrimony one Samantha Jane Gray of Glenwater County. The nuptials will be officiated by the Honorable Reverend Christopher Roy of First Baptist. The ceremony shall be open to the public, and all are free to attend as long as they are white.

WINTER 1866

FIRST BAPTIST — A QUARTER AFTER ONE

PAPA COULDN'T AFFORD A white wedding. He'd taken sick over the past year and never really recovered. He couldn't even attend. Claire was the only Gray family to witness Samantha marry the Captain, who stood next to the minister. Rugged and somewhat striking in his Confederate service uniform. His broad moustache waxed and splitting a pale face of handsome features.

Samantha glimpsed him from the vestibule. Her nervous belly churned with wild noises. It was loud enough her kid sister, Claire, heard it. She gave Samantha a concerned look and said, "That don't sound too good...you getting sick?"

Samantha shook her head and said, "Fan me."

Claire looked puzzled, turning around the church's anteroom, searching for anything to wave at her sister. Samantha closed her eyes to keep her wits. Breath quickened with shallow air. Finally, Claire found something and wafted it back and forth. This rapid movement cooled Samantha enough, her eyes reopened. She started to give thanks, but her jaw slacked instead. "You can't use the Good Book as a fan."

"Whaddaya want? It's December," Claire stopped fanning and scowled. "The only one hot in this pneumonia box is you."

Samantha took the Bible and fanned herself with it. "I think the corset's too tight."

"Think it's supposed to make you look like an hourglass."

"Then what's the bustle for—turn me into a footstool?"

"Ain't no one ever gonna make that mistake." Claire laughed, "You're too smart..."

Samantha blushed.

But Claire continued, "...thankfully I was blessed with Mama's good looks, so I don't ever have to worry about being smart."

Samantha's face fell. "Why, the very idea." And handed back the Bible. "Am I ready?"

Claire wrinkled her nose. Adjusted Sam's bonnet and gingham gown. "I'm so jealous."

Samantha gave her sister the side eye.

"I'm serious Sam. Won't be no handsome officers left by the time Papa allows me to marry one. He's gonna keep me too busy doing *ALL YOUR* chores. Wish I was the one he betrothed."

"Don't be so morose..."

"I'll never be as lucky as you, sister," Claire said, and frowned. "Ain't no one coming out of nowhere to save me from the spinning wheel."

Samantha lowered her voice. "I'm no old maid."

"Of course, you're not," Claire said. "But you gotta admit eighteen is cutting it close."

Samantha muttered to herself, "Oh, the chirps of little birds."

The doorway darkened. "Reverend Christopher says it's time to start."

Samantha exhaled nervously. She took one step and stopped—turning around to Claire.

"What is it? You can't keep the Captain waiting...he'll think you done run off."

Samantha took Claire's hands in hers and whispered close to her sister's ear, "Promise you'll forgive Papa."

Claire clucked her tongue. "Stop worrying."

Samantha insisted, "Promise me."

"A promise without trust is easily broken. Forgiveness can't be given...only earned."

Samantha, in no shape to disagree, added, "And you'll take care of Johnny, right?"

Claire straightened and smiled and nodded. "Even on your special day, your big ole heart wants to bleed all over the place. Papa and Johnny are not even gonna notice you've gone." Claire wiped away the bride's single tear. "Now let's go get you married."

It was time.

Butterflies floated Samantha down the aisle. She paid no attention to her surroundings. Didn't notice the sparseness of well-wishers in the pews, or how they whispered to each other as she passed. Keeping her eyes on the minister, because anytime she looked at the bridegroom, she knew she might faint. However, she *did* notice the Captain didn't look at her either. Maybe he was nervous, too. After all, they hardly knew each other.

While the minister spoke the solemn words, the man who had moved earth and sky to arrange this marriage to the famous and seemingly rich Confederate war hero, Captain Elrod Sinclair Jakes, stopped writhing in his sickbed. His moans fell silent. Air rattled from his opened mouth.

Captain Jakes repeated the Reverend's words. Then took her left hand in his. The gold wedding band glinted in the dim and weighed heavily on her finger.

Samantha looked at the man now pronounced her husband. His brown eyes watched hers water and flutter closed. The bride kissed her bridegroom, unaware Papa had died, and her little brother Johnny was now all alone with the corpse.

December 1866

THE NEW COUPLE STOOD for a grim-faced portrait. Smoke plumed from the photographer's flash. White hair emerged from under black cloth. The odd fella curled his thumb and index into the Old Kindred sign and packed away his curious tools. Samantha's husband gallantly turned to his newly minted sister-in-law. "Be no trouble at all, Miss Claire. Tis along our way to Sweet Pine. Glad to escort you home."

Why the very idea? Papa's cabin wasn't along the way. Far from it. Samantha knew this round trip would chew away nearly six hours. "Husband," gently touched his arm, "thank you kindly for offering my sister safe passage. But..." She made her case and added, "It would be well after dark before reaching Sweet Pine if we..."

"After dark?" He asked.

"Yes, husband..."

"Nonsense," laughed the Captain. "It'll be at least tomorrow morning."

"Tomorrow? Wouldn't that be an even longer journey?"

The Captain stroked his mustache. "Travel much?"

Samantha shook her head no.

"Then believe the time I quoted."

"Don't misunderstand...I do not dispute you." She lowered her voice, "Just thought we would be...as man and wife...spending this time alone together."

The Captain's face flattened. A slight shadow passed behind his eyes. "We shall have the rest of our lives to be alone together." His nostrils flared. "Be. No. Trouble. A. Tall."

Samantha protested as sweetly as she could.

"The road to your father's," the Captain spoke over her. "...splits just outside town." He opened the buggy door and offered her his hand. "D'ya know it?"

Samantha said she did.

"Recall then, one road follows the river a spell." He guided her to her seat and smiled. "The other rounds Burnside mountain." His gold tooth smile gleamed dully. "We shall travel whichever you know to be the shortest."

"Believe the shortest route runs alongside the Sabine River."

The Captain chuckled low and helped Claire into the buggy. "Mrs. Jakes, you are mistaken."

Samantha knew she wasn't.

"Nonsense," said her husband. "The river road leads nearly half a day away, before bending in the correct direction." The buggy squealed a complaint as the Captain's old, fat Aunt Aggie plopped down next to Claire. Their petticoats bloomed. The newly met pair wrestled the gowns into submission.

Claire politely smiled, "Awful cozy, ain't it?"

Aggie's face wrinkled. She leaned towards Claire, close enough to rub noses, and blushed. Breath held. Eyes bulged with intense pressure. Claire didn't dare look away. Not until the pink face winced and the old gal farted a high tuba blast. Aggie chuckled with relief. "Pardon my wind, dear. Happens whenever I get jostled. Take a morning constitutional daily but cannot shed this ailment. Dr. Holdfast believes it the result of a once rich diet turning poorly."

"It's not nonsense." Samantha spoke firm, "It's the gospel truth."

The door shut between them.

Samantha frowned and gripped his arm. "You're not joining us?"

Eyes narrowed as he plucked her hand by the wrist and called to his coachman, "June-bug."

"Yessa Cap'n."

"My bride demands we hurry home," he said. "One stop needed first. Her father's place—North of Thistlewood. You know the shortest route?"

The driver nodded, "Straight thru—but I reckon the shortest way be whatever you say it is."

"Very good Junebug. Make Buttercup take the Burnside road to Thistlewood or take ten lashes."

The driver agreed.

Captain Jakes donned his hat. "Ladies, I shall take my leave."

Again, Samantha inquired if he would join her.

His smile vanished. "You shall join *me* tomorrow morning at Sweet Pine...Godspeed."

The buggy-whip cracked. Buttercup, the mule, hee-hawed and pulled. With a heavy shimmy, they were off. Samantha watched her husband shrink in the distance. Her fingers waved goodbye. The Captain turned and spoke to the Reverend without acknowledging her.

Ploof! The photographer's camera smoked. White hair again emerged from under black cloth. His gaunt smile as inscrutable as the face of God. Samantha shuddered. The buggy rolled on. Mrs. Jakes returned to her fellow passengers—unable to ignore the nasty tug of disappointment. Awkward loneliness settled over her. All the pent-up excitement of the morning reduced to restlessness. She avoided eye contact—examined her hands—her new ring. It didn't shine. In fact, it was as cloudy as the sky above.

Brow furrowed. Breath held. One hand pinched the other, between her thumb and index so hard it purpled. Teeth clenched, biting into the sting of her disappointment.

Aggie spoke to Samantha's hands. "Elrod smelted both bands for this occasion."

"It's very beautiful," Samantha released the pinch. "I've never had a gold ring before."

"Cherish your first one, my dear," Aggie shifted uncomfortably against Claire. "You're a Jakes, now. You'll wear plenty more, I promise."

"Don't need more than the one," Samantha blushed. "Don't even need it, really. Our mama never had one."

"Nonsense," Aggie waved off the thought. "All Jakes men bestow gold on their wives: earrings, necklaces, bracelets, all manner of decorative chain. You shall refuse none of them, my dear. Family tradition."

Samantha pictured her thin frame being bathed in such treasures. Giddy with the thought of gold cascading off square shoulders and through fingertips, letting it collect on her naked body in some Sweet Pine bathroom. *A bathroom?* A fat smile curled her thin lips. *Never had one of those.*

"Speaking of traditions," Claire kept the air out of their conversation. "I do declare! Ever seen a more beautiful ceremony in your life?"

"My child," Aggie gushed. "newborns don't weep as much I did from start to end."

Claire and Aunt Aggie busied themselves with wedding chit-chat, make-believe futures about coming offspring, and the blessings of May-December unions. Samantha couldn't be bothered to join in beyond polite nods.

Her mind kept company elsewhere.

Why hadn't Captain Jakes joined her? This delay frustrated her to no end—yet Samantha remained intrigued. From this day on, she was Mrs. Elrod Sinclair Jakes, Captain in the armies of the Confederate States of America and heir to Sweet Pine; the third largest plantation between the Neches and Sabine rivers.

Being a military man, her husband knew the importance of planning and execution. She felt safe under his protection. And dared to fancy a future at her new home.

Aggie spoke as if reading her mind. "Sweet Pine is a marvel, my dear. As big as she is and not one draft to be found in the place. Other than the attic...and parts..." she paused for breath, "...elsewhere." Aunt Aggie cleared her throat and spat off the side. "Excuse me...Now what was I saying?"

Claire waited for Samantha to answer. When she didn't, Claire batted around Aggie's ball of yarn. "You were saying how *Sweet Pine* is quite *comfortable*."

"No, I wasn't," Aunt Aggie said flatly. "I said no such thing."

Samantha shared a glance with Claire, unsure of proper decorum. *Maybe the old dear was slipping into dementia.*

Samantha tried to remember the Gentlemen's Etiquette Book. But it was no use. She could not recall a fitting passage for dealing with old senile shrews incapable of controlling their farts. At least Aggie had been instructed in the ways of social providence. Which couldn't be said for Mrs. Elrod Jakes and her corn-scrub sister.

Mama had been a *school marm* until marrying Papa. And always encouraged manners befitting the gentry, without accepting certain conditions inherent in the curriculum: *Unless one lives within the walls and looks out plantation windows, you'll only ever see the world through your own dirty cabin glass.* Samantha knew at any moment, either Claire or her would say something unbecoming a young lady and spoil the day.

Aunt Aggie broke wind again. No apology this time. Luckily, a biting wind blew through. The trio bundled themselves under a red and pink quilt.

"Elrod's great-grandmother made this. Been passed down generations." Aggie said, then quieted—too cold to talk more.

Outside, the sepia winter of East Texas bumped along. Thick clumps of pines gave way to cleared fields dotted with oaks and sycamores. Where teams of un-freed and barefoot chattel reaped hay-grass. Moving in fractured unison with each sickle swish. All the while singing pentatonic field songs—swollen with melancholy and subtle codes about oppression. Armed oppressors sat seven hands high atop brown horses. Collars of thick overcoats pulled high against the cold. A testament to the area's committed resistance to the Emancipation Proclamation. Texans between the Neches and Sabine rivers were proud people and still refused all orders issued by the Yankee Republican government. The South may have surrendered in Virginia, but these surly folks just did not care.

The wind inside Aunt Aggie blew again. "You'll love Sweet Pine, my dear. I, for one, wouldn't want to live anywhere else. Been in our family since shortly before the Revolution." The old spinster clarified in case she addressed a dullard, "Before Houston beat Santa Ana. So many memories." More wind bugled. "Long before the troubles sent our young men to war, Elrod's grandmother hosted balls. Spared no extravagance—the absolute envy across Glenwater county. Of course, Sweet Pine has seen better days since then, but so haven't we all."

Thunder rolled overhead.

"Storm's a brewing," Claire said. "Hope it waits long enough to get me home."

"Coachman," Samantha spoke to the sky. "When we come to the split, please keep to the road along the river."

The driver didn't respond. Samantha called again, this time louder and with more insistence. After another moment, Junebug sighed, then spoke over his shoulder. "Cap'n said drive the shortest root. That's the only one I go."

"Yes, but that's not the sh..."

"No ma'am. I take only the short root. Cap'n won't take kindly to nothing different."

"He'll be none the wiser," Samantha said and laughed nervously. "He's not even here."

"Miss Aggie here," Junebug shook his head, "she won't allow it. And if'n she do, Cap'n know the truth shortly after. So, Mrs. Jakes, best we stick to the short root."

Aunt Aggie smiled with an eerie quiet. "It may require some adjustments but..." Her eyes fluttered as if holding back tears, "You're going to absolutely love living at Sweet Pine."

When the split came, Junebug pulled Buttercup as instructed. Already, a gentle mist sprinkled in from the west. The afternoon sun vanished behind menacing clouds. By the time the buggy reached Papa's sad and dilapidated cabin, cold rain showered them without stopping.

Claire was first inside. Didn't bother lighting a lamp. Instead, she went straight for a change of dry clothes. Papa's round-top trunk, the one used on *business trips* in their youth, creaked open and Claire retreated into the *shadows*.

Samantha helped Aggie down from the buggy. Then entered the hovel, "Papa?"

No one answered.

Removing her drenched bonnet, she called again. This time—Johnny wheezed, and she pinpointed the noise by the big brass bed. "Johnathan Samson Gray, you know better than to bother Papa—especially when he sick…"

A muted thump double-tapped the log-wall. More a signal than a noise, Johnny's only words. Two thumps meant yes.

She lit a coal lamp.

Immediate regret.

Johnny sat next to Papa in the bed. His scabby arms wrapped around his boney knees. Crying in toneless whelps like a newborn pup. Papa's face sagged towards the door. Mouth ajar—eyes heavy lidded and half-opened—only the veiny whites displayed. Samantha dropped to her knees on the rough-hewn floor. Her words, somewhere between a whisper and a shout, lost on a thunder crack.

Overhead, the maelstrom raged, indifferent to Samantha's terrible discovery, or the coming unfortunate events that would tear the Gray sisters apart, forever.

Early Summer 1867

CHANCE STEPPED INTO THE clear sunshine—felt no relief. The bloodshed was beyond anything he'd witnessed in the war—not even Andersonville compared. Hands shook slightly as he limped to his mount. Unspeakable pain ripped through his groin upon lifting his leg. He faltered. Andrews, the Tasmanian, already sat his horse. "How long 'til one of 'em sees you limping around, mate?"

Chance gripped the saddle horn in both hands. "Dunno what you mean."

Chance gritted his teeth. The second attempt found more of the same. He angrily clasped the horn again. Lifted the left boot. Stuck it in the stirrup. Took a quick breath. Pushed hard. Labored up and over. And painfully sat the mare.

"What you think they'll do," Andrews asked, "if'n you've taken lame?"

"Ain't lame," Chance protested. Even though part of him wanted to spur the horse and flee. After all, he'd been fingered in Nacogdoches by a riot survivor—his paper face would soon be wanted there as well as in New Orleans. While not impossible to outrun a bounty man's bullet, one traveled farther and faster, heavily loaded with gold. Chance didn't know people called that a paradox. If your gundraw was as quick as his, paradoxes wouldn't matter to you either. Besides, he owed it to his late cousin, Lloyd Ironsides. Running out the string was the only way he'd have something to show for their dismal effort. He could hear that water-headed buffoon's voice like it was yesterday—because it was. Granny said, *"The only cure for the curse of gold was more of the same."*

"Streets awful quiet," said the Tasmanian. "Weren't folks about when we rode in?"

Chance checked up and down the street—found no crowd. Not even a dog.

"Ever see a town this dead?" The Tasmanian took direction from the sun. Chance followed his gaze skyward and stilled. Maybe a mirage, he thought. Surely it can't be...across the street, above the General Store, a terrible shadow. Some broom handle swayed briefly, then vanished. Two more clustered on the opposite side. A lump formed in Chance's throat. "Blast your damn soul, Lloyd."

Precious seconds ticked away.

Already, the remaining Lovecock gang exited the bank. *So much for a slow evacuation.* Chance spurred his horse—right hand touched his Dragoon. Despite the anticipation, Chance's heartbeat remained slow and steady. Despite his feminine face—a warrior lived inside him. It wasn't his first brush with unmitigated death—prayed it wouldn't be his last.

Chance glanced around—no one else noticed the mousetrap, only the cheese.

Could've. Would've. Should've.

Frank and the woman stepped out as the first broom handle dusted. Window glass spider-webbed. Time slowed. The next shot also missed. Lost in the belly of ole Stone-Face. She deflated. The street erupted with the sound of gunfire. No way to count the guns involved without getting hit yourself. One of the Irishmen toppled from his horse. Two of his fellows could only watch with surprise, fumbling for their own weapons.

Doc Buie leaned far off his saddle, using his mount as a shield. The horse gasped and screamed as bullets peppered its broadside. Doc rode the frightened beast to its doom in the middle of the street. Once down, Doc pulled his Greener and sprayed the sky with both barrels.

Angel Ojete's teeth held his reins, a revolver smoked in each hand. He jerked his head and spun the horse in a frantic circle. Both guns blazed before abandoning the fight altogether.

The Wayne brothers emerged from the dust and smoke. A hell-bound Cerberus, wild and back-to-back on the same horse, Elias shot without aiming as Ezekiel drove full speed down the thoroughfare.

The thin bank teller—left to his own defense—slyly crumpled in the street where he stood. The Tasmanian saw the teller's cowardly charade and rode back to rescue their fool guide.

Shots rang from the balcony above. Chance finally drew his piece and triggered the sum'bitch. The Dragoon bucked twice. Shadows toppled from second-story windows meeting dead men in the street.

A round zipped past Chance's ear. His superior gun work drew too much attention. He swiveled around and emptied the Whitneyville.

Chance needed to flee.

Stone-Face's torso bouquet'd with blood. Frank returned fire over the woman. His human shield wilted heavily in his arms. Frank abandoned the shrew. Dove sideways. Found his horse in the confusion and ripped the Winchester from its saddle. The black beauty's knees buckled beneath it, leaving Frank exposed.

Chance started reloading his Dragoon. The horse swayed underneath. Chance feared it'd been shot too. But no such luck. It was only Frank Lovecock pulling himself onboard.

Frank yelled, "Drive this beast, you son of a bitch! *Drive!*"

The spare cylinder fell from Chance's hand and bounced beneath the horse, lost. Chance pulled the animal hard west away from the deadly shootout in Shermanberg. Where the late edition newspaper read: *Botched Lovecock Gang Ambush Leaves Twenty Locals Dead.*

LATE WINTER 1867

THE STAIRCASE GROANED WITH every step the Captain took. Samantha listened to her husband's drunken wobble. Pulled back the quilt and the nightgown off her shoulders—eager for his visit. After weeks of nonstop disappointment, would tonight finally be the night?

The continued delay of their union titillated Samantha to no end. Like discovering cheap books hidden in Papa's chifforobe, or naughty French tomes displayed openly in the Captain's study.

Tap! Tap! Tap!

Thumb marking anxious time against the gold wedding band. The material symbol of their spiritual vows. She wanted Captain Jakes to take her—biblically and crudely. They were married, after all, and this was the natural order of things.

Samantha refused to believe she'd widowed herself to a living man.

All dysfunction blamed on stress. Honeymoon cancelled. Papa's funeral arranged. Yankees invaded. Field chattels forced into freedom. Old Fat Aggie infirmed. Sweet Pine saddled with a trio of extra mouths to feed. The past fortnight alone could turn any saint into a sinner. At least, they drove her captain to drink away the part of the day he could not sleep away.

Mama's words between her ears, *A wife must gift her husband her obedience forever.*

On their only night alone together, the Captain commanded Samantha undress. She obliged, more than ready. Charged eroticism built with each awkward layer she removed: petticoat, bustle, both stockings. Her willful submission excited unknown urges inside her. Corrections came if he deemed her progress outside his tastes. Being a military man, the Captain expected obedience. His precision comforted her. No nerves, butterflies, or worry. Her man knew exactly what he wanted—and this fact made Samantha want him even more.

She'd never felt so safe. *And she never would again.*

"Kneel," he commanded, pointing not at the floor or bed, but a squat breakfast table.

She did her duty. Climbing on board. It wobbled. Her neck hair prickled in suspense.

"Hold your ankles."

Again, she obeyed. Thighs trembled. Expectations soared.

Unfortunately, Samantha's pleasure swiftly turned painful. Her husband lacked a soft touch. Fingers dug in. She winced. He grunted with displeasure.

Ugly shame came next.

"Disgusting," the Captain said, examining her nakedness as if she were unfed livestock. His mood darkened so fast. Bedsheets ripped. Furniture overturned and splintered. He fumed: "Your father, that black liar!"

Leaving her to clean the mess alone.

Why the very idea.

Outside her bedroom, the Captain farted, then slunk off.

Millions of tiny pins of disappointment pierced her heart. Lonely nights like these bred more things than any pair deep in copulation. Her thoughts—*too dark and dangerous*—she didn't dare verbalize her self-loathing. Ugly shame lingered the way folks gawked at Johnny. No matter what she tried, she couldn't get shed the poison. Books, once her refuge from harsh reality, offered no distraction. She'd allowed it to become a problem. *Her problem.* She wanted to feel loved, no doubt. But—this frustrating drip of unworthiness overfilled her bucket.

Only one way to keep it from spilling out and ruining everything.

Samantha flattened her right palm. Held it near her delicate cheekbone. Ignored it and imagined how she looked sitting posed like this—as if she were outside herself. Objectively seeing what others saw. The dryness of her plain face. The red acne bumps broke out no matter how many times she scrubbed with pigfat soap. Her thin frame with its tragically square hip to shoulder ratio—obviously allergic to feminine curves. Her bottom, she despaired, a fleshy cleft desert flatter than this book's cover. She opened hers and looked deeper at her own pages and found even more of herself to hate. This restless mind and its self-righteous vanity.

An unshakable loop:

She was important.

She was slight.

She was intelligent.

She was slime.

Her hand disappeared. The smoothness of her palm was replaced by the papery shell of a buzzing hive. Whoosh! Samantha awakened the swarm.

The angry hornet stung her nose. She winced. It stung again. The smack disrupted the quiet room. It smarted. She switched hands and gave the other side a taste.

Tears welled.

She wanted to kill the vanity, kill the shame, and kill the growing suspicion bubbling at the back of her mind.

Her Captain was stern, yet kind. *Slap!*

Her Captain was merely being generous with his affection. *Slap!*

Her Captain did not ignore his wife to dote on her younger sister. *Slap! Slap!*

Papa's words between her ears, *Needs must as the devil drives.*

October 1867

Territory of Lincoln — Near Red Carpet Country

Loose paper fluttered in the prairie wind. "Some folks got no respect for mother nature." Samantha spat off the side and shook her head at the dancing stationary. "Never understand folks packing things only to toss em?"

Neither the outlaw nor the wounded quartermaster spoke. The trio had ridden in silence since leaving Atoka in the Choctaw Nation. Hadn't passed another soul since crossing the Red River three weeks before. Some things are best left unsaid. Wise men and philosophers will quack on and on about matters beyond the comprehension of mere mortals—when, in truth, it's nobody's business. And Samantha was the kinda gal who knew how to keep a secret. And she aimed to take this particular one with her to the grave.

Finally, the outlaw spoke. "Shortcut worked better than I reckoned—Didn't expect the trail for another week."

The wagon drove on. The frontier inclined towards a narrow ridge. Buttercup slowed.

Ahead of them, prairie grass thinned into rugged patches. Exposing the reddest dirt she'd ever seen. As if eternally covered in fresh blood and growing strange sagebrush. "Do those bushes look queer to you? How the breeze whipsaws back and forth through branches?"

The outlaw glanced around. "Ain't no bush I ever seen."

The quartermaster said nothing because he never would again.

Samantha frowned. "That's what I was saying."

"No—"The outlaw stiffened. "I mean, it ain't no bush."

"Is you blind?" Samantha asked. "What else could it be all alone out here...alone?"

His eyebrow arched. "Thought a bookworm like you would recognize one when she saw it."

Samantha took another look. Sure enough, the pages turned freely—as if some invisible reader searched for a lost bookmark. Another lay open a few feet away. And another still lay paper side down. Samantha hopped from the wagon. Stooped and collected the thing. "Should be a crime to throw out perfectly good books."

The outlaw answered, "I know worse ones."

"Not what I meant." Samantha turned her back to them. "This'n here's an anatomy book. Hard to come by unless you're a surgeon or something." She flipped through the pages. "Must've fallen out on accident."

"Hard to come by you said?"

"Ain't ever seen one afore outside a library," Samantha said. "Especially not one out in the middle of nowhere." She collected another. "Make it two."

"Valuable?"

"Plenty if'n you aim to learn the mysteries of the body."

His attention dipped to Samantha's boots. He pointed, "Look out."

"What is it? A snake?" She hopped in a half-circle spin, avoiding the imaginary danger.

"Your stepping on the tracks," the outlaw lifted his finger in the distance. "You're a fool if'n ya think they was abandoned voluntarily."

She followed his view over the ridge.

"Oh my..." Her jaw slacked. "What a slaughter!"

The heavy books fell from each hand as she realized the awful truth. Dust clouded around her boots. The outlaw and the wounded quartermaster watched Samantha scrambling over the literary debris—desperate to rescue her sister, once again.

EARLY JANUARY 1867

SISTERS — A DIVISION OF LABOR

OH, THE CHIRPS OF little birds. You would've thought Claire grew up in a fancy French palace the way she put on airs. Of all the Gray siblings, only Claire seemed incapable of accepting the new normal. She complained daily. Everything scorched earth since the war ended. Any potential suitors never came calling. With zero prospects, Claire refused to complete a single chore without debate, and then performed said task without much effort.

And Samantha couldn't be expected to do everything required at Sweet Pine. The dump owned twenty rooms for crying out-loud, not including Aunt Aggie's cabbage stinking lean-to. She'd caught a bad cough from the storm—couldn't be bothered to do a thing for herself, now. Claiming the "vapors" at the slightest hint of manual labor.

Samantha needed help.

Claire's lazy sullenness was to be expected at her tender age of sixteen. Samantha hoped her captain was working diligently behind the scenes to betroth Claire to one of his fellow officers. If not...*how many more hints did she need to drop?* Marrying off Claire wasn't just necessary for Samantha's sanity, but also the right thing to do. She couldn't help but feel responsible. Blood being thicker than water in most right-thinking corners of this Earth. No one wants their sister to age into an unwed spinster. Particularly, one who already spun horrid stories about her new brother-in-law.

Oh, the chirps of little birds.

One day while Johnny played alone outside, Claire told Samantha she witnessed the Captain aim and fire his rifle. "He missed, of course," Claire had said. "But what kinda man would do such a thing? Shooting at a little boy. Specially one troubled as bad as our Johnny?"

Samantha only half listened. Too exhausted from housework and in no mood for Claire's rubbish. She preferred the book on her lap. The one found in the Captain's study. Written in a language she didn't know—filled with pictures of men and women. Some fully naked or barely dressed, or costumed in antique finery, donning wigs of curls and ribbon tails, and others bound at odd angles and held in submission, while erect men extended their fleshy shafts to all, no matter the receiver's gender, smiling and laughing in open relation, some participants freely intertwined into shapes of multi-limbed beasts, like some lascivious monster, culled and summoned from the shadows of your repressed libido.

Samantha caught Claire looking over her shoulder and slammed the book closed. Neither said another word. *Odd,* Samantha thought. Before moving to Sweet Pine, they would've greedily gone over each image, adding giddy commentary. Laughing and swearing each other to secrecy. Samantha knew they used to care, but apparently things had changed.

"If I stay much longer," said Claire, breaking the silence, "something bad will happen."

Samantha rolled her eyes and didn't respond.

Claire whined petulance, "Your Captain stares at me when you're not looking."

Samantha had heard enough and went to hide the dirty book back where she'd found it. But she stopped when Claire asked, "What about Aunt Clara? Could I go live with her?"

"No safe passage through the territories," Samantha said, arms akimbo. Picture book tight against her hip. "You'd most likely die before reaching Colorado. Besides..." Samantha heated her lukewarm words and consoled. "Dunno how I'd make it through the day without my sweet sister."

Oh, the chirps of little birds.

LATE WINTER 1867

AFTER DEAD SLEEP — AN EDUCATION

THE BEDROOM DOOR INCHED open. The lantern sent orange ribbons of shadow down the hall. Samantha's freshly slapped face sizzled from the self-abuse, and she crept forward. Stopping briefly outside Johnny's room, hearing only muted adenoidal snores. The kind kids make when sick. The only sound Johnny ever made. Now, passing the attic door. Drafty air chilled her barefeet. She remembered Aunt Aggie's confused boast about the comfort of Sweet Pine, then shrugged it off and moved on.

At the end of the hall, Samantha stopped. Heartbeat raced in her ears. Bump-bump-bump.

It couldn't be. There had to be a mistake. She didn't want to believe. Didn't want to admit her husband's trail of drunken noises led straight to Claire's bedroom.

Mama's words between her ears, *The key to a successful marriage, find bliss in ignorance.*

Vile curiosity turned the doorknob in her hand. Lamplight cast shapes on her sister's bed. Samantha squinted in the gloom and at once wished she hadn't.

Claire's feet hooked each ankle. Bare thighs absorbed the Captain's naked thrust.

"Get off her!" Samantha rushed forward. "*You've gone to the wrong room!*"

The Captain dismounted and stood. His war wound—a snaggled white scar—ran south from his chest to his wilting manhood. "No," he growled, "You're the lost one."

Samantha looked from her husband to her sister, and back again. Control lost. Primal rage blinded. The lamp-hand swung. Glass exploded on contact. Lamp oil ignited. Flames danced off his arm and across the worn carpet and headed for the bed skirt. The Captain yelped and fell to his knees to extinguish his burning skin.

When her vision returned, Samantha stood dumbfounded at the chaos she'd unleashed.

Already her little sister had jumped down—quilt in hand—beating back the flames. Samantha awkwardly started to help but stopped. Smoke hazed the room. Claire lit another lamp. "*Look what you've done to his arm!*"

"*His arm?*" Samantha asked, puzzled. "What about what he was doing to you?"

The Captain rose slowly to his bare feet. Stepped through the broken glass without a flinch. "You think you're worthy of an explanation...but you ain't worth the air you breathe."

Brows knitted. "But I'm your wife."

"Them's just words...," said the Captain.

"Go back to your room, Sam," Claire crept up behind him. "Don't *embarrass* yourself."

Samantha sensed no hint of distress in her words, only betrayal.

Claire caressed his face delicately. They kissed. Tongues and teeth hungry for one another.

Samantha's eyes drizzled. Crying so hard it was darn near impossible to stop. She didn't understand how either of them could do this to her and told them so.

"You think you're so smart," said the Captain. "Figure it out elsewhere and leave us be."

The only elsewhere Samantha knew flashed to mind as he said. "Return yonder to that chicken scratch mudhole I found you in. I've made my choice."

Claire clung to her brother-in-law. "Sweetheart, love, my king..." she cooed, "I'll stay with you forever and a day."

"Looks like she's made her choice too," said the Captain.

Samantha's eyes found her feet. *Turn damn you—walk away—wake Johnny and leave. Go anywhere but here.* She didn't move. Too heartbroken and shocked and angry and disappointed to do anything but stand there like a cuckquean fool.

"Three's a crowd," he said firmly. "Remove yourself or I will."

Her sister's voice cooed, "Sweetheart, love. I have an idea..."

Please wake up, Samantha thought, *you're dreaming. Please be dreaming.*

"Since she ain't got nowhere else to go..." said Claire, "she should stay here."

The Captain shot her a queer look.

"I mean, you ain't got no servants no more...and this is such a big ole house," Claire reasoned huskily. Fingers like spiders climbed his neck. "She may not know how to please a man's body—but she can cook and clean better than most negroes. She did it all the time for Papa."

Her prey slithered between her tickling hands. She cooed, "Free me for more pleasant chores. Don't you think my king deserves to be treated like one?"

"She can't be trusted." His burnt arm smoked. "This dumb cunt dunno how the world works. If'n she was a man—she'd be dead right now for what she done."

"But can't she earn your confidence..." Claire raked nails softly over his abdomen. "...somehow...some way?"

Her mouth neared his ear. Whatever she whispered stiffened him. "I keep close quarters with no one against their will, if they're white." He glanced at his arm. Cruel hands gripped his hips. Chest puffed with a gamecock's pride. He clucked. "Your sister thinks you deserve the chance to choose your own fate. You know where the door is...I care not if you find it and go, but don't darken it again if'n you do. But if you wanna stay in my house..." He crowed. "Wanna enjoy my company? Wanna empty my chamber pot. And wanna come when I call. Then you gotta prove your fealty to me."

Samantha remembered her wedding night when he commanded, "Kneel..."

Samantha felt herself—outside herself. Disconnecting her grasp of the physical world. Multiple maniacal sensations edged her wits towards oblivion. Wickedness seemed to wash over her. She wanted to punch the sinister leers from their evil skulls. Punch them until eyeballs leaked jelly down their chins. Playfully bathe in their blood. Chew on their livers, kidneys, and thumbs—spit em out for the coyotes to devour and scat in unmarked piles along a well-traveled path, only to be stepped in by some wanderer's boots, and scraped off with a stick. She wanted total annihilation. And worst of all, Samantha wanted to do all of this to her sister more than her husband.

Papa's words between her ears, *You reap what you sow, Sammie Jane.*

The idea hit her in a whipcrack. No over-thinking, beyond pure and crystal-clear acceptance. All tears dried. Heartbeat steadied. Knees bent at his command. Being a military man, she knew the Captain expected obedience.

He lowered his voice. "Now crawl to me."

Down on all fours now. One hand followed the other. She maneuvered over the broken shards of glass and arrived at their feet.

No nerves, butterflies, or worry.

The Captain directed her again.

She obeyed. Her pink tongue protruded beyond her lips. Drying in the open air.

Her man knew exactly what he wanted. She only needed to make him know she knew what he wanted, too. Picturing those crudely drawn women in those dirty books. Bent and submissive objects, mere smiling bodies used and abused and devoid of all personality. An erotic road map showed the only way out of her husband's maze.

And it strangely excited her.

Through small compliant acts of submission, she would earn his confidence. Through humiliating vows of admiration, she would survive this betrayal. Through total acceptance of delay, she would earn her revenge.

They were married, after all, and this was the natural order of things.

Without hesitation, she honored her husband's demands.

Samantha's tongue slowly licked clean the Captain's unwashed feet.

MID SPRING 1867

DUSK — BONES AND DUST

"DOCTOR HOLDFAST SAYS THE fever's gonna take Aggie. Two more days, maybe three—couldn't say exactly." Captain Jakes snarled, "Take this timber-stick and use it to right yonder crypt."

Samantha halted her floor polishing. Wiped her wet hands on her potato sack blouse. The only clothing he allowed her to wear. Eyes on the axe in the Captain's hands. When she didn't move immediately, he stooped, then stood. Silver flashed in a blink as he collected the trailing end of her pubic chain. The leash slithered against her thighs. Then he pulled. Tingles quickly turned to pinches. Hips propelled her feet forward in short, restrained steps. Iron shackles rattled at her ankles—just enough chain-link to complete her chores—as long as she didn't take big steps. A matching set of irons clapped around each wrist.

She flashed him a smile of faint promise—doing her best to conceal the discomfort.

"The sooner she's gone, the better," the war hero yanked harder on the newest present he gifted his wife. The finely crafted silver chain connected their wedding bands to her vulva. Hers healed within a week. His larger ring directly pierced the fleshy hood and remained swollen. "However, Aggie birthed Jake's blood—she's forever family—deserves her place among the others. Don't the dumb cunt agree?"

"Yes, sir, Captain Jakes," Samantha chirped.

She knew—he knew—she wouldn't complain.

"Everyone but Pa's down there. Old fool wanted to be buried in a pine box. Had one special built for the occasion. It sits yonder in the barn—never used. If he'd been so worried about his resting place, you'd think he'd've known better than to go gator hunting at his age. Guess it is what it is." He reeled in her pubic chain, hand over hand. "One day...many years from now...I and the dumb cunt's sister will join them."

All day Sweet Pine simmered with Texas heat. Now long shadows grew across the property. Samantha stepped out the back door—not a breeze to be found, nor a cloud in the sky. Sweat soaked the potato sack. She could see herself, outside herself, and not recognize this pale creature, no longer allowed to answer to a proper name. Snow White, Cinderella, and Sleeping Beauty never had their fairy tales dashed by Prince Charming. Happily ever-after never showed the next step once the couple left the story alone together. If Mama hadn't died, she could've warned Samantha—or at least told her the truth. This is what happens when the landed gentry marries beneath itself.

Why, the very idea.

A man raised with all of life's advantages and none of the shame.

"The dumb cunt better march double-time or all the light'll be gone by the time it makes camp." The Captain warned. "Tombs after sunset. Plays tricks it does. When Uncle John passed, Father sent two coons in to clear a shelf for his body. They didn't take rightly to it. Cried and begged to be whipped instead of doing their work. But something tells me the dumb cunt'll enjoy it enough to sing its praises tonight. Ain't that right?"

Samantha's little bird sang again, "Yes sir, Captain Jakes."

They moved on in the dying light.

Underneath the tater sack, Samantha's two piercings clinked together—a tambourine keeping time with each step. Incessant tingles edged her somewhere between pleasure and a snail crawling over a razor blade. Burlap sackcloth itched terribly, reeking of stale potatoes and swamp ass. Below her tethered snatch, Samantha's inner thighs chafed with ignored menstruations. She thought of Aunt Aggie. Her hidden warning about gifts bestowed on wives. *How many had Aggie found she couldn't refuse?*

After shuffling past Aggie's stinking shack, the broken corral, the empty stock pond, the rotting barn, and just before the land sprouted abandoned slave-holds and un-tilled fields, Samantha finally stopped at a stony mound crowded with weeds. She'd never been here before. Not one of the regular attractions on his usual walking tours of Sweet Pine.

"Hold the line," said the Captain and offered her his end of the silver leash.

"Thank you, Captain Jakes," Samantha obeyed and stilled. Making damn sure the handle stayed aloft where he'd left it in her hand. Her other hand supported her elbow, where the silver links cascaded, collecting briefly at her feet before looping north towards her equator. It dangled gently against her purple knees as she waited for further instruction. Each breath a rush of quick sensation.

Mama's words between her ears, *A good wife gifts her husband her obedience, forever.*

Shortly after Claire began showing, the Captain experienced second thoughts about his lawful wife's usefulness. Just another job Claire was no longer expected to perform regularly at Sweet Pine. Frankly, Samantha was grateful the bastard never planted seed where it could grow.

Above them, the sky reddened to its coming darkness. The Captain swung the axe side to side in wide arcs. Weeds flew in clumps until a low stone archway revealed itself. Further down, the Captain cleared stone steps until half the bastard vanished below ground. Satisfied with his work, his leg kicked. Heavy door hinges squealed open. All of the Captain disappeared this time. Reemerging with a rusty lantern. Then bladed away spent wax—adding a new candle. His dark eyes glowed in the flickering light of the struck match.

"Blacker than a negro's neck down there," he chuckled at his own cleverness. "Listen closely, There's six shelves. Three on either side. Carved into the clay. Don't remember who's who. Should be at least one putrefied to bone by now. If not, the dumb cunt'll need to scrape away the leftover meat."

Samantha nodded, "Yes sir, Captain Jakes."

He took the leash end from her hand. "Now pay attention to this next part...we Jakes save our skulls." Lantern hand gestured at the hole in the rocky crypt, before setting it down. "The dumb cunt'll see 'em lining the walls. Add the new one and pulverize the rest of the skeleton." The Captain's hands crisscrossed, winding the tether—tying it high until covering her throat. He asked, "Comfortable?"

The choker pinched. Breath made even more difficult. She thanked him for his kindness.

"Use the flat end to crush the fossils," he collected the axe. "The thin edge breaks the more troublesome femurs and hips."

Axe-handle extended towards her.

Samantha stared at it blankly. All she needed to do was grab it. Swing down and this would all be over. She pictured the dull blade splitting his skull in a gush of gore. While reaching for it, her thoughts ran. *He thinks so little of me he's giving me an axe—doesn't suspect I'd use it on him.* Samantha swallowed the lump in her throat. *Would she use it? Was now the right time?* She had desperately wanted this glorious moment to take place where Claire could watch. Then Samantha would decorate the little bitch with his steaming entrails and make her sing *Silent Night.* Could Christmas come early this year?

Before Samantha realized it, the Captain closed the door behind her.

Her world darkened.

Panic *screamed* through her mind.

MID SPRING 1867

LONESOME — A GRAVE

THICK AROMAS OF EARTH and rot stronger than spoiled chicken agitated Samantha. She fought the urge to vomit. Candlelight danced across generations of dead Jakes, but Samantha didn't really notice. Too afraid to open her own eyes. Heartbeat raced. Skin shivered. Yelping in fright when tiny claws crawled over her bare foot. The lantern nearly dropped. Nerves rattled. Papa's words between her ears, *when trouble comes, Sammie Jane, you can't waste time on fear.*

Samantha mumbled broken bible verses and lifted the lantern. She summoned the courage to open her eyes. It came slowly. Light flickered across earthen walls, where carved primitive visions of fish men with arms and legs had been carved. A veritable school of them. These figures encircled a nightmarish image. Some kind of bear with clawed arms outstretched—a giant spider for a head. Legs intertwined scruffier than a hermit's beard. A multitude of eyes stared into her. Samantha looked away from one horror to another. Light fell on the nearby shelf, illuminating the remains of a face covered in papery dust. Long, scraggy hairs twisted and curled from each nostril. Moss-green fur covered the edges of sunken eye sockets. Something black and vile scuttled from under the papery eyelid on a dozen tiny legs.

Samantha shrieked and again looked away—the scene didn't improve—nightmarish visions burned to memory. A terrible state of things. Breath pumped ragged in her lungs—somewhere between laughter and a scream. She felt outside herself, and didn't recognize the girl lifting the axe and blading away the cobwebs. Bringing the lantern towards a shelf and gasping. Spiders fled the light over the dusty bones of what was once a man.

Samantha remembered her Shakespeare. *Alas, poor Yorick...something, something...a fellow of infinite jest...something, something...the end.*

WHACK! Samantha buried the axe in the corpse's chest. And pulled. Bones dragged off the shelf, clattering to the dirt floor. Clenched her eyes and teeth and screamed. Both hands lifted the axe overhead. One swing parted spine and skull. It bounced aside, spinning upside down, looking at her—looking away—looking at her again.

"You shouldn't have such terrible thoughts about your Master." Claire appeared, an apparition forming in a pile of Jakes' bones. The vision laughed and said, "The Good Book teaches women to cleave to our husbands and love, honor, and obey them." *WHACK!* Samantha drove the axe-handle forward into Claire's forehead. The bitch vanished. *WHACK! WHACK!* Bones fragmented and spun and vanished. Samantha did it again and again and again. The dark crypt blurred red—like closing your eyes on a sunny day. No way to keep count of her swings—*WHACK! WHACK! WHACK!* She panted over a pile of broken bones. Yorick's skull mocked her in the Captain's voice. "The dumb cunt'll sing its praises tonight. Ain't that right?"

Samantha raged and flung the axe and missed the offending skull entirely. Colliding instead against the wall behind. It happened so fast. A single stone gave way. The rusty axe had hit just right and gone through the hole.

Sometimes it's better to be lucky than good.

Samantha attempted to swallow. Mouth dryer than a probate will reading. She lifted the lantern at the false wall. In the dark abyss—something glimmered. She hesitated, then stepped closer.

"Oh my god!" she exclaimed.

SPRING 1867

Night — The Best Laid Plans

MOONLIGHT BLUED THE SWEET Pine stable. Rot pocked the leprous whitewash. Inside, shadows loomed at strange angles. The scent was thick with moldy hay and animal dung. A welcome relief from the stink of the crypt. Samantha barely notice the difference. Too busy avoiding obstacles as she crept inside. The stable's lone occupant, Buttercup the mule, whinnied unseen. She felt along the wall towards the dead-end corner. Once found, fingers reached for grip. Her shackles rattled as she lifted the coffin's lid and made her deposit.

Samantha knew she needed to hurry.

Papa's words between her ears, *The Goddess of Fortune favors the bold.*

She crept by the big house. Listening to her betrayers humping upstairs. The bastard called aloud the names of Confederate heroes. Claire answered with moans beneath him.

P.T. Beauregard! Ugh! Jefferson Davis! Yes! Joe Johnston! Don't stop!

Samantha shuffled on. Not waiting around to understand why a man would call the names of other men while topping a lady. As long as they made time with each other, Samantha could make the most of hers.

Pubic chain slipped from around its coil around her neck. Trailing behind her back to the crypt. Ignoring the dead and primitive etchings in the clay, she went straight to work.

Gold glittered in the lantern's light. Each bar and coin stamped: C.S.A. and a collection of numbers.

This would make her fourth trip between the two places tonight.

After discovering the Captain's hoard of Confederate gold a week ago, she'd snuck out every night since. Even then, she still hadn't made a dent in his stash. More than half remained hidden behind the false wall. Mountains of treasure and nearly ten rotting bags of coins. And Samantha Jakes aimed to steal every penny.

Once that business concluded, she would calmly go into the Captain's study. Collect the lone edition of Encyclopedia Britannica. And force her husband and her sister to beg her for mercy. Little did they know none would be coming. After satisfying her revenge, Samantha and Johnny would ride out of Sweet Pine and never look back.

She even considered burning the dump to the ground.

She refilled her arms and moved on. Despite her footsteps clinking like coin purses, the night remained eerily quiet. Heartbeat quickened near the big house. She had hoped to hear more of their humping. Unfortunately, tonight it seemed he'd exhausted the list of names already. It usually finished right around *Robert E. Lee* or sometimes *John Wilkes Booth*. The eerie quiet sent panic through her spine. Hopefully, the Captain slept. But she heard no snores. Glancing again at the upstairs window, she saw it was closed. Thank God for small miracles. The stable remained another fifty yards away. Each new step deliberate and slow until clearing Sweet Pine's back porch.

The path ahead vanished as moonlight clouded over. The sudden darkness cued the night to life.

Papa's words between her ears, *When trouble comes you can't waste time...*

She moved on—best she could. Stumbling blind over uneven ground. Lost in the dark familiarity of a well-worn path. It was only a matter of time before her shackles snagged a root, and...Samantha went sprawling. *Splash!*

Foul moistness slapped the breath from her. Gold slipped away—sinking beneath the mud.

Samantha popped up, coughing—at least she knew she wasn't lost anymore. *But the gold?* Fingers combed the mud. Cold and somehow empty. She'd never find it splashing around in the dark. Getting to her knees, she froze when she saw it.

The glowing cigar was supposed to be sleeping off the drink and fornication and... "Awful dangerous to take a swim in the cesspool, especially at night. Never know what kinda critters a-crawling around. Ain't that right, ye dumb cunt?"

Clouds above cleared—they could see each other clear enough now.

"I'll be ginger headed," He approached. "Who'd have thought the cesspool would improve the dumb cunt's aroma?" He laughed tight and demanded her tether. With no other choice, Samantha obliged. He reeled her in as easily as he would a hooked catfish. Orange cigar tip burned bright. She could feel its heat as he spoke smoke, "Tell me why the dumb cunt's here right now."

She'd prepared for this moment. Had conjured a plausible excuse. But instead, her plan fell immediately apart. She feebly muttered, "I heard a noise."

The night around them seemed to go on forever. Creatures of the night calling to each other in loud indecipherable noise. Vile muck slick between her toes, fingers, and her vulva rings. Each wet crevice sheltered multitudes of filthy danger. His cigar darkened, then glowed orange and he commanded, "Strip."

Samantha did so.

"Cold out tonight, ain't it?"

She nodded, "Yes, Captain Jakes."

"Here," he said, "...allow me to warm you."

Hot pain sizzled. Shooting stings across her chest. Embers crushed against her left nipple. The stink of burning flesh. She held her tongue. Mutes made less sound as her mind raced elsewhere. Christmas mornings with Mama and Papa. Sunday picnics in those cool breezes before a Texas spring became hellish summer. But it was no use. Finally, she broke. A soft, lone whimper escaped her lips.

"Did I say the dumb cunt could speak?"

Embers fell and scorched the top of her feet. He pressed his cigar against the other breast. Pain spread and throbbed, and his mouth found hers. Teeth bit into and chewed her bottom lip. Taste of blood flooded her mouth. Another solitary moan came. Hairy fingers found her throat and squeezed. Air compressed from her lungs. Suddenly, he broke their connection. Rocked his head back and spat in her face.

The Captain laughed with cold menace. "Tonight, it will learn silence, or it will die."

EARLY SUMMER 1867

DAWN — THE TAO OF GUNPOWDER

TODAY WAS SAMANTHA'S NINETEENTH birthday. She knew exactly what she wanted—a good escape. Reading had always been her happiest way to pass the time. She thought of the Captain's bookshelves. The four-volume set of Encyclopedia Britannica missed three books, but it didn't matter to Samantha—one of the few unmolested tomes left behind in the Captain's once proud library.

According to the gospel of the encyclopedia, *The Taoist heathens believed in the Three Treasures: compassion, frugality, and humility.* Samantha could not avoid the latter. Her weary head drooped. Bells jingle-jangled. Snapping her upright on her knees. She sat on her heels. Blood-shot eyes reopened—not awake or asleep—somewhere between dimensions. Sleepy tingles climbed her legs. Her soap-bubble head floated over the iron-collar. Designed for those of us with unbreakable spirits. Her's faltered. *Did the sun rise in the west and set in the east? Was up really down and right really left?* If the Captain deemed it so, then the only answer was *yes*.

According to the gospel of the encyclopedia, *The Taoist heathens believed in a simple path to join the greater universe and merge with the infinite. They called this the Tao or "The Way."* Even neglected books contained useful information. Samantha understood information bred ideas. Ideas created actions. Combine all three with an extravagant indifference and steady disgrace, and Samantha knew you could build something truly dangerous.

One only needed the patience required to suffer.

Sweat pooled underneath her. Securing her at the foot of Master's bed. The one Samantha used to sleep in alone. Back when she was allowed such privileges. Her collar guaranteed only the purest form of ruined sleep. Four iron ramrods jutted straight out beyond her shoulders—wide enough she could never lay down. To make things worse—clustered grapes of sleigh bells dangled from each rod. The slightest movement—the tiniest nudge—and the tinkle-tinkle-tinkle would chime-chime-chime.

Being a military man, the bastard was a lite sleeper—and didn't take kindly to being awakened before reveille. The evil contraption, just another punishment for being out of bounds. Now she knelt here, condemned to wait and beg for more humiliation. Her escape plan—far away as if in a dream—plenty afraid she'd lost the opportunity to ever leave Sweet Pine.

If she didn't earn her revenge soon, death would come before her next birthday.

Why the very idea?

According to the gospel of the encyclopedia, *The Taoist heathen did not believe in Jesus Christ to achieve salvation. In order to achieve ideal perfection, they preferred acts of self-discipline.* He'd left her alone in the crypt. She knew—he knew—she'd stay put. And when she didn't, his chronicle of cruelty followed. It took everything Samantha had to keep wits about.

According to the gospel of the encyclopedia, *The Taoist heathen's endless search for the Tao's enlightenment accidentally stumbled upon a different discovery altogether. No one knows exactly when, but all sources acknowledge the Taoist heathen were the first to discover gunpowder.* In the bed behind her, Claire's belly inched out from beneath the bastard. Little sister's soft bump brought with it such vile cravings. Pecan pie drenched in pickled vinegar or tightly folded sheets of stationery paper soaked in eggs and pan-fried. Samantha had seen her eat it. Chewing away happily, as if eating a roast pig. Neither sister ate proper meals anymore, which was especially troubling since one of them was now eating for two.

In the backyard, not more than five days ago, Samantha watched her sister drop to her knees and shovel handfuls of dirt into her mouth. Now Claire stood before her and stretched—arms out—wrists bending in front of her as she looked Samantha over with both pity and disregard. Floorboard creaked beneath her feet. Young knees popped corn as Claire finally knelt beside Samantha and yawned wide. "No matter how much I sleep, my back and feet won't stop hurting."

According to the gospel to the encyclopedia, *The Taoist heathens originally used gunpowder as medicine. They believed it could extend a person's life if ingested orally once a day.*

Oh, the chirps of little birds. Samantha didn't respond. No secrets held from the Master.

"Did mama ever say carrying a baby would hurt *this much*?"

Mama's face and voice long gone from memory. Less familiar than those bloated bodies in the crypt. "Every child's a blessing."

"A blessing?" Claire asked slowly. "What if the baby is sired by the devil himself?"

"All part of God's glorious plan..." Samantha refused the bait. "...sorry about your feet."

"Dunno if you've noticed, but..." Claire fingered one of the collar's bells tentatively—a soft jingle-jangle filled Samantha with dread. "God ain't been around lately to make no plans."

"Don't say such evil things." Samantha rattled off the actor's script. "He's with us now more than ever. Like the good book says about Joab."

Claire wrinkled her nose, "That the one about a flood?"

According to the gospel of the encyclopedia, *to fuel a gunpowder explosion, the Taoist heathens mixed charcoal, sulfur, and saltpeter. Add friction liberally to ignite a spark and...kaboom!*

Samantha shook her head at her sister. "God and the Devil bargain for Joab's soul. If he suffers—Satan says he'll turn from God."

Claire rubbed her nose, "Ain't bargaining like that wicked sinful?"

Samantha nodded.

Claire yawned and scratched between thighs free of modification, "If it's a sin, then how is it ever okay?"

Samantha shrugged. "Joab loses his family. Suffers poverty and want. But Joab keeps his faith and perseveres. Therefore, God wins the devil's bargain and rewards Joab with a new wife and a new house and more babies—living happily ever after. And the devil gets cast back into hell where he belongs."

"The devil can't be in hell..." Claire dug a finger into her nose—uncorked it for closer inspection before rolling the snotty discharge between thumb and index. "...if the devil's asleep on the bed right now."

Satisfied with her handy work, Claire extended her fingertip at Samantha's broken lips. And clucked her tongue. Samantha eyed it with dread.

Samantha's mouth tightened. "Don't do this?"

"You ain't eaten nothing but Master's seed in days." Claire giggled, "Ain't you hungry?"

Samantha sucked her teeth.

"Go on now," said the coquette. "Before I wake him, cause you called me a dirty bitch and tried to escape again." She laughed and added, "Wonder what he'd make you eat after that?"

Samantha looked at the stranger she once knew. "What's stopping you from spreading that lie anyways?" The bells *tinkled-tinkled-tinkled.*

According to the gospel of the encyclopedia, *the load procedure of a smoothbore flintlock musket included three steps. Step one pours the powder charge down the muzzle. Next, patches a lead ball, and then rams it down the barrel until the ramrod stops.*

"You hurt my feelings," Claire said, and frowned. "It could be worse, you know...he could've thrown you out. You ain't been beaten with an ugly stick or nothing, but you don't turn heads either. Someone as painfully plain as you would've been your ruin. I couldn't let him do it. And you still ain't thanked me for *saving* you."

According to the gospel of the encyclopedia, *the invention of the percussion cap improved the efficiency of firearms. Thereby cutting down each load time. An experienced musket man could load/fire/reload between five and fifteen seconds.*

Claire wanted grace? After everything she'd done to her very own sister. Knifed in the back and through the heart at the same time. Papa's words between her ears, *Some folks have, and some folks have not, but all reap what they sow.*

The bells on Samantha's collar jingle jangled. Claire leaned in close and poured in more poison. "...what about Johnny? Hmm? He got needs we can't tend to. No one pays him no never-mind. He stays dirty as a piglet...eating slops."

Icy tinkles as Samantha spoke cold. "He's not as hungry as you, sweet sister."

Claire paused. Her evil smile dipped. "Whaddaya mean?"

"You a might peckish these days?"

"I can admit," Claire said, "I have my moments."

"Yeah," Samantha said, head lulling slightly, "I've seen em."

Claire's smugness deflated. "Seen what?"

"Go for any long walks lately?" She whispered. "Maybe out where the clay's the reddest?"

Claire darted her brows.

"Down on all fours..." Samantha's dry lips cracked as she smiled. "Shoving handfuls of dirt in your mouth...Can't taste too good. Eating dirt. I couldn't understand why someone would do such a thing. Then it dawned on me. Of course, I'd want to prepare for my grave too if I were incubating my own doom."

Claire blushed with rage.

According to the gospel of the encyclopedia, *Texas Ranger Captain Samuel Walker wanted a more powerful, repeating handgun for close combat. For this purpose, gunsmith Samuel Colt developed the Colt Walker single action revolver. Each chamber held a doubled powder charge and weighed close to five pounds. However, if mishandled or overloaded, the Colt Walker's cylinder would rupture easily and need repair.*

Why the very idea?

Samantha's eyes leaked as she remembered books contained information. Information bred ideas. Ideas took actions, like hollowing out a thick encyclopedia slowly with a tiny shard of broken glass to hide a cherished family heirloom. Papa's Navy Colt waited on her there. A birthday present ready to be unwrapped and unloaded into the Captain's face. Then Samantha would reload and find her sweet-sweet sister.

According to the gospel of the encyclopedia, *1851 saw the release of the Colt Revolving Bell Pistol of Navy Caliber. A cap and ball revolver that fired six thirty-six caliber rounds. It weighed significantly less than the other contemporary pistols and could be loaded with a combustible paper cartridge. Its reliability and aggressive marketing led to it becoming one of the most popular firearms of the nineteenth century.*

From outside the Master's bedroom, there came a loud crashing sound.

JUNE 1867

MIDDAY — NEAR SWEET PINE ROAD

THE LOVECOCK GANG, OR what was left of it, fought against punishing briars and poison ivy leaves as big as pennants. Horses abandoned to enter the pine thicket on foot. Each stuttered step rubbed unrelenting pain between Chance's legs—deadly certain any cure would be worse than the cause. Off in the corner of his eye, something moved. A familiar shape. For a brief moment, he thought it waved. The blur vanished when he turned his head. As if it had never been there. Chance cursed the pain tricking his vision.

At the clearing's edge, the bank teller pointed, "That'n's the place."

Doc Buie surveyed the crumbling mansion. Then glanced at Frank. They shared a moment of telepathy. Frank whistled low, then Doc Buie announced an action plan. Chance heard his name combined with Andrews, but not the rest. If he followed behind the Tasmanian, at least he'd keep from going sideways of Frank.

Chance did just that, best he could, until they emerged along the edge of a worn and forgotten horse pen. Dung patties dried to brittle cakes. No living horse kept here for months, maybe years. Last one probably slaughtered with the same vainglory used for the war. They followed an overgrown fence to the back of the house and stopped under an opened window. Above them, the sounds of a kitchen. A woman hummed a familiar tune and rolled biscuits. Air thick with fried eggs and bacon. The smell triggered Chance's belly rumble, loud enough to give them away.

"Silence that noise, pretty boy," Andrews growled with disgust. "About to have enough loot you'll be up to your balls in meat pies, with a harem of big titted bitches to serve em." Chance heard something from above and waved his hand to silence the fool. The woman called for somebody. Chance didn't catch the name, but he heard, "*Fetch some water.*" In the short distance away towards the woods, Chance noticed a well-house.

The back door opened.

The outlaws pressed themselves against the wall.

The Tasmanian went for his gun.

Chance barred his arm to stop him. "Easy...he don't see us."

A boy mindlessly plodded out. An empty pail dangled from each hand. The boy made the short trek towards the well-house, unaware he was being watched. With the backdoor still open, the Tasmanian whispered, "Get the water boy, I got the biscuit roller."

"Shouldn't we wait for Frank?"

"Opportunity's knocking," said the Tasmanian. "That boy'll see us and sound the alarm."

"Ain't no reason to kill a kid."

The Tasmanian squinted and said, "You'll kill your cousin, but not a stranger?"

"Lloyd had it coming," cold sweat ran down Chance's forehead. "Someone was bound to lose a bullet in him."

The Tasmanian looked him over queer. "Would you prefer I lose a bullet in you?"

"*Mine eyes have seen the glory of the coming of the lord,*" the boy sang to himself. Well bucket clanging against stone as it rose. The rope pulled hand over hand. Not once did he hear the shadows closing in behind him. "*He is trampling out the vintage where the grapes of wrath are stored.*"

Some folks are born with all the luck in the world.

"*He hath loosed the fateful lighting of his terrible swift sword.*"

Some lucky folks never look death in the eye. Shuffling from the mortal coil in a dream.

"*His truth is marching on.*"

How long does it take a life to flash before eyes? Especially one so young.

"*Glory, Glory...hallelujah!*"

Chance stepped forward. Boot-heel crunched in the slag. The songbird slowed, then stopped. Chance touched his Dragoon.

The rope fell free.

Should've. Could've. Would've.

EARLY SUMMER 1867

SWEET PINE—THE LAST DAY: PART ONE

JOHNNY GREY BOUNCED DOWN the staircase in a tin washtub. Each impact reverberated through the house. If Johnny could've hollered with joy, he certainly would've. A tremendous ruckus. On the last step, Johnny took a bad bounce. His strange teeth clinked as the boy spilled across the floor—skidded to a hard stop against the far wall. Dusty portraits of the Captain's family rattled on impact. A multitude of painted eyes watched the boy seize with quiet, panting laughter. A scabby lesion above his left eye oozed brown splatters and puss. Dirty hands clutched again for his makeshift sled to do it all again.

The bells on Samantha's collar tinkled, *"Go make Johnny stop Claire. He'll wake the...!"*

Before Samantha could finish, a blur sailed between them. It crashed, spraying the wall with whiskey and broken glass.

Behind them, the bastard sat upright on the bed. Murderous rage behind two groggy red eyes. His unshaved mouth snarled, "I've done told ya bitches...keep that freakshow from disturbing my peace."

Claire fluttered her eyes at him. "My king, he's just a boy. I'll speak to him now..."

"Now?" He growled, "Now's past the talking time."

Red long-johns moved heavily for the door. Claire stood and caught his wrist. For a moment, everything paused. Claire spun her web. Whatever she cooed at him next, Samantha didn't hear. But Captain Jakes wheeled around fast. The suddenness startled Claire. The gal yelped between his meaty hands. Her feet left the floor. The Captain screamed, "Too late to interfere! I'm settling outstanding accounts today!" He growled. Head butted forward—cracking Claire's face. She crumpled silently to the floor.

Samantha, sensing this as her only chance, stretched out to intercept him. Her chained hands weakly reached for his knee and only found his ankle. With great effort—she pleaded, "Oh my god! Please don't hurt him! He don't know no better..."

The Captain swung. Fists and sparks exploded across her vision. She fell forward. One of the long barbs caught the floor. She gulped for air in an awkward pose. Unable to balance herself against the metal cutting into her throat.

At the top of the stairs, Johnny gripped the sides of the tub. Shifting his weight back and forth. Scooching closer and closer. All he needed to do was find the edge. And. Gravity did the rest.

Woosh! The boy clattered down the kaleidoscoping world. Clackata.-Clackata-Clackata. Everything vibrated in waves. Clackata-Clackata-Clackata. On the last step, the tub took another bad bounce. Johnny felt his stomach climb higher than his throat. He flew—like the birds outside. The ground faraway. Rashed and boney arms flapping over hardwood shadows. Slower than a lesson learned the hard way, the boy finally stopped flying. Portrait eyes followed him as gravity regained control. A well-crafted and beloved canvas lost its frame.

Both fell to the floor with a loud rip.

Johnny's unfortunate face poked through the tear at the lady's neck.

"Look what ya' done to my mother's portrait!" The Captain bellowed.

Johnny, dazed, blearily saw a red blur rushing down the staircase.

Panic seized his tiny mind. The boy fought free of the picture frame, leaving a trail of tatters as he dashed away, honking louder than a frightened goose.

Claire spoke through her hand in disbelief, "He hit me?"

One of Samantha's iron rods had pierced through a floorboard gap. She struggled to stand, but nothing could release the pressure blocking her throat. One hand waved for help.

Blood spilled from Claire's broken nose. Down her lips, her chin, and spilling on her pregnant belly. Sweet Pine's real princess erupted with indignant rage, *"He! Hit! Me!"*

"Don't leave me like this, Claire!" Samantha croaked with her last breath. But there was no calling her sister back. Not now—maybe not ever. Claire stormed off towards a fight. All of Samantha's fight slowly drained. Her brown hair sagged against the wedged collar. Pressing against her windpipe. The world blurred around her. *If you let go,* Samantha heard through the gathering darkness, *you'll finally see Mama again.*

July 1867

THE BELL ABOVE THE front door clanged. Some fool
made a fatal mistake and opened it. All hell broke loose.
Black powder exploded at everything that moved. A white
shirt reddened. The fella in it dropped down the staircase
harder than a boy in a basket.

Frank checked his cylinder. "Do inventory. Take a
broom to the place. Any dandy-dude ya find..." He reloaded, "...dead or alive, show em the light."

Gunfire was constant as the Lovecock gang moved room
to room, collecting women and smoking the men on the
spot. The Wayne brothers emerged from upstairs. Each
held a young girl against their will. No more than six or
seven years old—still clad in nightgowns despite the length
of the day. The brothers dumped the kids beside the red
shirt man. Soon they were joined by their mother, an older
sister, and a housemaid. An Irishman produced a length
of washing line cord and bound all together at the wrist.
With enough line left over to include all ankles save for the
oldest daughters.

She wouldn't be subdued so easily.

Her foot found the red-headed brute's knee with
enough spite it temporarily hobbled him. She cursed and
kicked again. Her nightgown fell open from the effort.

The Irishmen took her ankles—each in hand. The older sister fought it, but she soon tired. Ankles met her earlobes. The Irishman boomed wild odes to his homeland as he mounted. Unmoved by loud shrieking protests around him. First one hand and then the other clutched the girl's neck. He squeezed and snuffed her screams. Her eyes bulged. Face radiated sunset heat and broadcast panic. The mother cried, "Stop! *You're killing her!*"

A fellow countryman stood nearby, awaiting his turn, and took the initiative. The mother's nightgown flipped over her head, and she went face down to the floor and his knife cut through her bloomers easier than a Christmas goose and the two men cheered each other on as they enforced their advantage. These horrid battle whoops were barely audible over the cacophony, rattling through the rest of the house.

Elsewhere, the killers moved lighting quick. Drawers spilled what-not everywhere. Cabinets rifled through and abandoned with doors ajar. Upstairs, Kid Nobody knifed each mattress, emerging like a savage demon clouded in feathers. On the landing, Angel Ojete dueled with a grandfather clock. Broken gears and chimes punctuated the chaos. During this vulgar display of power, Chance limped in.

Frank saw him and spat and called above the noise, "Where ya been, pretty boy?"

Chance's mug was paler than a piano's keys. He saw Frank's gun pointed loosely in his direction and then met the boss's eyes. "Andrews told me to see to a boy."

"Boy?" Frank answered back.

Chance nodded towards the well-house.

Frank stroked his talisman. "Go and fetch him. We're collecting skulls."

Chance started to move then turned back.

"Bring him in here?"

"Aye."

Chance stammered, "I-I-I...can't."

Frank turned his head. "*Can't?* Can't never could, you *will* or you *won't*. And if you won't, then we have a *serious problem*."

By now, Doc Buie returned, dragging a dead girl by her blonde locks. Dropped her next to the growing pile. Her ears, breasts and nose long gone.

Chance swallowed. "The boy's down a hole. You want him—fetch him from the well yourself. I ain't going back out there."

Frank clucked his tongue.

Doc Buie raised an eyebrow. "*Why'd you put him in the well?*"

Chance let him have it. "Had to act quick. Figured if I shot the bastard, it might make too much noise. Instead, I sent the bally fool to Jericho." He gestured to the walls. "Now? Dunno why I even bothered. Ya'll could wake Lazarus."

Frank snorted a laugh and revealed his missing back teeth.

"*How deep was it?*" Doc Buie raised the other eyebrow. "What I mean is...How long until you heard the *splash*?"

"Dunno," Chance spat, "Reckon he's still falling. Didn't wait around to learn different."

Frank and Doc shared a suspicious glance.

"When we conclude our business," Doc Buie said, "show me this well-house. May have a few more things to stash."

"Find it yourself. Straight out the back door. Can't miss it." Chance licked his dry lips. "Like I said...ain't going back out there."

Doc and Frank lingered on Chance. Doc Buie exhaled knowingly, "Killing people ain't as easy as you thought it would be...huh pretty boy?"

Chance cocked his head—cold steel for eyes. "No..." Chest pumped air. "Actually, the opposite. It's too easy." Eyes met Frank's. "Now where in tarnation is this gold we've been promised? Ain't that the whole reason for this horseshit?"

Doc Buie laughed heartily, "Think we're about to find out."

Angel Ojete appeared at the top of the staircase. "We've turned this place out. Other than a few heirlooms, *there's no gold.* Not like the rumors said."

Doc Buie flashed anger. "Where's that broom-tail banker?"

The teller had stashed himself near a far wall. Figuring it was a safe place to observe the chaos. Upon hearing his name, he stood. Doc Buie pulled him over to the clump of survivors. "Ask these bitches where the chiseler keeps it."

"M-m-miss..." the teller's voice cracked. "Give'em what they want."

One of the Irishmen refastened his suspenders and pulled the mother's nightgown off her head so she could answer. Then extended more chivalry by helping her sit upright.

The teller asked about the Captain's gold. The woman refused to answer. The teller tried again.

She shook. Traumatic rage boiled in her face. "Dunno of any gold."

The teller asked again. The mother spat in his face. "Look around you. Look at this place. Do you think if we had any gold, this place would look like this? The Yankees took everything. You evil jink-gobblers took the rest."

"Now miss," Doc Buie chimed in, "we have on good authority the Captain recently transferred his accounts...here."

"The Captain?" The woman asked, confused, "Do you mean *Captain Jakes?*"

"The same."

Tears welled in her red eyes. Lips trembled as she spoke, "For some no count son-of-a-bitch you've broken into our home and ravaged our family!" She laughed pure spite, "Dunno whose authority said this was the Jake's place, but they was wrong-wrong-WRONG!"

Chance's guts bubbled with dread. He knew it before she said it, "Our. Name. Is. *Cobb*. Captain Jakes lives on the opposite end of Sweet Pine road."

The teller's mouth yawned surprise. All eyes bore witness to his shock. The teller bolted—straight at the front door. Angel Ojete's gun gave chase—peeling off three rounds in quick succession. *Blam! BLaM! BLAM!* The third caught the banker's hip and sent him bleating like a goat to a worn rug. The door—his escape—only an arm stretch away. Angel Ojete, flanked by the two Irish assholes, approached. The teller's hand found an Irishman's boot-heel. Agony screamed. The boot twisted. There was a pop. Fingers separated from knuckles. His executioners, leaving no good deed unpunished, took it personally and their time finishing him off. The louder he screamed, the worse it got.

Then it happened.

Wood on the front door splintered.

All heads snapped in the direction of the noise.

It happened again. Followed this time by breaking glass.

One of the Irish rapists grabbed for his throat. Eyes wide. Blood gurgled between fingers. Confusion gushed across his face. The celt sank just as another round ripped through the house. It deflected off a column and buried itself just above Frank's black hat.

Their leader found the nearest window. Slammed his fist against the wallpaper. Turned to them incredulously, "Boys...don't know how but them bushwhackers found us."

Chance's world shrank as every gun in Shermanburg, Texas, took aim at one of the houses on Sweet Pine Road.

Early Summer 1867

Sweet Pine — The Last Day: Part Two

Hateful sounds echoed up the walls from downstairs. Each vicious lick of the razor strap was unaccompanied by a scream. Samantha teetered—edging closer to that big sleep.

"He's killing him Claire..."

Only a *few more* seconds now and finally sweet release. Samantha hadn't wanted her demise to come so soon. Especially not like this, here—*in the very middle of the Jakes master bedroom...*

Eyes blinked open. Everything rushed into focus. Electric and primal—her heartbeat marched against her eardrums. An arm twitched. Then flopped over in one last desperate attempt to save the rest of the body. Her fingers inched under her jaw and collar. Just enough to open the windpipe again. She braced her body against the apparatus.

"I'll be jinxed," Samantha croaked. She looked around in disbelief. "Middle of the room?"

There was only one explanation.

The bastard hadn't been exceptionally drunk the night before. *Could she be lucky enough for an oversight?* Being a military man, after all. Everything structured with clockwork precision. Even his nightly intake of whiskey. *Had he forgotten to lock her chain?*

Opportunity knocked—it wasn't much—but enough to answer the door. Bunching her knees to her chest, she reeled in her permanent tether. Silver coiled below the golden rings without stopping until...*she couldn't believe her eyes.* The fabled loose end rattled free between her fingers. A third wind inflated her bladder. Something else filled it with grit. What was once weary, awakened. Samantha gripped the stuck iron rod and rocked back and forth. Back and forth until the motherfucker budged. Slowly, with each thrust, the rod budged a little more.

Captain Jakes panted over the limp boy. The bastard spat and yanked up one of Johnny's legs. The boy trailed the bastard down the hall. Unconscious head knocked each step up the creaking staircase. Steady bouncing brought the boy somewhat back to life. Head swam—dazed and confused. Tiny body—all of it—hummed in a tabernacle of pain. No fighting this trip down the balcony boards, towards the attic door. Where Captain Jakes flung him into darkness.

Click! The Captain turned slowly around. When he saw her standing there, he stiffened. She always had that effect on him. "A gal in your precious condition shouldn't be lifting such *heavy* things."

"You broke my nose," Claire shouldered the shotgun awkwardly.

"If your nose is broken, Honey Pie," a shadow passed over his face. "Guess you shouldn't be sticking it where it don't belong."

He moved towards her.

Claire's voice cracked. "Take another step and I'll *shoot!*"

The Captain laughed. "Don't believe you will, darling."

"Swear you'll be graveyard dead!"

Her words meant nothing. "Hand it over now and I'll forgive this trespass. A woman blessed with child often becomes hysterical. *Loss of all rationale.* You can't help it none. Tis the curse of your sex. Mankind pays dearly for the sins of Eve. Always has..." His face flattened. "Now gimme that dod-gasted boomer."

Claire screamed only vowels and squeezed the trigger.

Click! Click! Nothing but clicks. Claire's face contorted. *Why hadn't it gone off?*

The Captain laughed louder than a battlefield. "You think I'd keep a loaded gun with your idgit brother running around free as spring jack rabbit?"

He snatched the long gun faster than Claire could react. Its buttstock struck her chin. Feet lost the floor. Spittle and blood flew. He raged and yanked her by the hair and wrist. Feet flailed beneath the nightgown. Sparks flew across her vision. The Captain's fingers dug into her hair. He pulled. Claire was dazed. She saw the ceiling change to dark and dusty boards. All light disappeared as the bastard shut the attic door—locked it—and brought the buttstock down hard. The brass doorknob rolled away.

In the darkness of the attic staircase, Claire slowly realized what had happened. From behind the attic door, the

Captain mocked her futile screams for help and farted an exclamation.

Samantha heard everything perched next to the wall. Trying her best to keep perfectly still. She didn't want the *god forsaken* bells chiming. The Captain was shuffling back towards the bedroom. Prepared, she figured, to dish out more punishment—exert more ruthless control—torture her until he felt satisfied.

Little did he suspect, Samantha wouldn't play along *anymore.*

Footfalls slowed to a complete stop just outside. Close enough, Samantha could smell his musk. "What in the blue hell?" He murmured over the liquid puddle on the floor. She couldn't tell if it was enough room or not. Her frantic mind raced. All she needed was one clear shot. If her aching muscles faltered or if she missed entirely, it would close her storybook for good—*no doubt about it.* The chamber pot weighed heavy between her sweating palms. She'd coiled her silver pubic chain inside the pot to weigh it down. It had worked a little too well, as she now feared losing her grip.

"Piddle? What in the hell..."

Papa's words between her ears, *When trouble comes, Sammie Jane you can't waste...*

She went for it.

In one fluid move, Samantha lifted the makeshift cudgel overhead and twisted around the doorway. Bells chimed her arrival. Already some of the loose contents cascaded out. But it didn't matter. Past the point of no return. She shouted and leaned into her forward momentum. Swinging the heavy basin down with all her might.

The bastard saw it coming a split-second too late. Porcelain and chain-links exploded on impact. Two white shards cut paper thin lines in the pads of each hand. Her front foot slipped out from under her. Sending her sprawling over Captain Jakes and the nasty mess. Just managing to catch herself on the balustrade from toppling over and falling. Quicker than a flash, she scrambled awkwardly back around to face him. Head swimming from exertion—catching her breath—hands bleeding on the banister. Captain Jakes remained face down in the urine-soaked wood.

Maybe it's a trap, she thought. And waited for him to move. When he didn't stir, she asked, "Master?"

No response.

She said his full name.

Still nothing.

Samantha shouted, "You alive bastard?"

Not a flinch.

Tentative relief washed over her. After months of unspeakable humiliations, now Samantha would taste the revenge she desperately craved.

The pubic chain trailed as she raced towards the Captain's study. The Encyclopedia Britannica lay exactly where she'd left it. Its secret remained unmolested inside. Samantha pictured herself opening the attic door and immediately introducing Claire's pregnant belly to Papa's Navy Colt. Her sister and the Captain's evil spawn would die a slow and painful death, together. *It would have to be slow,* Samantha thought, *the only way to forgive all that had happened.* She watched with glee as her mind conjured images of Claire's deceptive ass writhing in agony. And Sam, laughing with cold menace, would ask, *Who's the dumb cunt now?*

July 1867

Trapped — Beg, Borrow, or Steal

LOCAL BOYS SURROUNDED THE Cobb plantation. Laying siege all afternoon. Now, the Gatling Gun smoked emptier than a drunken promise. Sunset pierced the dump with forty-five caliber shafts of light. Dread filled each outlaw inside, unable to hide completely among these odd shadows. Outside, some fool lit a torch. It touched another and then another and now flames on sticks encircled them. Too many to count without leaving yourself open for a musket-man to say both hello and goodbye with one trigger pull.

Chance checked his revolver in the dim—one round left.

A grumble outside told Chance the mob had wearied of the standoff. A fat fella stood on a wagon and called aloud, "Frank! Come out now with ye hands up or prepare ye soul for hell."

"C'mon along with it!" Frank hissed. "I'll set a table for all y'all sons-of-bitches!"

Frank stroked the talisman around his neck and whistled at Doc Buie. Who nodded, then looked down with delirious glee. The last surviving hostage—a girl of no more than six, still just a baby—knelt trembling at his boots. Her exhausted face, reddened with teary wet, could not be clearly seen in the gathering dark.

Light flashed as Angel Ojete handed over his blade.

Chance closed his eyes. No need to witness her senseless slaughter. Could've. Would've. Should've. If he wasted his last bullet on Doc Buie, he and the little girl would both be slaughtered for the trouble. Careers cannot be made, nor retirements enjoyed by martyrs. The dying days of Andersonville could not quench the bloodthirsty Captain Wirz. Everyone was worthy of the rope if he judged it so. Cousin Lloyd's fresh memory asked, *"Can the Good Lord above send you to hell for all you didn't do as easily as all you'd did?"*

Doc Buie's voice bellowed skyward. Strange incantations followed. Something about "demons...dark lords...an abyss...a sacrifice...a rescue."

Chance's reopened eyes blinked in terror.

Angel Ojete, Kid Nobody, and Frank encircled Doc and the little girl. Whimpering in the shadows around their boots. The men chanted. Low, at first, but building to a definite crescendo. Limbs gyrated with Pentecostal abandoned. Eyeballs, heavy lidded, and blacker than a volcano's obsidian glass. Mouths foamed with passionate glossolalia.

It happened so fast, Chance felt out of his own body.

The little girl yelped. Doc Buie stiffened. Blade slashed.

Chance heard himself holler, "Let her go!"

All heads snapped in his direction.

Goosebumps rippled. This was it. Doom had hunted him for twenty-four years, and now it stepped forward to collect his pelt. Chance clutched his Dragoon's handle, ready to pull it for the last time. Frank's dark face passed through pinholes of light as he approached. But it didn't see Chance. Those black eyes never wavered as they reflected torch light flickering through the broken window.

Frank whistled triumphantly, "Finish the ritual Doc and let's light a shuck! The Calvary's here."

Torches congregated in the front yard. Tension, which had been high since the night before the ambush, erupted into a scuffle between the bushwhackers and a newly arrived platoon of Union blues. From what little Chance could tell, their dispute involved the posse's use of the Gatling gun. Apparently, it had been borrowed without asking and the Yankees wanted it back. Not caring alick about the Lovecock gang or the path of destruction they'd left behind in Shermanberg.

Some damn fool took umbrage at the Yankee's rudeness. Couldn't these bastards see they were in the middle of something important? Well, one thing led to another, and someone slapped down the gauntlet. Which created a peculiar miracle for the Lovecock gang.

A bold bushwhacker unloaded at a cavalry officer. That was all she wrote. The stand-off's stand-off erupted into all out combat. Chance found his knees. His knees found the floor. Stray bullets ripped through. At once, the torches flew. Bouncing around the two-story tinderbox. Everywhere flames rose. Smoke thickened. Chance hacked and choked and crawled low to escape it. He saw Frank, Doc Buie, Angel Ojete and Kid Nobody fighting over the little girl's dead body. Their mouths smeared dark with the child's blood.

The Wayne brothers appeared above, holding a rug. Using it for cover, they drew iron. The outlaws breached the back door. All around them, the Civil War raged on again.

Chance followed the Wayne's outside. Un-aimed bullets zipped overhead. Over his shoulder, Andrews stumbled into view. If Chance had known it was the last he'd see him alive, he'd have given him the finger. Scatters of gunfire ripped through the Tasmanian. A tangled marionette jerked by strings, side to side.

Behind them, fire engulfed the house—four dark shapes moved through the flames—beams overhead snapping and breaking as the roof caved. Sparks followed black smoke skyward.

Chance limped for the woods. Each step gored his groin. He concentrated on a distant beacon of hope. Ahead of him, tiny specs of light flickered. Maybe a house, or a nearby community. Something better than the flaming wreck behind him.

Chance stepped forward in the darkness.

Boots never landed. Head and feet tumbled through empty air. Plunging him—end over end—then a cold *splash! Could've...Would've...Should've.*

Early Summer 1867

Keys twisted in locks. Shackles fell free. Wrists, ankles, and neck itched in the warm air. Samantha opened the Captain's closet. Fingers traced the gray wool of his service uniform. It still looked new—dang near store-bought. Had it never seen a battle? Tailored for a man, the coat actually complimented her lack of figure by sculpting her narrow shoulders. And the best part of the Captain's coat, Samantha thought excitedly, was an abundance of pockets. She wiped a bloodied hand across the mirror to see herself better. Who stared back, she wondered. And lifted her silver chain for closer inspection. She considered her options. None jumped out as easy or preferable.

Papa's words between her ears, *Needs must as the devil drives.*

Hands ran front to back, wrapping silver around her waist. Safe keeping until it could be removed later. She tied it off in a half-seamstress knot. Then stepped one foot at a time into the Captain's trousers. Unlike the coat, these needed suspenders and had no pockets. Except for the girlish length of her dirty hair, she might pass for a rumpled soldier. Not nearly as rumpled as that lost Yankee who wandered in hungry three years ago and stole more than a bowl of stew.

"Move back or die where you stand!" Papa's Navy Colt bucked. Wood splintered behind the smoke. A slight tingle buzzed between her legs. Samantha waved all of it away and saw she'd missed. About a finger width from the deadbolt. *It's to be expected,* she told herself. After all, *you hadn't fired a gun in about a year and a half.* The Yankee's dirty, leering face sprang from memory. Samantha shook it off. And cocked the gun again—aimed higher—barrel floating slightly to the left. The unbalanced Colt heavy as the adrenaline surged, then ebbed—fatigue setting in. Holding it with both hands, she squeezed once more.

Misfire. "Damn..."

Muted shouts from the other side.

Samantha called back, "Hold your horses!"

Barrel dipped as both thumbs worked the hammer.

Kablam!

Another tingle, pleasantly warm, tickled her belly. Samantha enjoyed this strange sensation. But when she inspected the door, disappointment came. The bullet had missed again.

Grip tightened. Trigger pulled. She swooned as if falling from the rush between her thighs. The bullet hit the iron knob plate. Ricocheted at a strange angle. And vanished somewhere in the walls of Sweet Pine. The spasms, three this time, subsided. She caught her breath. "Dueces."

If she kept wasting bullets, she'd have none left to shoot Claire. Frustration boiled. Now her barrel stuck directly against the wall. Both of Samantha's hands clutched the pistol. Eyes closed. She squeezed.

Kaboom!

It kicked back so hard she nearly dropped the hot iron. That strange pleasure surged. Samantha couldn't help herself and moaned. The ravaged door squealed open in response. Samantha ejaculated victoriously. One hand held aloft, punching through the gunsmoke.

The good feeling didn't last.

Claire's swollen nose emerged in her afterglow. Her voice was just as crooked. "Who in the name of God do you think *you're shooting at?*"

Samantha raised the Colt and spoke firm, "Hands over head, bitch."

Claire's eyes dimmed into points. "You wouldn't dare...not your own sister."

"Not just you." Samantha levelled the hog's leg at Claire's midriff. "Now do as you're told."

JULY 1867

Pre-dawn — Cold Water

Mud squeezed between Chance's fingers. This wet animal clawed itself onto the riverbank, emerging with Darwinian prehistory, and flopping on his back—coughing and choking yet somehow still alive.

The outlaw gulped big air. Completed a crude inventory and wiggled his toes. Thankfully, boots remained on both feet. When he reached for his gun—nothing. Lost and already rusting somewhere beneath the Sabine River. Chills vibrated his flesh. Fatigue jumbled his mind. Eyes closed. *Only for a moment,* he thought, *gotta keep moving. Don't pass out...Don't pass...don't...*

He sagged asleep.

Beyond the ether, a familiar voice said, *"Can the Good Lord above send you to hell for all you didn't do as easily as all you did?"*

Chance raised on his elbows—groggy eyed and head still between dimensions. *"Lloyd?"*

"Don't be sore, Chance..." his cousin said, "had a gal at the livery write home to Granny."

"You shouldn't've wrote no letter."

Clouds parted above. Moonlight shone. Chance rubbed his eyes. Unsure why his dead cousin now stood in the river.

Lloyd's voice was soft and watery, "...had a gal at the livery write home to Granny and told her what we was a-doing. Didn't want her worrying..."

"Must be dreaming," Chance tried to stand, but his groin howled. Chance collapsed. Found a nearby stick and let it fly—expecting it to sail straight through the illusion. To his horror, the stick broke in two on Lloyd's left shoulder. Both halves splashed into the drink and washed away in the night.

Chance sucked air. Lloyd's boot diggers remained bone dry, floating above the surface. "*Can the Good Lord above send you to hell...*" Clouds recovered the moon. The world fell silent. "*...for all you didn't do as easily as all you did?*"

"He made all the rules..." Chance said. "...so, I reckon he can do whatever."

Somewhere a cricket chirped, then another, and another. Soon the riverbank's natural symphony returned. It made him feel less lonely yet did nothing to calm his nerves.

The sun and moon began their inevitable exchange of places. First light gave him a better view. Chance rolled on his belly—crawled over to a deadfall tree—climbed on and sat and felt skewered. Took a quick breath and fought against the pain to remove his boots. Upending each one to drain in turn. Tossed the pair aside. Next came his shirt. Sopping wet and clingier than a homely gal. Lloyd spoke behind him, *"Don't be sore Chance..."*

Neck hair prickled. Couldn't turn around. Too afraid to see the hole between the eyes. The very same Chance gifted Lloyd two days ago.

"Shouldn't've wrote no letter..." Chance's eyes locked on moving water. "...but I'll forgive you...if you'll forgive me."

"Can the Good Lord above..."

Chance cursed and grated and yanked the wet shirt off. "Put you out of your misery, didn't I? You'd show a lame horse mercy, wouldn't ya? I ain't the one who squealed about Frank's plans. That's your burden, not mine."

"...just as easily as all you did?"

Shirt stretched between hands. Water bubbled and squeezed with each twist. "I swear cousin," Chance rang out his shirt, "Done ya a straight favor. No way in hell's half acre Lloyd Ironsides could have handled Sherman-berg. Slaughterhouses are more humane."

"Can the Good Lord above send you to hell..."

Chance gripped both knees. "If this is about that little gal...you're right...should've, could've, would've...alright *ya happy?"*

Lloyd's mantra repeated again and again *and again.* Echoed Chanting. Glossolalia of a million tongues fluttering incessantly. Chance feared he'd go insane. A heartbeat, not his own, went *bump-bump-bump.* He wanted to draw iron and blaze at will—shoot the very dawn from the sky. But he knew he couldn't. Trapped here by circumstance—by breeding—by his own poor choices. Knew he wasn't more than human. A small thing whose days were numbered. One day, maybe now, death would stop lending more time. And at that exact moment, two things would occur: regret for a wasted life—*every minute*—and Chance would want another of his namesakes. And second lives were rarer than albino midgets. The outlaw folded his arms and gripped his elbows. Cosmic weight heavy on his soul. "I'm sorry for shooting you, Lloyd...And...for not helping that little gal. I made a mistake."

Still the cousin droned on. This hellish hum cast a heavy spell of static noise. An ancient and primally cosmic roar. As if buried under the ocean for eons.

"What about that boy? Huh Lloyd? They wanted me to execute him...but I didn't...got him alone and told him to run for help. And sure as shooting, he done it. You can't haunt me for that one, Lloyd. *Confessed everything! Sent him screaming for the law!* Saved him by gum."

A different voice spoke and startled Chance. He didn't want to turn around.

"Thought we heard someone's jaw a-wobblin," Elias Wayne drawled. "Fancy finding it to be yours, *pretty boy.*"

SUMMER 1867

DIVISIONS OF REVENGE — SWEET PINE IN THE AFTER GLOW

SAMANTHA LED THE BITCH to the barn. Inside, Buttercup whinnied at their intrusion. She pointed the gun at the far corner. Claire walked over and stood there, dumbfounded. After a long look, she spoke to her feet, "This thing meant for me?"

Oh, the chirps of little birds.

Samantha gestured for Claire to open it and said, "Not everything is about *you*, sister."

"Whaddaya want with this dusty old thing?"

Samantha laughed. "Don't you recognize it?"

Claire swore she didn't.

"Mama's inside," Samantha said. Keeping her face as flat as possible. "We can't leave her behind. She's going with us."

"Mama? Going?" Samantha's plan slowly dawned on Claire. "You're crazy."

"Thinking California," Samantha said. "Or maybe Colorado. Mama would've wanted to be buried near Clara—near family."

Claire's curiosity opened the lid. And her jaw dropped. "Oh my god."

Samantha Jakes nee Gray stood over her husband. Papa's Navy Colt wanted her to pull the trigger. It called in an oily twang, *Please Sammie, squeeze me tight. Make the gunsmoke come. You deserve it. Go on, it's your birthday.* Shooting the gun did feel extremely good. Better than riding an untamed mustang through the woods and over the ether. Papa's words between her ears, *Careful what you wish for Sammie Jane, you might just get it.* Terrible advice, she reasoned. Isn't getting what you want paramount to suffering? Isn't this what the Taoist heathen always wanted? Pull the trigger and blast off into enlightenment.

Why, the very idea.

Three words, 'not like this,' eased the hammer back down. Click! Click! Click!

The potency of Papa's Navy Colt was beyond her wildest imagination. A bullet to his sleeping skull was too easy. She thought of Johnny. All the hurts. His lacerated body. Her own vile modifications. His triumph of will. The man at her boots deserved to die. And she deserved to guide him there.

Beneath her coat, the pubic chain rattled. Inspiration came. The thirty-six found Claire.

Claire knew—Samantha knew—she wouldn't refuse.

Samantha didn't know how long it took to maneuver the bastard into position, but once the labor and delivery ended, the light outside begun to die. Had the whole day passed already?

"You just gonna leave him here?" Claire asked. "He'll starve to death. *You can't Sam!*"

Can't never could, you will or you won't. Samantha didn't say a word. Simply unbuttoned the trousers and let the silver cascade down. The fine handcrafted metal shined between her fingers. Stretched between hands.

Fear and loathing in Claire's shaky voice, "What are you fixing to do?"

Samantha twisted her wrist. Caught Johnny's misshapen eyes, somewhere between an acorn and a goat. She knew—he knew—she knew what he wanted.

Samantha smiled, "Johnny Samson Gray...this first lick is for you."

Chain twirled. Whipping through the air overhead. Arm swung. Metal flashed. Whip cracked. Joy blossomed. The Captain barely quaked as red chain links marred his naked back. Claire protested. Her thin pleas felt so good, Samantha did it again. It was her birthday, after all, and each whiplash exploded inside her like dynamite.

JULY 1867

CHANCE TURNED SLOW AS the sunrise. "Elias...Ezekiel...glad to see you made it out alive."

Elias Wayne stepped forward. Unsure if they shared the sentiment. "Go on...you was a-saying something about confessing? Ain't that right, brother? Was just a confessing loud as all get out."

The bigger one scratched his neck beard, "How it sounded to me alright."

Elias slapped the back of his hand and rubbed, "D'ya pull horns, pretty boy?"

Chance shook his head. "Dunno what you mean."

Elias grimaced and slapped the back of his neck. Looked briefly at his palm before wiping clean on his shirt. "Your dumb face may work on womenfolk and lecherous punks like Doc Buie. But I seen through it from the start. You ain't no rough-and-ready nothing. And worst of all..." His arms outstretched, "We could all be dividing shares right now and getting our pricks licked by big-tiddied whores..." His hands squeezed at large invisible breasts.

Ezekiel guffawed, then slapped his own neck twice.

Elias sneered, "...instead we're getting our blood sucked by river skeeters cause you and your water-headed cousin started listening to angels on your shoulders." Elias shook his head. "What should honest men do with those who ain't trusted?"

"Depends," Ezekiel slapped at a mosquito that landed on his cheek. It left a smear of blood. "Some would say kill em where they stood. But I prefer letting em live."

Elias raised an eyebrow at Chance, "Awful charitable of you, big brother. You wouldn't punish an oath-breaker?"

"Now I didn't say that," Ezekiel chuckled low and pulled his knife. Angling the blade at Chance and drawling, "I think we should make it so no one ever mistrusts your dumb face again."

Instinctively, Chance stood—reached for his hip. His shooting hand came up empty. Pain sizzled through his torso. His knees weakened. He was in no shape for fight or flight.

"Unarmed's a bad way to keep living," Elias snickered. "You doing the honors?"

"Nah," Ezekiel said and offered him the knife handle, "pretty sure your spelling of traitor's better than mine any hour of the day."

Ezekial Wayne was incredibly quick for a large man. A big blur seized Chance between hairy biceps. Criss-cross-apple sauce behind his neck. A hold he couldn't get a wiggle on.

"Now stay still," Elias smiled. "Wouldn't want my hand to slip now, would ya?"

Chance spat, "Drill your hole *AND* the one that made the two of you!"

Elias's face contorted with savage glee. "Oh, I'm gonna enjoy this...so much so I may not know when to quit." Gripped Chance's chin tight. Knife—nose high. Elias's eyes were deader than your cherished baby-doll's. An apex predator who'd caught the scent of blood.

Chance could only dangle from Ezekiel's grip. He braced for the coming sting. Felt the blade tip press his forehead. Lloyd's voice chanted loudly in his ears, "Can the good lord..."

"Do it brother!" Ezekiel cheered. "Show em the price squealers pay to stay alive."

The lunatics laughed as if—knowing their victim excited them more than meeting a stranger. Chance's spine felt the big fella's stiffening erection. Were they both aroused each time they put the hurt on someone? If so, it wouldn't have surprised Chance. Why else would they love it so?

A peculiar noise halted Elias from digging in. He turned riverside and said, "Company."

Chance couldn't move his head well. He heard a strange panting. On the periphery—he saw what could only be described as a small child, perhaps a boy—flailing wild and mute as the current pulled him swiftly down river.

December 1867

Slag crunched under Samantha's boot-heels. Breath fogged over her shoulder. She moved steadily through another crisp Colorado dawn—coming face to face again with pure danger. She'd barely bested him before. Frank Lovecock rasped, "Don't uncork no bronc. Your boy's safe. For now."

In the gospel, according to the Gentleman's Etiquette book, *make your share of conversation modest and brief, and avoid long speeches and tedious stories.* Samantha spat on the crumbled rock path and said nothing. They'd hear from her soon enough. Pictured the barn. Trader Sheridan's old dynamite sweating inside Mama's coffin, keeping all that glitters company. Shrapnel for the bomb.

"D'ya hear me, Mrs. Jakes?" Frank fumed and stroked the talisman. "Boy's just fine. But won't be long if'n we don't settle terms. Now I want what we come fer."

In the gospel, according to the Gentleman's Etiquette book, *Speak of yourself but little. Your friends will find out your virtues without forcing you to tell them, feel confident that it is equally unnecessary to expose your faults yourself.* Frank's hand rested near his pistol. "Shouldn't have come to this...you should've parlayed square back in

Dallas. Everyone would still be alive if'n'ya hadn't made me chase you across God's country."

"That's your mistake, Frank," Samantha smiled. "No one told you to follow."

Frank whistled low. "Let's not drag this out any longer. When I give the signal—the boy dies. You've lost. Hand over my gold, right now, and he lives."

"What's to keep you from killing him afterwards?" Samantha just needed to keep him talking. Lovecock hadn't noticed the periphery. Hadn't smelled the smoking fuse. Wondered if he would before...*kaboom*.

Frank squinted and hissed, "Gonna have to trust me."

"Show me he's alright," Samantha licked her dry lips, "and I just might."

Frank stuck two fingers in his mouth and whistled. Behind him barn doors opened.

Samantha's blood chilled—bless her heart—the patron saint of lost causes. Been exalted as such ever since failing to put a bullet in the Captain's cruel face. If she killed Frank now, would she be officially canonized with redemption and break the devil's hex?

She'd been prepared to die since leaving Dallas. Now—second and third thoughts.

She might save the boy's life, sure—but could this sinner be forgiven for not saving her own?

JULY 1867

NOTHING LIKE NEW FRIENDS — A GOOD SAMARITAN

SAMANTHA LOST CONTROL OF the mule. The rest of the wagon followed. Crashing through patches of saplings, lurching over stumps, and rattling the teeth of everyone on board. Whip-thin branches lashed out, then vanished from all sides. Buttercup cared not. Flat ground disappeared beneath its hooves. That sinking feeling swelled. Down they slid into the muck of the river the natives named Sabine. Muddy water sprayed on impact. The mule heed and hawed and stamped its hooves.

Something upset it good.

While the dumb beast bucked and cried, everyone heard a loud cracking pop. A wagon wheel snapped, dipping the rig riverside. Mama's coffin shifted and collided against Johnny. Tumbling the boy out of his bedroll and into the drink. *Splash!*

"The river!" Claire screamed, "Sam! It's taking him!"

Papa's voice between her ears, *when trouble comes Sammie Jane, you can't waste time on fear.*

The boy thrashed. Head dipped below only to breach again and grew smaller and smaller as the current pulled. Her little brother couldn't swim a lick. Samantha had seen enough and dove in fully clothed.

Cold water slapped the exhaustion from her. Fast current gave no chance to plant feet and stand. His head was now barely a bump on the river. *Gotta move quick or you'll lose him.* Samantha paddled in quick arcs. Her boots kicked. Dawn and darkness battled across her vision. The current took them both around a bend of willows and slowed. Here her boots found the shallows. She got to her feet and yelped with fright. "Don't hurt him!"

Some giant stood calf deep in the river. Johnny thrashing between his arms. Neither of them was sure of the other's situation. The giant reared back to slap Johnny and Samantha bounded out of the water. "Please don't hurt him."

The sudden appearance of a person startled the giant, who nearly dropped the boy.

Johnny saw his sister and began reaching for her from behind the burly arms.

Samantha approached slowly. The giant scowled, "This...thing belong to you, Mister?"

"He's my brother," Samantha said. "And I'm a girl."

"Sorry, um...couldn't tell," then added, "This thing's someone's brother?"

She wanted to thank him for his help, but two shadows emerged behind him. Forming a strange triangle. The talker was just a smaller version of the giant and the other'n—wore the perfect face of a porcelain doll—feminine features so striking Samantha couldn't look at him. Her heart might burst. She'd never seen a man so beautiful in all her life. A moment passed, and she recovered. "Um...Thank you for saving him...our...our wagon it—"

Mr. Giant still hadn't let go of the boy. Johnny rasped and jerked wilder than an awkward puppy squirms. The giant looked over his shoulder at his smaller double, then back at her. "Why's he sound like that? He crippled or something?"

"Please...you're hurting him," Samantha said and felt in her pocket for Papa's Navy Colt. The heavy piece remained stowed right where she'd left it. Although she reckoned after the swim, the powder was too wet to do her any good.

"Despite your britches, you's a lady?" The small giant stepped forward. and smiled, but not with his eyes. His voice sounded roasted, ground and strained with chicory darkness. "You heard the lady Zeke, best put him down now."

His eyes never left Sam's. Zeke eyed Johnny and let him go. The boy thrashed over the water to Samantha. Thin arms hugged his sister's waist. She ran a hand over his misshapen head. From what she could tell, the boy seemed fine—Johnny's tolerance for misadventure continued to impress. With his arm in her hand, she said, "Thank you—we'll be on our way..."

"Hold on now," said the smaller man. "We didn't mean to startle you none. Especially, since it seems you's had such an awful fright yourself. Made mention of a wagon, did ya?"

Samantha glanced quickly between the three. Stepped back without answering. Feeling their eyes crawl over her.

"Zeke," said the small one, "step back, brother. You're making the lady nervous." He then doffed his dirty hat, in a move of borrowed gallantry. "Forgive my brother. He don't know much but what I tell him. I know he looks big and scary, but he's a gentle lamb in a grizzly's fur."

Hat hand landed on his chest, "Eli Wayne, my brother Zeke, you've met." He nodded over his shoulder. "That's our associate Mr. Glass." He laughed but didn't blink. "Do you believe in Jesus Christ?"

Samantha found the question odd but said she did.

"Mighty fine. Always good to find Christian charity, especially out in the wilderness." He paused. "You see, we're pilgrims." He elbowed the brother. "Heard there was some trouble this a-way and since we've dedicated our lives to serving the good lord above. He spoke to us..."

"He sure did," Zeke agreed. His eyes were on the boy.

"...told us head to Texas. Promised we'd find his path by serving others."

"Best of luck to all three of you," Samantha stepped back once more. The current bubbled around her and Johnny. "The proud South needs more folks like you."

"It's my brother's size, idn't?" Eli Wayne asked ruefully. "I thought the South wouldn't judge a white man the way they do up north. Don't fret, he's used to it. But just cuz you used to something don't mean it don't still sting." Eli shook his head slowly side to side. "Gentle souls heal quickly. We meant no offense to you and your...um, brother."

"I'm sorry," Samantha apologized, hoping it would free her from the situation. "Again, thank you kindly for your trouble...we best be getting on."

"Now hold on—hold on," Eli showed her his palm. Glanced at his brother and back to Samantha. The light of an idea behind his dark eyes. "Wasn't I just saying we needed a sign from the good lord to tell us which way to go next?"

Zeke nodded with dead-eyed slowness. "You sure were, brother."

"And next we know, here comes a child of god around the bend." Eli brayed with laughter. So loud it could be heard down river for three miles. He stepped towards Samantha. "I believe things happen for a reason, don't you?"

Samantha didn't respond.

"It would be our great honor..." He quickly added, "No, privilege—to assist you today."

Nowhere left for Samantha to retreat without the current dragging them both to Beaumont. She quickly scanned the riverbank behind the trio. A chill went up her spine in the simmering Texas dawn. "If you're traveling pilgrims like you say..." Samantha asked, "where's your horses?"

Eli nodded knowingly, but never took his eyes off her. "Our pilgrim's vow to only do good deeds is extended to beasts of burden as well. God blessed us with two feet a-piece, so we walk. Allow us to help you along—and I believe the good lord above will bless our hearts with salvation."

Papa's words between her ears, *only a fool refuses straight help when a curl binds.*

The gal and the unfortunate walked some distance ahead. Elias considered this safe from earshot. His knife gleamed. "Play along, pretty boy, or we finish what we started."

Ezekial guffawed, "My brother'll core your apple if'n ya don't."

"Want me to say thanks?" Chance eyed Elias's knife.

"Say nothing," Elias scowled. "Be as dumb as that gal's little idgit. If anyone asks. You're a pilgrim. I'm a pilgrim. This is a dad-blasted pilgrimage. Ain't no bag of nails. Understand?"

Chance hesitated. Elias took the silence as acceptance of terms. Turned to follow the urchins splashing ahead. Chance's voice halted him. "I ain't as useless as tits on a boar, you know."

Elias spat, "Sure as hell can't stay quiet, can you?"

He lowered his voice, "Following them kids without a plan is plumb bad." Chance showed them his palms in quiet protest. "Care to lemme know your first mind on the matter?"

"Why?" Ezekiel leered down, "Alerting the law again, fancy face?"

"Hush, Zeke," Elias stopped for a moment in thought. He checked over his shoulder, "Pretty boy's gotta point." He turned back to Chance. "Bitch's gotta wagon and a mule. It ain't classic Latin or nothing. We do what we do and take it off her hands—go find Frank and the gold."

You could hear the trouble before spotting it. Jackass was hee-hawing and kicking wildly against the leaning flatbed, unable to pull free from a busted wheel—like a snail trying to escape a crushed shell.

"Zeke!" Elias motioned for his brother to follow him towards a nasty mess of hooves and near swears. Chance hung back, happy to let them deal with the problem at hand. He knew one thing to be true: no matter what the brothers said or did, they were not about to let him, or anyone, leave this river valley alive.

"Snake-bit," Elias said after his brother had corralled the animal. "That's what done it."

"Ah!" A girl with a broken nose spoke as if she understood, "Snake-bit?"

"Just above yonder hoof," Elias pointed, "see the bloody swelling."

Chance ignored their animal husbandry. Performed his own survey. The wagon was in fine shape except for the heavy load. The axle stuck in the soft riverbank where the back wheel had slid off. Snapped off spokes jutted in various angles from the rim. But it still seemed usable. Then he saw the girl. Her nose may have been broken, but no doubt about it, the gal looked like heartbreak. She asked the dangerous outlaw, "Is it gonna kill our sweet Buttercup?"

"Depends on the snake doing the biting," Elias smiled. "Know much about snakes, young lady?"

The gal shook her head.

"Outside the one in the Good book," Elias leered, "I couldn't tell you a water moccasin from a cottonmouth. Miss...?"

She introduced herself as Claire and added, "You've already met my sister, Mrs. Jakes."

The ether vibrated between the strangers.

Chance cut his eyes at the Wayne's. Elias clicked his teeth, *"Jakes, you say?* Not married to Captain Jakes, is ya?"

All eyes landed on the gal in the Confederate coat.

Samantha buzzed with electric nerves. Hadn't expected to be found out this quickly and fumbled for words, "Why...y-y-yes...Know my husband?"

The short pilgrim licked his lips. Eyed his compatriots. "No ma'am. Just a famous name around these parts." He made an honorable gesture. "We shall attempt repairs." A lion roared in his grin, "And God willing, get you home by this afternoon."

"We're not going home," Samantha blurted out and immediately wished she hadn't. "I mean, not the route we're headed."

Eli gave her and his compatriots a side eye.

Samantha darted hers and spoke half a truth. "Our dearly departed mother. We're taking her for her final rest in...in..." Before Samantha could think of something, Claire blurted out, "We're going to Colorado territory. Boulder, to be exact. If you come across the good Captain—let him know you saw us, will ya?"

The trio glanced at the leaning coffin still strapped to the wagon's flatbed.

"A-mighty long journey," Elias said, rubbing the mule's flank. Scratching his fingernails as if trying to clean them in the shaggy brown coat. Fella seemed to be working things out. "You're going to attempt such an adventure without an escort?"

Samantha's face fell. Her hand touched the coat pocket. "Beg your pardon?"

"Meant no offense," Eli laughed, "And I'd never consider calling a lady a liar, but..."

"Sir, take much care with your next words," Samantha breathed fire. "You are speaking to Mrs. Elrod Jakes. And I will not be accused of such indecencies. Now my brother and sister and I, indeed, have a long journey ahead. We'd like to be on our way as soon as possible. You said you were willing to help...so help us, please."

Eli chuckled and patted his brother's shoulder. "Say no more, ma'am. It'll be our pleasure."

Mrs. Jakes led Claire and the unfortunate over to a shady spot under a tree. As good a perch as any to bird-dog the work. Elias pretended to point at the wagon's what-not, "Bitch still watching?"

Zeke nodded.

"I'm not a big believer in divine providence, but," Elias had that look in his eyes again. "...dumb luck sure feels good sometimes...don't it, boys? Can you imagine the look on ole Frank's face when we bring him the Captain's wife?"

"You think she's really a-married to that rich bastard?" Ezekiel asked.

"You saw the look on her face, didn't ye?"

"Aye," Ezekiel nodded.

"She may be homelier than pony's asshole," Elias said. "but the other'n...would go for three dollars back in Crescent city. If her nose weren't broke, that is. Hell, I say we each take a dollars' worth taking turns on that piece of slit, then kill her last."

"Look more like refugees than landed gentry," Chance said. "Dunno where they come from, but they sure as hell didn't hang fire to get here."

Elias shoulder-checked again. Mrs. Jakes was watching. He nodded and smiled, then said, "I don't give a dern about their tarndiddles." He spat into the river. Eyes shifted between Chance and his brother. "Let's get this wagon

fixed. Unload the um," He nodded at the coffin, "cargo."
His eyes found Chance. "The wheel at your feet, pretty
boy? Is she passable?"

Chance gave it a once over. "Missing a few spokes, but
the ring's still Simon pure. Mud the axle. Might hold the
better part of a day. Until we reach a smithy, that is."

Elias snapped, "Well, light a shuck then and hand her
over?"

Samantha watched the men conferring amongst themselves, pointing fingers, shaking heads, and what not. She
felt the nagging sting of anxiety as her mind raced. The
morning's events had given her a bad jolt. To think the last
two days had shown more promise than she could recall
since marrying the Captain.

Dread mounted. Exhausted eyes burned. Couldn't remember the last time she'd even slept.

Claire spoke low in Sam's ear, "Have you ever seen a
more beautiful man in your entire life?" She squealed,
"He's prettier-n-me!"

Samantha looked over at Johnny and frowned. "Best
get that wet off him. Don't need pneumonia on top of
everything else."

Claire added, "Get out your wet clothes, too, then, sister."

Samantha shot her with a look. "That dog won't hunt."

Claire rolled her eyes. "That's not what..."

Samantha wheeled around quick, "What's the big idea
giving away our plans to strangers?"

"Didn't know what else to say," Claire smiled. "You weren't doing nothing...as always."

"From now on—keep your mouth shut. Ain't no one's business what we do."

"You know we won't get far," Claire giggled.

"Hush your mouth."

"This whole trip's been cursed from the start," Claire smirked, voice rising. "I got a bad feeling about those men. You shouldn't have taken the Captain's gold. It's why we crashed. It's why that stinking mule's gonna die on us. You're too dumb to recognize—"

"Enough, Claire," Samantha reached out and gripped Claire's chin. She pulled her close. "We ain't at Sweet Pine no more."

"Last time I felt like this, you didn't listen then either." Claire huffed, then pulled free, "And look at all the mayhem you've caused."

"It is what it is," Samantha said. "Should be thanking me. You've still got blood in your veins. I ain't done with you yet." The thought of revenge curled her dried lips. "No ma'am. Not even close."

"Trust 'em being that close to Mama's coffin?" Claire folded her arms. "What you gonna do if'n they look in?"

"Trust 'em until I reckon I can't. Think we're safe enough." Her smile disappeared. "These simple pilgrims ain't about to upset the wife of the famous Captain Jakes. You heard em. About time the perks of being married to that son-of-a-bitch paid out. Besides," Samantha patted the pocket of her coat. "If they get too curious and wanna resurrect the dead, I'll introduce them to Papa's thirty-six." Samantha met her sister's glare with her own. She demanded, "Now get Johnny's clothes dried."

Claire started to complain then thought better of it.

Johnny didn't make it easy—he never did. Finally, she'd stripped him naked. Brownish-maroon bruises were spotted all over his shivering frame. A leopard's rash across his back was crusty with scabs. Claire wrapped the pink quilt around Johnny's bare ass and made him sit.

The trio watched the men struggle with the wagon.

"The pretty one must be the smart one," Claire said and giggled.

Samantha asked, "How can you tell just from looking?"

"Easy," Claire smiled. "He's letting the other two do all the work."

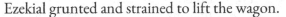

Ezekial grunted and strained to lift the wagon.

Elias held the wheel, waiting to rejoin it to the axle. "Little higher Zeke. Almost there."

Ezekial's neck cords tightened. His dark face blushed. He shook and sweat poured from his temples. Those big hands drained of color.

Elias cheered him on, "C'mon lift!"

The wagon was too much. Ezekiel gave out and dropped it. Tired hands found his knees, bending him over, trying to catch his breath.

Elias spat, disgusted. "You getting soft on me, Zeke?"

"Too heavy," Ezekiel rasped. "It's that coffin—gotta lighten the load—I can lift for certain, then."

Elias squinted. "Wanna dump the dead bitch out now?"

"Don't care how it's done," Ezekiel said, straightening his spine, slapping at his neck and then again on his arm. "Gogswobbing skeeters! Eating me alive."

"Alright brother," Elias set the wheel down and grabbed one of the coffin's handles. "Pretty Boy gonna hafta help, too. No way the Wayne's can do this job alone." They waited for Chance to limp along. Then the outlaw trio counted to three and heaved, but the damn thing wouldn't budge. "Hell, this dead bitch weighs a ton. Mr. Handsome's gotta get on this end with me—Zeke, give it a push from your side."

The bigger Wayne shook his head. "Dunno if'n that'll work either."

"Why the hell not?"

"It's an uphill incline." The big man heaved again. Inside the wooden box, something rattled.

Chance stopped pulling. Whatever was inside clinked like metal on metal.

Elias frowned, "Don't sound like no dead mama, does it?"

Chance shook his head once. *"Maybe bones?"*

Ezekiel slapped his neck. "Dog-gone river skeeters."

Samantha's eyelids felt heavier than a hangman's duty. She blinked quickly. Keeping them wet enough to stay awake. Hands found each other. Teeth gritted. She pinched the web between her thumb and forefinger. The pain was dull. But she was too tired to feel anything.

"Sam," Claire said. "They're moving Mama's coffin."

Samantha's hand found Papa's Navy Colt. She kept both in her coat pocket. Feet moved one after the other. "Please be careful with our mother. She had a tough life, deserves to make it to her final resting place in one piece."

The coffin was laid down roughly on the riverbank. Eli licked his lips. A hungry wolf ready to run down a rabbit. Samantha thumbed back the hammer in her pocket.

"Beg your pardon Mrs. Jakes," said Eli. "Just needed her out the wagon—that's all."

"See you put her back at once."

"Oh, we will," Eli smiled. "Have no fear. Could you offer us a hand, maybe? Hold the mule steady. Don't want this jackass too spirited once the wheel's back on. Might roll over and break my brother's foot."

Samantha hesitated but moved for Buttercup's muzzle, nevertheless.

Zeke lifted the wagon, and the other two replaced the wheel. Samantha stroked Buttercup's cheeks. A fly crawled across his eye. She shooed it away. Just in time to see the men lifting the coffin again and returning it safely to the bed. She sighed with relief when they didn't bother sneaking a peek.

A shadow fell over her. It was the giant. He leaned down and took the leather reins. Eyes deader than Aunt Aggie.

Chance's heart kept steady time in his chest. Glanced around for a rock, a short log, anything possible. The Wayne brothers ignored him to focus attention on the Captain's wife.

"Cannot thank you boys enough," Mrs. Jakes waved her siblings over. "I'll make sure my husband hears of such good Samaritans. Feel free to stop in at Sweet Pine anytime. You shall always be welcomed."

"Mighty kind of you," Elias stepped in front of her. "We plan on doing so right now."

"Sweet Pine is half a day away." Mrs. Jakes stepped back. "We have other travel plans."

"That a fact?" Elias closed the gap between them.

"Yes," Mrs. Jakes sidestepped.

"Funny thing about facts," Elias said. "They don't ever change. But yours have—now."

Samantha backed into the giant. Rough hands squeezed her shoulders. Arms held down by her sides. *"Lemme go!"*

Eli grabbed Claire. Knife blade gleamed at her throat. "We're gonna play a little game, Mrs. Jakes. For every question you get wrong—I cutoff one of your sister's body parts."

The threat struck her funny. She cackled with wild defiance, "That the best you can do?"

Eli raged, "I'm serious, Mrs. Jakes."

"Go ahead and hack away," Samantha laughed again. "I'd say start with the bitch's tits. Then you can go ahead and cut out her kid while you're at it."

"Sam!" Claire cried, *"Don't do this!"*

The pilgrims looked at one another, confused. Samantha saw her chance. The giant howled. Boot-heel collapsed his knee. He let go. Ground slammed against her. Spine rattled. Papa's Navy Colt entered stage right.

Eli shouted, "She's gotta gun!"

The giant saw it one second too late. The report echoed off the riverbank and across the water. Zeke's watermelon burst into red mist. Blood sprayed Samantha's face. The Giant timbered. Samantha's instincts rolled her sideways. Thumbed the hammer back. On the second click, Eli attacked. His right leg swung. The pistol spun away on the far riverbank. He fell upon her. Samantha struggled against his weight. Johnny saw and jumped on the pilgrim's back. Eli twisted, thumping the boy off like a flea. Papa's Navy Colt returned. Firmly in the hand of her savior—the outlaw.

"Drop the blade, you son-of-a-bitch." Chance stuck the barrel of the thirty-six in Elias Wayne's ear. "Do it now, or I'll spray the scat you got for brains all over your brother."

Elias stiffened. Eyes flashed hate. Knuckles tight and whitening around the Bowie's hilt. He growled, "You cornhole dandy—"

Chance didn't wait for him to finish.

Kaboom!

Clouds of red misted everywhere. The last Wayne brother rocked sideways—dead before he fell at the lady's boots. Chance wheeled around smoothly, leveling the pistol at Mrs. Jakes. "Been done talking to him since yesterday. Now he knows it too."

Blood dripped from the bridge of her nose, narrow cheeks, and the gun barrel. She didn't flinch. Unafraid of the bolt aimed her way. Her fierceness took Chance aback slightly. In the past five years, he'd witnessed a generation of young men blubber for their mamas. Courage can find you even in the middle of nowhere. Off to the side, the looker and the unfortunate huddled together, shrieking in fear.

He spoke through his teeth, "Make 'em quit that noise."

Mrs. Jakes remained as flat as the rest of her. Chance repeated himself. A lone eyebrow twitched, but everything else remained the same. He hated to waste time like this. Not with Frank Lovecock out there somewhere. He fired into the sky, "I said, tell them fools to quit that noise."

Mrs. Jakes gritted her teeth. "Hush, Claire, make Johnny do the same."

It took a minute for them to calm shrieks to whimpers. Like most girls, Mrs. Jakes never took her eyes off him. Black powder smells burned his nose. He asked. "You hurt?"

She must be hard of hearing. "I asked you a question."

Her eyes squeezed into slits. "What do you care if'n I am?"

He lowered the pistol. "Then you'll be able to help me hide these bodies."

"Hide em?" Mrs. Jakes asked.

"Yeah. In half a day—vultures'll lead someone right to em." He expected hesitation. But instead, she took to it. Helping him strip the corpses and submerging them in the river with a stone. When they finished, Chance said, "Ya look smarter than the average Buffalo gal. If you are as I reckon—you won't refuse my offer."

A fellowship of Katydids vibrated songs in the near-by reeds. When Mrs. Jakes still hadn't answered, Chance asked, "Didn't you hear me? I said I wanna make a deal with ya."

Ten seconds of pregnant silence counted down between them.

Mrs. Jakes chose her words slowly. "What. Sort. Of. Deal?"

"I know what's in the box," Chance said. "Belongs to Captain Jakes, don't it?"

"It did," Mrs. Jakes said. "Mine now."

"But how much longer?" Chance's free hand gestured across the river. "They's coming. Go by the handle of the Frank Lovecock Gang. Ever heard of em?"

Mrs. Jakes hadn't.

He pointed to where they sank the deceased. "Them two's part of it."

Mrs. Jakes's eyebrows darted, "And you ain't?"

"No, I was..." Chance said. Sticking her gun into his belt. "But I'm quits now."

"Quits?"

"I got what they was a-looking for. I know how they conduct business. And you and yours..." Chance nodded at the two urchins. His forehead wrinkled like a puppy dog's—a tick developed in childhood—displayed whenever negotiating with a woman. On rare occasions it disappointed, but those were far and few between. Since he had harbored no desire to kill three kids, Chance hoped his hound dog sincerity worked its charms now. "Agree to terms...y'all keep some of your treasure."

"Whaddaya mean some?"

He knew it would only cost him three more bullets, and he'd have all the gold to himself. But Lloyd's voice echoed inside his skull. He spoke over it, "I ain't greedy. Right now—Frank and the boys are probably at your husband's place hazing the tenderfoot. And anyone else misfortunate enough to be home. Only a matter of time before they catch the scent and follow it here. And believe me sister...when that time comes, you wanna be three counties ahead."

Why the very idea?

Samantha hated Claire. The little bitch had been absolutely correct. She could barely keep her mind right and look at the dusty knuckler at the same time. Mr. Handsome wanted to make a deal—Okay—But his math was too ugly.

"You'll be under my protection until you settled—wherever. For this service, I take half."

Samantha laughed.

The outlaw frowned. "If Frank, or Doc Buie, or Kid Nobody, or that bastard Angel Ojete finds you," said the outlaw. "They'll take the gold and your tongues. Dunno what for. Don't ever wanna know, for that matter."

"You're in their gang, but don't know what they want tongues for?"

He wiped sweat from his forehead. "Met em in New Orleans—at some cracker-box voodoo brothel."

"Voodoo?" Samantha asked, slightly amused.

"Been riding with 'em a few weeks now," the outlaw said and leveled his brown eyes at her. "I've seen things. You're gonna have to trust me. You don't wanna see them too."

Samantha looked at this puppy dog and felt warm all over. She couldn't help herself and asked, "Think you're man enough to escort us through the territories? We wanna find the Oregon trail and head west."

"Comanche land?" Asked the outlaw. She waited for his response. He mulled it over and said, "For half that box, I'd escort you through hell and back with a kerosine lantern up my ass."

Samantha shook her head. "Too high a price."

"Looking at this wrong," he said and knelt with great effort. As if bending his knee were too much agony. A face as perfect as his couldn't hide the pain. Brow made that puppy dog crease again. Morning caught his hair. An auburn halo glowed. "You ain't no barrelhouse tart—got yourself some raw courage—ain't no one can deny it. But I know how much my life's worth. D'you?"

Samantha sure as hell did.

"To double-cross Frank Lovecock and live to tell about it, I stand on my price."

Samantha scoffed.

The outlaw added, "I promise you will be under my protection...until the air leaves my lungs."

Claire and Johnny stood near Buttercup and Mama's coffin. It wasn't the best situation, but it was what it was. Samantha asked, "How long to reach the trail west?"

"Dunno," said the outlaw. "Already middle of summer and your mule's snake-bit. You'll need at least a horse. Maybe a couple oxen to make it to Missouri before the snow falls."

"Snow?" Samantha asked. "Hadn't even considered it snowing."

"Winter's coming, Mrs. Jakes. You wanna see the other side of it, you'll need to trust me."

Samantha hesitated.

This handsome stranger wanted her answer. "Do we got a deal or are we quits?"

Samantha's eyes imprinted the symmetry of his face to memory—rugged yet soft. If she could bottle and sell it, she'd never need the Captain's gold to be rich. One dirty hand outstretched in agreement. The outlaw, her savior—the man with the beautiful face took her hand in his.

July 1867

Somewhere in Sweet Pine a tea kettle screeched. The rusty whistle popped opened the Captain's bloodshot eyes. His brain swirled between dimensions. Skull throbbed. Back ached. The worst hangover Elrod had ever known.

He recognized the room at least, though he didn't ever remember seeing it from this particular angle. Something crunched between his fingers. A paper slip reading *Gone to Oregon* went in and out of focus.

It didn't make any sense. *Which one of the dumb cunts forgot the tea pot?* "Somebody take the danged kettle off the stove!" His shout echoed through the house and out the open door. More curses flew when Elrod learned he couldn't roll over. Someone had shackled his feet around the bedpost, leaving him face down. And he had a pretty good idea of which dumb cunt had done it. "I'm gonna kill that bitch."

He pulled against the short chain. An unnatural chaos looped together like a black widow's nest. The Captain could only get to his knees. This is how he looked when the whistling stopped, and Frank Lovecock found him.

His familiar voice rasped, "Quartermaster?"

Four mirages appeared in Sweet Pine's master bedroom.

"We had a deal, Quartermaster."

The Captain didn't respond. Already Frank's pistol was out against the Captain's aching skull. Teeth clenched as Frank thumbed back the hammer. "Where's our gold?"

He spat, "Your half's at the bottom of the Colorado river where you left it." Stars jumped across his vision. Pistol-whipped, the Captain teetered over. Frank stood him and hissed, "Always had funny ideas of what was fair. Ain't in the mood for none of 'em now. Where's our gold?"

The Captain, bound at the wrist, was unable to stop his bleeding nose. "Come for half of mine, have you?"

"Half?" Frank said. "We followed your stink across two states. Didn't cross a devil's trail for only half. You're handing it all over Quartermaster."

Captain Jakes showed his palms. "Ain't got it here."

Frank nodded once and aimed at the Captain's left hand.

Kablam!

Elrod's thumb exploded. He sat there, looking confused. Too shocked to scream. Finally, he grabbed for the missing digit and fell back. Blood darkened his long johns. Frank stepped on Elrod's throat and growled, "God blessed you with twenty-one appendages. And that's one. Now tell me what I wanna know. Or Doc Buie'll fetch his medicine bag and start sawing through bone."

July 1867

The wagon pitched and rolled over the grooved ruts. Chance's guts gurgled so loud Mrs. Jakes laughed and spoke at her elbow, "You smell it too, huh?"

"Smell what?"

"Don't know, but something's cooking. Ain't none of us ate since..." Her voice trailed off.

Chance couldn't remember when he'd eaten either, but it weren't his belly rumbling. No, this troubling noise came from the hips. He felt a push coming on and prayed it wouldn't foul the air. The scent finally caught his attention. "Smell it now...sure as shooting."

"Gotta be close," said Claire. "Smell like chili to you? Think they'd spare a bowl?"

Chance didn't know. He brought the mule to a stop outside a hut carved into the riverbank. A little path, imprinted by countless crossings, led to a door made of stiff animal hide. To get there, you had to pass a cookpot over a campfire. "Wait here. I'll see what vittles I can rouse."

Mrs. Jakes insisted on coming along. The enticing smell grew stronger as they neared. Chance got a few feet away and listened. A strange chittering like giant pine beetles chewed behind the door. He stopped and held a hand aloft. Mrs. Jakes stopped too.

The noise continued, unaware of the pair outside. Mrs. Jakes started to speak. Chance touched his own lips. Slag crunched under foot. He found a gap between the door and the wall. It was dark inside, but movement could be seen. He pushed open the stinking door. Light fell on something grey inside. It skittered. He stepped back.

"What's wrong?" Mrs. Jakes asked.

Chance turned to shoosh her. Then he saw him. Clutching knotty firewood between his dirty arms and limping down the path. The grey hermit wore a scraggly beard of Spanish moss. Watery eyes blinked at the intruders. The beard parted and groaned, "Trespassers!"

Behind Chance, the chittering increased excitedly. Chance looked away from the stranger—only for a split second. The quicksilver knife appeared. Logs dropped. Hermit lunged for the gal. Chance pulled the pistol and fired. The hermit tumbled backwards into the water and out of sight.

Chance shouted at Mrs. Jakes, "Snatch that cookpot!"

Together, they raced back to the wagon, clambered aboard, and rode on. Down the road, they collected magnolia leaves. Formed them into crude bowls and doled out five portions of delicious smelling chili. Using shaved pine bark as spoons. They ate in silence. Chance could not place the flavor exactly. The hunks of meat reminded him of chicken. And the only spice seemed to be salt. A hint of vinegar...no...iron in the aftertaste, as if blood had been used to thicken the rue.

"Gross," Claire cleared her throat to remove a long black hair.

Another moment passed and Mrs. Jakes chirped at her bowl, "Is it an uncooked onion?"

The sister shook her head and said, "More like a small toenail."

Chance lifted his own woody spoon and gazed in horror. A hunk of meat amongst beans and rue. Small and curved like a child's finger. Skittering sounds churned his stomach. A hint of bone peeked from inside the flesh. He dropped the pine bark spoon into the makeshift bowl. The offending digit sank out of sight.

"Ain't hungry no more," he offered up his portion. The others gladly accepted. He looked away. Chance said nothing.

Could've. Would've. Should've.

After a time, they rode on.

Mrs. Jakes finished her bowl. Belched louder than the man she resembled, and immediately passed out against the coffin. The mule limped ahead. Chance's neck hair prickled. That feeling like being watched. Glancing over his shoulder. Unfortunate eyes off-set strangely at different angles. One green, one brown, both un-curved. Sores the size of Muscatine grapes pimpled his entire head. Making the sandy brown scalp lumpy, like a briar patch hound infested with ticks.

"Is you touched?"

The boy wheezed with excitement—as if a stranger had never spoken to him before.

Chance cautiously asked, "Having some kinda fit, boy?"

Teeth like a lumberjack's two-handle blade clinked.

"Johnny Grey don't stare." The younger sister climbed over the coffin towards them. Shoeing the boy away from their driver. The boy scuttled closer to the Captain's wife. The sister remained. Eyes sparkling over a purple nose. "I do apologize—he's curious about strangers."

Chance gave him another quick look. "Know what's wrong with him?"

"Mama said he's a blessing," Claire shook her head and giggled. "Then she got sick and died. Mama used to have this bottle of mint oil she'd rub on them boils. Make them go away. But could never make 'em stay gone." She wetted her lips and checked for clearance. "Do you mind if I sit?"

"It's your wagon…" Chance squinted. "I'm just driving it."

Trouble lifted herself over the divide. "It's not our wagon. It belongs to the Captain."

Chance clicked his cheek at the slowing mule. It barely responded. The wagon rocked on.

"All of this…" Claire gestured behind her, "belongs to Captain Jakes."

Chance slapped the reins. "Don't see your meaning."

"He's very rich," she said, eyes fluttering like a moth in a spider's web.

Chance skipped her nose (the only thing seemingly wrong) down her face to watch her pouty lips say, "If you turn around right now…I'm sure he'd be happy to reward you if'n you take us home." Her soft hand found his knee. "I'd be happy to reward you too, with whatever you'd like until I'm returned safely to Captain Jakes."

Chance glanced at the hand on his knee. "Aye, this Captain…?" Chance pointed with his chin. "He the one who busted your nose?"

The gal didn't flinch. Not only was she trouble—she was also dangerous.

"Sounds quite the gentleman," Chance said. "But you ain't got nothing I want in trade."

"She's not really his wife," Claire bit her lower lip. "I mean they's married, but..." Her fingers traced circles on her belly.

"Is she really your sister?"

The gal shrugged.

"Our deal's for half the coffin?" Chance said. "Doubt you could do better."

Desperation crept into her voice, "You won't get half."

"That a fact?"

"My sister kidnapped us. At least I'm not here of my own accord. If my captain must come looking for his property, he won't be in a forgiving mood."

"Don't see his name on nothing but your sister. And she don't seem keen to keep it much longer." Chance spat off the side again. "You call yourselves sisters—but I don't see any resemblance."

Fingers tickled his neck. "Thank the lord for small blessings...don't you agree?"

The outlaw remained rigid.

"You dunno him like I know him," her mouth hot against his ear, humid with poison. "My king'll stop at nothing to get me back."

"Sounds like you're in love, or..." Chance eyed her with pity, "...a complete fool."

Claire doubled down. Lips pursed tighter than a skinflint's asshole. Hand traced circles near his craw. This bitch was in it to win it.

"Talk is cheap," Claire pressed against him. Teeth nibbled the soft of his neck. Little hairs stood at attention. Gooseflesh rippled. In spite of this, Chance pulled away slowly. She purred, "Be a dirty shame for the Captain to ruin a face as perfect as yours."

"Many have tried already," Chance said. "None done it yet."

Her hand traveled inward. She breathed heat. "No one can show you as good a time as me, handsome."

"Flattered, but..." Chance shrugged her off. "Ain't no lover boy."

An awkward moment passed. Then another. And another.

"My charms ain't never..." Claire recollected her hands, "...been refused so roughly."

"Don't feel bad, kid," Chance said. "It ain't you...it's me."

Overhead, a collective of black birds swarmed the sky. They made no attempt to perch or land but flew on—wings flapping with a zealot's glee. Their song—frightened and unwavering. Chance and Claire watched this undulating cloud disappear in the distance.

"That's odd," Chance muttered. "Awful late in the season for them some-bitches to migrate."

"Know a lot about birds, do you?" Claire asked.

"Enough to be dangerous...you?"

"The only birds I know are cocks," Claire giggled. "But you done missed out on that lesson."

Chance smiled at her and brought the mule to a stop and swung his legs stiffly over the side. Needing to keep his rump-splitter as far away from her as possible. Near a strand of oaks, the katydids quieted on his approach. He dangled his worm. The stink of infection wafted into the summer air. Yet nothing came out. A common trouble usually brought on by sensations of being watched. Neck hair stiff in the eerie quiet. Chance glanced to and fro. Saw nothing but woods and Claire pretending not to look.

"C'mon damn you," Chance commanded Old Rowley to uncork. Bladder needed to leak so bad his kidneys ached. Guts bubbled like a witch's cauldron. Could sense the edge nearing and yet no fiddle-diddle. He cursed it once more and demanded the levee break.

Yellow eventually trickled. Still, he felt no relief. Something dammed up his waterworks. Shaking it did no good. But something twitched. A drip became a leak. The leak mercifully became an awkward drizzle. Any relief turned uneasy. Chance winced as invisible razor blades slashed his nethers. Watching in horror as the urine clouded over orange, then dimmed to brown, before changing into a crude oil, blacker than an ocean's trench.

Lloyd roared cosmic static from deep beneath the aquatic abyss.

August 1865

"No matter what you think you hear...*don't breathe a sound.*" Samantha Gray closed the attic hatch. Johnny and Claire's young faces vanished behind rough-hewn boards. Seconds before, they'd been playing with jacks and dolls. Now she prayed they wouldn't be found. Papa's voice between her ears, *when trouble comes Sammie Jane, you can't waste time on fear.*

In one move she stowed the attic ladder under the big brass bed and opened Papa's chifforobe. Papa always kept the box in the corner. The brass hinges ached on opening. Her brow knitted. She gasped, "Where is it?" The empty box made no sense. Papa never took it hunting or at least he hadn't before...*Could he have left it on the...*

Behind her, the cabin door opened. Her search for Papa's Colt Navy momentarily postponed. Samantha smiled at the bandaged hand holding a revolver.

Samantha asked, "Can I help you?"

The Yankee stepped for the stove and sniffed the cast-iron pot. "You alone gal?"

"Yes...I mean no. I mean..." Samantha's words stumbled out. "My husband'll be back soon...fetching firewood."

The Yankee snorted with contempt. "Don't believe you."

She tightened. Don't *let him rattle you.* "Which part?"

"Which part..." He mocked. "First off, you ain't got no husband. No shrapnel on your finger."

Hands found each other.

"Secondly," said the Yankee. "Why leave for firewood when there's plenty in the bucket?" Boot tapped the full kindling pail beside the stove. His glare lingered on her thin frame. "How old is you?"

Samantha's hands moved to her chest. "Twenty-two."

"Cut the horse shite," the Yankee smiled with teeth blacker than coalsmoke. "Don't look old enough to grow cunt-hair, let alone be no twenty-two."

Why, the very idea. Mama said some gals developed slowly. And just because she'd turned sixteen didn't mean she'd bloom overnight.

"How old is you, *really?*"

Rumors of Yankee deserters had frayed the area quilts for weeks. Even the Brumley's oldest daughter, Harriet, claimed one such brigand had ravaged her for close to three hours over a fortnight ago. But considering Harriet Brumley's beau got his fool-self killed at Sabine Pass, Samantha felt Harriet was just desperate for attention. Why, the very idea. She'd never known anyone willing to admit to God and everyone a stranger knew them biblically. It's one thing to pretend shock when it involves your neighbor's daughter. Something else entirely when...

"Does my age matter?"

"Curious why you're out here all alone. Place looked deserted."

Belly butterflies flew with worry. "Plenty old enough to be alone."

The Yankee sneered, "Bet you'd like to think so."

Samantha looked at the floor.

She knew—he knew—she knew what he wanted.

Papa wasn't due home for another day or so. Claire and Johnny couldn't stay in the attic for long—too hot. Especially Johnny. One only needs look at him and know trouble. Strangers hated him on sight. Some folks remained polite enough, but you could tell they deemed Johnny's very existence an affront to their own decency. After Mama died, Papa had forbidden Johnny from going into town. Papa had said, "Johnny might break the rope around his waist, run into the street and get trampled to death." But Samantha really thought Papa couldn't handle heads turning wherever they went. That feeling of being watched. As if Johnny's condition was a direct reflection of Papa and his business. And she could never understand that about her Papa. He had two little girls before Johnny, and we turned out fine. She figured it's tough for fathers when sons disappoint. Made even worse when other people can see it too. The way they whispered.

That feeling...like being stared at.

The Yankee closed in. "Ain't heard a kind word in ten since getting stuck in this godforsaken country." The bearded chin titled back. Nose hair rustled with each deep sniff.

An idea sprang to mind. "Hungry?"

Tired eyes opened.

"Seems you caught me at the right time," she fought back nerves. "Making stew."

The Yankee squinted. One boot stepped back—then another—then he stood beside the stove again. His eyes never left hers. Waved a hand over the pot. "Fire's out."

She chirped, "Would you be so kind as to restart it?"

The Yankee didn't budge as he stood blocking the kindling pail.

Samantha clucked her tongue. "Mind stepping aside?"

The Yankee's rotten teeth clicked, but he didn't move.

The bastard was only going to play by his rules. And furthermore, expected her to enjoy his game too. His proximity to both the stove and firewood created only a small opening for Samantha to reach through. She knelt before him. The dirty face leered down. "Go on gal," he said, "fetch that wood."

She reached, but the Yankee's boot-heel slid it further away.

When trouble comes, Sammie Jane, you can't waste time on fear.

Samantha felt outside herself, watching as she reached further back. The brute pushed his hips forward. Foul crotch reek wafted from his soiled trousers. Samantha choked back sick and grabbed a log. If she'd had any advantage at all—she'd have broken it to splinters on him. She pulled away fast. His filthy left hand clutched her wrist. His pistol hovered at his suspender buttons. Her arm was toothpick small between his thick fingers. She feared he'd snap it in half. But instead, gently helped guide the log inside the stove's open maw. He shook her wrist, dropping it into a puff of grey ash. Then he returned her hand to the pail. They repeated the motion. He led this dance until the stove overflowed.

"Matches?" asked the Yankee, more than satisfied with how things had proceeded.

Samantha's eyes darted to the shelf on the wall behind the stovepipe.

The Yankee followed her gaze. "Fetch 'em too then."

He let go. A noise thudded above. The Yankee's eyes snapped to attention. The coonhound in him froze, waiting to hear it again. Samantha thought quick—grabbed for the matchbox, hitting it just enough—matches spilled on the floor.

"Clumsy me," she laughed. "I'll collect the Lucifer's."

She stooped and gathered the tiny red tipped sticks.

"D'ya hear something?"

She shrugged, then struck a match across the front of the stove. It sparked, then died. A thin, smokey ribbon unwrapped in her nose. She tried again. More of the same.

"Why the very idea," she said, laughing it off nervously, hoping to regain his full attention.

If only she could get him outside. Or better yet...find mama's medicine. The salts she kept for her monthly visitor. She'd take one and sleep for a day or two, then she'd be as sweet as pecan pie. Her and papa could laugh together again. Samantha always liked it when her parents acted so happy. She wished she could still remember mama's laugh. The first memory she lost. Mama's whole voice disappeared next, then her smile. Gone too was the woman who'd once sang soft hymns to her children, and taught Samantha how to read, how to make dresses from sacks, and how to cook, sew, and mind her manners. That woman disappeared—replaced with a silent shell—a dying meat bag sweating with fever for fifteen days without food or water. Papa said he couldn't stand for her to spend another night shaking and suffering, so he collected half the bottle of salts. Commanded his oldest daughter to see to the young'uns outside until he said different. Samantha didn't know how long they waited before Papa emerged and announced mama had gone to live with Jesus. Samantha couldn't help but feel she'd lost both parents when mama died.

Samantha found another match. She went to strike again, but the Yankee found her wrist again, but this time he squatted beside her. Pulled her closer. Her knuckles inches from his chest. He looked from her hand and back at her face. His invitation smoldered.

Smoother than a lake breeze, the Yankee glided her hand to a button on his coat and flicked her wrist. Match sparked. Smoke haloed. A cute enough trick, Samantha chortled. Together they lit the fire in the stove. The smell of burning wood filled the cabin. "What's in the pot?"

"Carrots, taters, some corn...needs salt."

The Yankee's lip curled. "No meat?"

Samantha shook her head. The Yankee followed her out. White leghorns scratched in the dirt. Samantha leaned forward. Pushed air against her cheek, chick-chick-chick! Snuck towards the nearest fowl. A hen lifted her head—jerked it sideways—eyed the girl, eyed the dirt, eyed the girl again, then escaped her grasp. Undeterred, Samantha reset and called again. Chick-chick-chick! Ten fingers twitched. White wings flapped—the hen jumped. *"Dang!"*

The Yankee spat and asked, "There a problem?"

Samantha waited...and waited...and—*Chick-chick-chick!*

She dove. Brood cackled in fright and flight. Samantha beat the dirt in mock frustration. "Double-dang! Dunno if I can catch..."

The Yankee thumbed the hammer and fired. The explosion was enormous. One hen disappeared. The others scattered in the cloud of feathers. Samantha, so shocked by the gunshot, peed herself.

"Caught one," the Yankee licked his lips.

JULY 1867

A RIVER CROSSING — THE TAO OF GUNPLAY

KABLAM! GUNFIRE ECHOED OFF the far riverbank. Samantha awoke from her nightmare. Head snapped to attention—all alone with mama's coffin. She looked around dazed until hearing the gun report echo again.

The myth, the legend herself, didn't recognize the place exactly, but saw a river. *Was it the Sabine or the Neches?* She clamored out the wagon. Ignoring the black necrosis of Buttercup's swollen wound and followed the sound of voices. She smelled the gun-smoke and parted a clump of reeds to see better.

Why the very idea?

Jealousy heated her skin when she saw the two of them close together.

Claire giggled between the outlaw's arms, helping her aim Papa's Navy Colt.

"Turn my back for one minute," Samantha raged, "and you've armed my bitch sister."

"Four days," said the outlaw—taking back the gun and opening the cylinder. "...didn't know if you'd ever wake up again."

The amount of days didn't make any sense. How the hell could she sleep so long? How many days had she been denied it before their escape? Samantha didn't have time for math. She pointed at the brown water. "We ain't even left the Sabine yet!"

In truth, they'd reached the Trinity river during her long nap. The outlaw smoothly informed her of the facts.

"Only twenty miles or so outside Dallas." Claire batted her eyes. Cue a familiar tone, "*Ain't that right, Chancey?*"

Samantha's rage steamed. "Dunno what this little bitch told you. But I'd think twice before allowing her access to Papa's gun. Might go off in your back when you ain't looking."

The outlaw didn't speak. Replaced spent cartridges with fresh. Snapping it closed.

"Just a little target practice," Claire purred. "Just passing time till the ferryman comes."

On the other shore, a wide bottom ferry floated outside a leaning shack. Both looked bombed out and abandoned, and Samantha told them so.

"Barge ain't been stowed," said the Outlaw. "And the horse is still inside."

Samantha couldn't see or hear no horse and told them so.

The outlaw nodded, "Reckon the ferryman gone off drunk somewhere's."

"I thought you was in a hurry," Samantha said. "Thought hellhounds were on our trail."

He spun the cylinder. "Our mule's exhausted and sick. Didn't think it'd last this long. Did you, partner?"

"Partner?" Samantha repeated as the outlaw put on a show, spinning the pistol on a finger.

"Careful," Samantha scolded. "It's a...a...prized family heirloom."

Chance was incredulous. "The mule?"

Claire mocked her with laughter, "Chancey just got done saying how badly calibrated Papa's pistol was. Told him how it ain't been put to much use until recently. Ain't that right, sweet sister?"

"Nothing wrong with Papa's Navy Colt," Samantha said.

The outlaw cocked an eyebrow. Her knees wobbled slightly. Her rings clinked.

The outlaw pointed the pistol across the river. Primed the action and fired. Smoke plumed. A corner of the lean-to splintered. The unseen horse whinnied at the noise.

"See," Samantha pointed. "Hit it just fine."

"I was aiming for the window."

"Maybe you're just a bad shot," Samantha felt her chain pinch. She scratched her craw.

He scratched his chin. "Boy!"

"His name's Johnny," Samantha corrected and pulled more at the pinching chain.

The outlaw said his name. Their brother bounded over, excited and drooling.

"Pick up yonder rock," Johnny followed his finger to a rounded river stone the size of a box turtle. Stooped and collected it.

"That's right kid. When I yell *AIR—want* you give it a toss." The outlaw mimed what he wanted the boy to do.

Johnny breathed through his mouth and didn't respond.

The outlaw asked the girls, "Can he do it?"

"He ain't blind or deaf...just dumb," Claire giggled.

"Alright then...Johnny Boy." The outlaw stuck the pistol through a belt loop. Shooting arm hung free by his hip. "Give it a toss."

Johnny held the rock and didn't budge. The outlaw raised a brow at the ladies. Samantha snarled, "That ain't what ya told him to do. Give him the right signal and see what he does."

A soft smile dimpled the outlaw's cheeks. Samantha's heart fluttered. She stopped scratching herself.

The outlaw nodded at Johnny, *"Air!"*

Johnny let it fly.

The outlaw unsheathed the pistol and fired. The twang of contact whistled overhead. The river stone spun towards the water from which it came. The outlaw slapped the hammer rapidly with his left hand. Bullets skipped the rock over the river before sinking from view. The outlaw blew smoke from the barrel and reloaded.

Samantha suddenly felt hot all over as he flicked his wrist, twisting the handle around and holding it towards her. "Try for yourself if you don't believe me. I had to aim a foot away from the target."

Samantha scanned his words for a trap.

"I trust you as much as you trust me." He broke their shared silence, "Go hit yonder window."

Here was a man who knew exactly what he wanted. And Samantha was going to obey. The pistol felt heavier in her hand than she remembered. Hammer clicked back. She sighted down the barrel. Tongue poked out a corner of her mouth. She pulled the trigger back. Dust plumed to the right—far off from the ferryman's shack. Her breath hitched at the pleasurable sensation; a light sweat broke over her skin.

Claire clapped her hands and taunted, "Was you aiming for that clump of willows?"

Spasms inside her came in waves. She bit her lip because she couldn't speak.

"Hmm...guess I was wrong then," said the outlaw. "Maybe it don't need recalibrating after-all. By all means...squeeze off another round."

Pleasant sensations finally ebbed to nothing. Samantha glared at her sister in the afterglow. She quickly leveled the pistol again. Squinted down the barrel and pulled. Papa's Navy Colt bucked in both hands. Unable to conceal the moan escaping her lips. Tingles reached her earlobes. A shake trembled through her.

The outlaw saw it, "Everything okay, miss?"

"Missed again," Claire sang aloud. "I think Chancey's right about calibration. Just needs a lighter touch." She stroked her hair and played with the ends. Eyes batted at the outlaw. "From someone who knows how to handle a hot ramrod."

The outlaw refused to acknowledge the tart. "Hand it over and I'll fix it myself."

Samantha leveled the pistol at her spasming waist. "What if I wanna keep doing it?"

The outlaw smiled seriously, "Haven't given you no reason not to."

Samantha's knees weakened. This beautiful man with the puppy dog eyes scratched behind his ear, confident he wouldn't be shot. "Wanna hang on to it—fine. But let me offer some advice. Your feet are all wrong."

Samantha didn't understand.

He approached. Gently nudged her dusty boots wider. Matching her stance to his. "Shoulder-width apart."

The outlaw closed in behind her. Hands caressed her arms. His pretty mouth next to her ear. Breath hot on her cheek. Her rings tinkled. All the hair raised on her arms. He whispered, "Relax. Can't hit a target if you're worried about missing it."

Gooseflesh rippled over her arms as his hands passed her elbows. Found her wrists. Then shook them softly. "Loosen your grip," he whispered. "Let the thirty-six be an extension of your arm. Not something you're holding."

Samantha couldn't focus. Butterflies fluttered. Claire stood opposite and jealous, and Samantha never wanted this moment to pass. The outlaw whispered, "Your finger never squeezes the trigger."

"No?" Samantha laughed, then asked. "Am I supposed to use my teeth?"

"No ma'am," said the outlaw. "Feel my hands?"

He traced her arms towards her chest. She felt them run down to her hips. Strong, manly fingers gripped her hips. "Keep the pelvis tight...this is the only place you squeeze. You got it?"

Smanatha nodded. The outlaw whispered into her ear, "Fire when ready."

Samantha swooned. Her heartbeat raced. The gun orgasmically bucked like a wild mustang. She caught her moan this time with her hand over her mouth and collapsed against him. Unable to stop the climaxing tingles washing over her in long waves.

Across the river, the lone windowpane shattered.

Everyone but Samantha cheered.

Her heavy breath finally subsided. She leaned in. Her voice was half a pillow-whisper. "See what you mean about squeezing with your hips. May need to do it again."

"Again?" the outlaw asked. "Right now? I think you might've had enough."

"Yeah," Samantha said huskily. "Make sure I'm not just getting lucky."

"You ain't lucky," Claire said, killing the mood. "Hand it over and I'll show you some shooting."

Samantha saw that self-satisfied smirk and fired at Claire's bare feet.

"Jesus!" That famous Claire temper steamed. "See what I mean! Nuttier than a shithouse rat!"

Samantha fired again.

"Quit it!"

"You done talking," Samantha said and cocked back the hammer. "Or do you wanna keep dancing?"

Claire pleaded for the outlaw to make Samantha stop.

The outlaw glanced from one to the other and said, "The gun belongs to her."

Samantha blushed. Desire rushed through her veins. First opportunity she got, she aimed to squeeze her hips again alright. Make her savior—the outlaw—the man with the beautiful face holler aloud the names of famous traitors until his Dixieland burned down and limply surrendered, just like Robert E. Lee.

Summer 1867

The Dark Thirty — A Storm Near Sulphur Springs

Just before sunset, black clouds gathered. The road ahead dimmed. Samantha couldn't shake the notion they'd traded one hell for another.

"Should we be worried?" Claire asked the ominous dark above.

The outlaw remained quiet.

"No," Samantha said, "it'll pass. Look how fast those clouds are moving."

Within a quarter of an hour, the hellish maelstrom arrived. Pelting them without mercy and putting out their lantern. Rain veiled Samantha's vision. Couldn't see an arm's length in any direction. Next to the coffin, Claire and Johnny bundled under quilts. The waterlogged fabric sagged and leaked. Thunder clapped overhead. The limping mule whinnied and bucked. Unshod hooves kicked against the wagon's footboard.

The outlaw jumped from the driver's seat and disappeared. Capillaries of light flashed overhead. Oh, how the sky did roar. One blue flash connected with a nearby tree. *Key-rack!* Orange sparks exploded. A branch sheared off and crashed. Fire glowed briefly, then died out wet.

Everyone yelped in fright. The outlaw emerged from the outer dark. "We gotta find cover! Help me pull Buttercup!"

Papa's voice between her ears, *Needs must when the Devil drives.* Mule hooves clattered against the seat—knocking Samantha down as she stood—barely missing her knee. She dropped off the other side.

He held the mule's snout. "Blind him or he'll wreck everything."

Samantha reached into her coat pocket and pulled out a handkerchief. Immediately the cloth weighed heavy with wet. The mule shook its dumb face side to side. She fought against the deluge, and somehow managed to knot the fabric over the mule's skull, but the thing jerked away before she could tighten it. Her balance faltered, and she went sprawling. Static discharged through the ether. Between the flashes, Samantha spotted a weeping willow tree. Had to be close to a hundred years old. Big enough to cover the wagon or a small cottage.

"Over there!" She pointed, "Chance! Pull it over there!"

The darkness asked for more information.

"Just a stone's throw away." Samantha said before realizing the outlaw couldn't see a thing. She grabbed him and caught his waist. Even through his wet clothes, he felt warm in her hands. It didn't feel peculiar at all. He felt right—Samantha pressed against him, and together they fought the mule. One hand firm below his navel. The other gripped his gun belt from behind. If they weren't in such a squall, Samantha might've fully enjoyed the embrace. She guided them towards the willow's low swaying branches.

They switched places so he could hobble Buttercup.

The outlaw commanded, "Get them kids under the wagon. It ain't safe here."

The willowy pendulums above provided some cover, but it didn't matter. The wind changed direction in a blink. Pelting them sideways. Claire and Johnny found their sister's hand and followed it under the wagon. Samantha angled the quilt. It blocked the rain fine until the wind shifted once more. Now it swirled around them in a vortex.

The outlaw still hadn't come back.

Johnny's rusty air-pump squealed, wrapping his arms around Samantha so tight she couldn't catch a good breath herself. Wedging an arm between them for leverage. "It's going to be alright Johnny boy. Storm'll pass any second."

The boy whined like a wormy pup. Lightning crashed close. The trio yelped and Claire joined Samantha's other side, in spite of herself.

"I knew we should've been worried!" Her little sister said something else, but Samantha couldn't hear over the growing noise. The wind wailed death around them. Huddling together, Samantha held her siblings tight. Above them, the wagon rattled. The wheels shimmied in place. As if something big wanted to lift it and toss it aside. Buttercup screamed. Air rushed over them fast.

The outlaw emerged, "Get low!"

Claire jumped down, and Samantha pulled Johnny to her. He wheezed in fright under the wagon.

Then she heard it. Something more than thunder or wind, and yet equal parts of both. A hungry beast hunting in the dark. Curiouly, Sam crawled from under the wagon for a better look—and immediately wished she hadn't.

"Get back under there, you fool!" the outlaw shouted, but the words didn't register—lost in the rising wind. Water whipped upwards. Samantha couldn't pry her eyes from the dark funnel, like a lady's stocking in one of the Tinker's dirty books, twisting through the trees. Rattles of snaps and cracks and crunches roared at her from the pines. Tornado threats are a way of life for every East Texan. However, it took eighteen years for one to finally arrive at Samantha's door. All around them pell-mell debris flew.

Something dropped close nearby and splashed in the dim. Its shape resembled some kind of large seed pod. Too close for comfort. Samantha crouched with the armadillos. Hands covered her neck. Squeezing in on herself. Another heavy something flopped even closer. The tornado spun everything it had at them. Despite the deafening roar overhead, she thought she could hear a cow mooing. Samantha tilted upwards to steal a glance at the flying bovine. Lightning struck again in a long-crooked arc, sending her eyes downward again. In the brief light, Samantha glimpsed the strange fallen fruit. And recognized it at once. Time slowed.

Why the very idea?

Samantha screamed, but it went unheard over the cacophonous storm.

Lightning flashed grim shadows inside the eye-sockets—hollowed out by crows. Frayed and unwinding rope remained tight around its tiny neck. Little fingers curled forever into stiff and bloated fists. Whatever sex it once owned had been removed—leaving a wide and gory gash between its fattened legs.

Samantha sawed back on her hips—scrambling away from the dead baby.

"Where the hell are you going?!" the outlaw shouted after her. Samantha didn't answer—unaware she backed towards the coming tornado. Eyes glued to the tree of unspeakable horrors she'd mistaken for a weeping willow. Men, women, and children, three generations' worth, swung to and fro from the branches above. An entire family dangled from the weathered nooses. Colliding with each other as they flopped in the churning wind. One of the adults broke free—hurled into the atmoshpere.

Air pressure dropped. Samantha felt it in her ears. Hailstones bigger than boiled eggs rained down as if being laid by unseen birds. Trees splintered around them as Samantha's pubic chain came unmoored, snaking out from under her shirt, and floating over her shoulder. Samantha closed her eyes and turned to reel it back in. But the myth, the legend herself, couldn't keep her curiosity at bay. This brave gal of only nineteen years stared unblinking at the massive column of destruction twisting in front of her. Her tether, as if out of pure conditioning, offered itself to its new master, the tornado. Samantha realized too late. Teeth clenched. Hands gripped. The serpentine silver flashed in front of her, curling with unrelenting force, pulling her towards doom. Boots slid in the mud beneath her feet. It was taking her whether she wanted it too, or not. Each chain-link slipping one at a time through her fingers. Shirt buttons popping as it breached. Dead bodies and splinters whirled around her. Through gritted teeth, she screamed, "God! Not like this! Anyway, but this..."

The tornado bellowed, unconcerned with the tragic events that brought her here. And then it happened. The twister spoke with the Captain's voice. It commanded her to obey.

Why the very idea?

Samantha stared it down. If it was going to win, it was going to have to fight her for it. Pressure tingled between her legs. If this tornado was going to bend her knees, she was going to make it suffer. Chills rippled up her spine. If it was going to make her submit to its will, it was going to bleed. Electric vibrations edged her nerves. Samantha pulled back on the unmovable chain with all the strength she had left. Heels dug in. Lightning strobed like a photographer's flash. Time elongated. The tornado looked into the abyss that was Samantha Jakes, and a curious thing happened.

The pubic chain lifted in her hands, then fluttered to the ground. First one eye opened and then the other. Samantha's jaw sagged. Truly mystified as the funnel kicked skyward and dissipated. Debris like rain fell for several more minutes until the calm darkness of night returned.

"You alright?" The outlaw struck a match. It sparked briefly, then went out. Too wet to light.

"Is it over?" Claire asked from under the wagon.

Johnny wheezed with excited fear.

"For now," the outlaw said and went to strike another match.

"Don't..." Samantha said.

"If you can see in the dark Mrs. Jakes, by all means lead me around to make us camp."

"Camp?" Samantha reeled in her chain and wrapped it around her hips. "We make no camp."

The outlaw bristled. "Storm's knocked down trees—washed out bridges—no telling what other mayhem left on the road. And it may not be the only one touching down tonight."

"Don't care," Samantha said firmly. "We're not staying here."

Behind the outlaw, the sky popped with distant lightning. She counted to ten before she heard the thunder. The outlaw grated, "I just got the mule hobbled."

"Then you'd best unhobble it," Samantha said. "I want Dallas County by daybreak or the terms of our deal's quits."

"Our terms quit when you're delivered safe and half the treasure's tucked in my steamer. By my side. Westbound for Californy." The outlaw protested more, but Samantha wouldn't hear it. Her mind was already made up. The outlaw struck another match to light the lantern. Samantha blew it out.

"How the hell are we supposed to go anywhere in the dark?"

"That's the only way I've ever known to go," Samantha said and felt blindly for the wagon. She got in next to mama's coffin. Opened her coat and snuggled Johnny against her flank inside. The boy trembled with cold. Samantha, having just played chicken with Mother Nature, felt absolutely numb.

The outlaw clucked his tongue and went to work in the inky black. Soon, he rejoined the rest of them. Buttercup snorted and pulled the wagon with a jolt. They slowly rolled away from the storm, the hanging tree, and a past that would remain unforgiven.

October 1867

A Savage Butchery — The Other Side of
Red Carpet Country

ONE CAN NEVER APPRECIATE the power of a cool breeze until it's gone. Above Chance, the Oklahoma sun blazed. He slowly climbed out the wagon. Mrs. Jakes had already disappeared over the ridge, towards the massacre. He drew one of his new pearl handles uneasily. Limping over the endless red dirt country. Handmade arrows dotted the battlefield like strange feathered reeds. Scattered all around lay the scalped and the dead. Everything was coated red from dust, making it near impossible to avoid hidden slicks of blood. A little way ahead, Mrs. Jakes stumbled through a family of buzzards, who merely flapped their wings in response and carried on eating.

"We need to keep moving," Chance cupped his mouth and hollered. His voice was flat across the prairie. "The savages may come back. You don't wanna be here if'n they do."

Mrs. Jakes didn't answer.

He called again. She kept on—frantically ignoring him—with each overturned corpse. Her desperation escalated. Couldn't for the life of him understand what the gal went on about. Black flies buzzed over their smorgasbord. In a day or two, these dead bodies would spring to life with maggots. Some steers lay in the muck nearby. Hooves as stiff as the arrows stuck in their hides. Chance spoke aloud to himself, "From the looks of it...this here train got itself pinched from both sides." The weight of his words settled. The rugged landscape owned matching rock formations. Plenty of places to hide. "Damn fools had no chance to circle the wagons nor build a defense..."

Mrs. Jakes wailed like a new widow.

Chance turned his head just in time to see her falter to her knees. Arms hugged tight against herself and crying, "It's not fair!"

Because it never is...

Chance's guts bubbled as he limped towards her. Realization washed over him, hotter than the still air. He doffed his hat and rubbed away the sweat. Stood just a little behind his benefactor and asked, "Which one? Which wagon did you send them out on?"

Mrs. Jakes took her time to pick one of the wrecks of splintered wood and torn canvas. Chance didn't look. Didn't want to see the unfortunate boy's mutilated corpse. If one felt sorry for Johnny when he was alive, Chance doubted there'd be any relief upon seeing him dead. However, after much searching, neither Claire nor Johnny could be found. Dead nurses, on the other hand, lay scattered about like playing cards in a jail cell.

The sun burned bright overhead. His shadow darkened her white hat. After everything they'd been through, he felt he should say something, but like a jilted lover, he let the silence remain undisturbed.

"Shouldn't've done it..." Mrs. Jakes finally said.

Could've. Should've. Would've.

Across the painted prairie. Off in the distance. A strange silhouette advanced slowly over the Red Carpet Country.

Rattling like a tinker's cart. Heading straight for our trio of travelers and the night that would finally destroy the Gray family for good.

August 1867

Dallas Star-Herald Tribune — Vol. 12 No. 75. 2nd Edition

In the gospel, according to this newspaper: Avery Sanderberg Wholesale Druggist and dealer in patent medicines paints oils glass dyestuffs, etc. Number thirteen Magazine Street, New Orleans.

In the gospel, according to this newspaper: Max Shreck's pulmonary syrup, seaweed tonic, and mandrake lozenges. Dr. Shreck's principal office and laboratory is at the North-East corner of sixth and commerce street in Philadelphia, PA. Where all letters are advised, or business should be directed. He will be found there every Saturday professionally to examine lungs with the Respiratotatler of which costs three and one-half dollars. All advisory statements are free. The History of Dr. Shreck's own case and how he was cured of consumption. Can be found on page three of the *Star-Herald.*

In the gospel, according to this newspaper: Kolakowski's Wholesale dealers in boots, shoes, and brogans, hats, caps, etc. Number ten magazine street, between canal and common, New Orleans. Opening second branch in the growing incorporation of Dallas in Texas.

In the gospel, according to this newspaper: Jeremiah Cleveland Forester has announced plans to resurrect the Houston and Texas Central lines for railroad construction. Mr. Forester believes connecting Texas with the national lines will be a boon for our fledging economy and do much to heal the wounds of the troubles and create industry.

In the gospel, according to this newspaper: Sperm oil services needed, contact Rosie Felcher of Dallas. Inquiries should be made in person at the Garden Bloom just outside town.

In the gospel, according to this newspaper: P.H. Goodnight, importer and dealer in foreign and domestic hard-ware, stoves, tinware, tin plates, sheet iron and zinc, bar and slab iron, nails, castings, hollow ware, etc. Tremont St. Galveston, Texas. I keep constantly on hand a full stock of tinner's tools and machines.

In the gospel, according to this newspaper: A painful rumor is in circulation here to the effect that Colonel A .B. Mahfood living in Borland's crossing or Red River in Cook County, was murdered one-night last week by a company of robbers, his house sacked and some $800 in specific, stolen. Colonel Mahfood has ever been held in the highest estimation in this section of the state and his death will cause widespread grief. We sincerely hope this rumor may prove false.

In the gospel, according to this newspaper: Competent cowpokes and punchers wanted/needed for late season overland cattle drive from Ft. Worth to Chicago. August through December. Serious inquiries only.

August 1867

Samantha had never seen this many people in all her life—at least not at one time. A trio of scuffed refugees stepped into the muddy street. The outlaw pulled the brake. The mule bristled against the stop and whimpered loudly.

All around them the street ebbed with crowd flow. A nesting doll family of blondes crossed the street. Samantha waved and asked, "Where's everyone going?"

The bigger blondes kept their heads down and ignored Samantha. All except the last one. A sandy-haired cherub offered her a gap-toothed smile. The girl's warm face could melt snow in winter. So cheery, in fact, Samantha smiled back without much effort. The little girl beamed excitedly. "They's hanging a nigger. Two of 'em. I ain't ever seen one dangle afore, let alone two."

Samantha's face fell.

The more the mob grew, the more it hurried. Spectators pushed forward and shoved back to muscle claims on the best available spots. This wasp nest hummed. Excited tension passed person to person. Anticipation tightened everyone's focus on an old tree near an impromptu courthouse. The ropes were already knotted and strung, awaiting their victims.

The outlaw let the last of the stragglers pass before slapping the reins to put the mule to work. Samantha stuck a hand out, "Hold on a second."

The outlaw stopped the rig without looking at her. Samantha didn't notice this because her eyes remained on the tree. "You ever see a live hanging?"

The outlaw didn't move. His eyes straight ahead. "Once. At Andersonville."

Samantha joined her siblings on top of Mama's coffin. The trio huddled close for a better look. Samantha asked, "Where'd you say you saw a hanging? Andrewsville?"

The outlaw remained unmoved. "Andersonville."

"Where?" Samantha asked and blocked the noonday sun with her hand.

"Further East," He said. "Last stop before the train arrives in hell."

The storm had almost blown them away, but hadn't touched the bustle of Dallas. Everything had the feeling of a camp instead of a city. Vendors erected mildewed canvas on pine stakes. Crude stalls to sell even cruder wares: Twisted rag dolls, pig fat candles, and heavy tin toys, each vied for money in this sudden marketplace. The almighty dollar says wherever you gather in my name—there shall I be, also.

Johnny's breath whistled.

Claire pointed, "They're bringing 'em out."

The spectacle unfolded, the crowd chattering with anticipation as a fat fella emerged from a metal box. His wrinkled beige suit pulled a pair of negroes across the courthouse yard. Their dark skin was covered in ruptured lesions. Telltale signs of abuse. Bound feet shuffled beneath them. The crowd cheered at their appearance. The tall negro smiled a simpleton's smile. His future might've been explained to him, but Samantha wasn't sure. The condemned man's expression reminded her of Johnny. The thought filled her with dread. She felt the noose on her own neck as it slipped over his.

"I wonder what they done wrong to get em hanged?" Claire asked.

Samantha didn't answer. Whatever he'd done probably didn't justify what was about to happen.

The official in the beige suit raised a hand and quieted the crowd. Most leaned forward to hear the charges read. Samantha was too far away to hear. A photographer's camera flashed white smoke. The fella cursed the infernal machine. Apparently, the shot was premature. He demanded a few more minutes to reset. The official in the beige suit ignored the photographer and kicked out the stools. The pair dropped. Cheers erupted. The condemned kicked wildly and more photography smoke plumed.

Samantha turned away and closed her eyes. The outlaw asked, "Glad you seen it now?"

Samantha shook her head.

Next to the wagon, a gentleman with a shock of white hair asked, "Care for a postcard?"

Samantha looked into the man's strangely familiar face. "Do I know you, sir?"

"Perhaps," said the man with unblinking eyes. "Maybe you once sat for a portrait?"

Samantha remembered the last time she was photographed and the company she kept.

"What are you selling, sir?" Samantha asked.

"Cherished memories," said the photographer. "The moment of death captured by my glass and printed here on this postcard. Send it express to family back home wherever that may be. Show em the excitement of a big city. Make them green with envy. All the miracles of a modern world."

"Selling pictures of dead men?"

"Small proofs they were once alive." The photographer chuckled, "Existence can be a terrible thing, don't you agree?"

Samantha wrinkled her brow. "No, thank you."

The photographer bowed and turned to another in the crowd. "Care for a postcard?"

The outlaw asked, "Can we go now?"

"Guess we better," Samantha cleared her throat, "before this crowd disperses."

"These folks ain't going nowhere," He said. "Not without a souvenir. If those bucks were half as stout as they looked, it could take all day for each to die." Clicked in his cheek—slapped the reins—the wagon rolled on.

"The hotel I know's just outside town," said the outlaw.

"Hotel?" Samantha asked leerily.

"Well...it lets rooms...hourly. Hoping they'll make an exception for an old friend."

Claire tuned up from the back of the wagon, "Where are you taking us, Mr. Glass?"

"Every journey," He didn't bother looking at her, "needs a friend." He glanced sideways at Samantha. "Mrs. Jakes, I'm taking y'all to a damn good one. Probably the only one I have left."

August 1867

Madame Rosie Felcher toed the edge of the porch. A fancy gown squeezed her into the shape of a wine goblet. Her bosom overflowed with busted biscuits. Above her veil, a rat's nest of greying blonde hair, mother-of-pearl clips, bright variegated feathers, and a pizazz Samantha had only seen in the tinker's dirty books. She lifted her veil beneath a freshly painted sign which read *The Garden Bloom.*

"How long's it been, Mr. Good-face? Five years?" Madame Felcher fanned herself. "The war certainly didn't hurt your best asset. But the rest of you could sure use a wash."

Why, the very idea. Jealousy greened inside Samantha. Here stood a woman who'd fully harnessed her feminine power. While Samantha stank of road sweat and swamp ass.

"Only three years Rosie." Samantha's savior, the beautiful outlaw, blushed. "And it's good to see you, too."

"I see you've brought the whole fam-dam-ily. Who's the short fellow with ya?"

Chance rubbed his chin and introduced Samantha as Mrs. Elrod Jakes.

"Oh...I blame the pants for my mistake," Rosie said and stuck out a sparkling hand.

Samantha eyed the diamond rings cautiously.

"I don't bite, sweetheart," Rosie said and smiled, but not with her eyes. As soon as their fingers touched, Felcher added, "Been known to nibble from time to time."

"Charmed," Samantha said and let go.

Madame Felcher's smile found Johnny, then quickly searched for someone else and found Claire. "You poor thing. When's they letting you out of confinement?"

"Not till December..." Claire touched her belly, "...is it that noticeable?"

"Don't see it down there, child." Madame Felcher let Claire rattle her jewelry. "Your glowing cheeks can be seen a mile away. Just a trick of the trade. Easier than most things to know when a gal's found unwanted trouble."

Felcher's smile found Johnny again and quickly looked for Chance. "Where's that water headed cousin of yours?"

"Lloyd didn't make it."

"Damn shame," Madame Felcher said. She collapsed the fan. "Gals are gonna be so disappointed. Not too bright, but...you don't have to be if you're keeping an elephant's trunk in your dungarees." She pictured it, then fanned again. "He will be missed. Lloyd the one wearing that pinewood suit?"

The whorehouse madam nodded at the only other thing in the wagon.

"Pinewood?" Chance looked over his shoulder, "Oh no...that's..."

Samantha cut him off and spoke about Mama.

Madame Felcher asked, "Is the poor dear embalmed?"

Samantha shook her head. Not knowing what the word meant exactly, but not about to let this bitch know she didn't know.

"Alighty then," Madam Felcher wrinkled her nose. "Poole's as friendly as any fella who deals in death." Her diamond ring pointed behind them. "You'll find his place at the other end of town, near the church. The one with the cemetery."

Samantha furrowed her brow. "Who's Poole?"

"A grief merchant," said the Madame. When Samantha didn't respond, Felcher added, "The undertaker, child. I respect the dead...just don't allow them in my establishment. House policy. Tough for a man to snatch a piece of ass while a corpse rots and watches. Not to mention my gals...Chance knows how superstitious they can be."

Chance started to speak, but Samantha cut him off again. "That's alright ma'am. It was a pleasure making your acquaintance." She turned for the wagon.

Chance caught her by the arm. Whispering, "Why the clouds, sunshine?"

"Dunno this person," Samantha whispered back.

"Show her there ain't really no dead body."

Samantha wasn't about to show her goods to God and everyone and told him so.

Madame Felcher cleared her throat. "While it's always a pleasure to receive old friends. I can't run a charity when I'm supposed to run a business. So, if you could..."

"Just a moment, Rosie." His smile vanished at Samantha. "We need a port in the storm."

Claire spent her two cents with folded arms. "I got a bad feeling about this place."

"Relax, both of you," Chance grated. "I trust Rose Felcher with my life."

"Don't mean I gotta," Samantha snorted. "The troll said it herself. No one crosses her bridge without paying a toll."

"Small price to pay, I say," Chance pleaded with his eyes.

Claire sniffed. "I say a real friend wouldn't require payment at all." When both Chance and Samantha remained silent, she added, "I'm just saying."

"Whatever Rosie wants in trade," Chance said. "Pay it. Greed sure don't look good on you."

"Ain't greedy," Samantha protested. "I can't afford to be stupid. Sure...this bitch'll cut her friend a deal. Then what's to stop the two friends together cutting me out?"

Chance clenched his teeth. Fire blazed behind his eyes. "I'm a man of my word."

"Ain't met a man yet worth the breath it takes to say one."

If he could've gotten away with it, Samantha knew he would've broken her nose. This promise of violence tightened her chaps beneath the dirty shirt. Adrenaline surged. Heartbeat galloped. Jaw trembled. Part of her wanted him to smash her face in. Desire tingled up her chain and around her waist.

"Can't spend the entire evening waiting..." Madame Felcher cleared her throat again. "So, if there's something I can do for you. Now's the time..."

Chance wagged a finger to buy more time. "Whatever it costs...pay it from my half."

Samantha gestured towards the hotel. "You'd cut into your share just to stay at this dump?"

Madame Felcher stood close enough you could smell lavender. She spoke, "Since both of you learned to whisper in a sawmill, I want to make something absolutely clear. If my friend's paying for the room, then he's the only one getting one."

"Don't mind Mrs. Jakes, Rosie," Chance said. "She's just partial to her mother. Could you perhaps, for old times' sake, allow us to store the coffin here? Feel free to double the price."

Madame Felcher shook her head. "Can't allow it. Despite your reasonable request." Her eyes shifted. "The price would just be too high."

"I'm sure whatever you set is reasonable," Chance nodded.

"I wasn't talking about my room rates."

"Miss Rosie..." Chance said, laying it on thick, "since we're friends. I'd be mighty obliged if you'd extend our friendship to my companions."

Madame Felcher looked them up and down. "Just need the one room?"

"Two please," Chance said and thumbed at Samantha. "Just friends."

Madame Felcher figured it in her head, "How many nights?"

"No longer than a week."

Madame Felcher laughed. "The Garden Bloom's not keeping a coffin for more than two days."

Chance smiled, "Two days is plenty."

Madame Felcher matched his with her own and said. "Be two dollars American."

Samantha perked up. "Why so low?"

"That's the friend price, since Chance asked so nicely."

Samantha smiled. "Thank you for your kindness."

"Kindness?" Madame Felcher scoffed. "Your's'll be six dollars."

Samantha's face fell, and she demanded to know why.

Madame Felcher rolled her eyes. "Simple math. Chance only got the one head...while you need to sleep three."

"Stay if you want, Chance," Samantha said, turning again for the wagon. "Me and mine aren't welcome here."

"Goddamn, Chance," Madame Felcher laughed. "Dunno what relation you two share, but she ain't got the brains God gave a monkey."

Samantha wheeled around—fist on hip. "You don't know who or what I know."

Madame Felcher sneered, "I call 'em how I see em."

"I won't have my book cover judged by some whorehouse floozy...And I am smart!"

Madame Felcher laughed. "Any gal who gotta advertise such facts is only selling fiction to herself because no one else is buying." The Madame cocked her head, "How I earn a living should be no concern to a waif gal with no figure...who looks and smells like a man whose rolled in the cesspool. Especially if that same bitch is troubled by such ugly luggage."

"Leave my brother out of this!" Samantha felt Papa's Navy Colt in her pocket.

Madame Felcher raised her eyebrows. "I was referring to your mama in the box...but if you call a spade a spade, we can agree." Madam Felcher frowned at Johnny. "That thing's...um...your brother?"

Claire and Samantha nodded together.

Rosie studied Johnny a beat, then added, "Sure, he's a sweet boy. Unlike your bitch sister, I meant no offense. If

Chance and I didn't go back so far, I'd bid you good day right here, right now."

Chance clucked his tongue. "Sorry about this Rosie...Mrs. Jakes and I are business partners." His voice rising as he looked over his shoulder at Samantha. His words drew lines in the sand between them. "If I'd known it'd be like chewing buffalo-turds, I wouldn't have come a-calling."

Samantha glared at Chance then spoke to Rosie, "Could you please take us all in for three dollars?"

Madame Felcher fanned herself. "At least this gal knows her own worth." She scowled. "What did you call me a second ago? A troll? Ha! I've been called worse. But you're right about one thing. You gotta pay my toll as listed. Six dollars American or fare-the-well."

"Fine!" Samantha stiffened. "But at that price, my mother stays in the room with us."

The Madame's breath hitched. "You'll keep it in the barn out back and like it!"

"Rosie..." Chance flashed his failing charm again. You could feel the tension releasing along the thin line between confidence and arrogance. Both the Madame and Samantha soaked it in as he spilled the secret. At least there was one thing both women could agree on. When he'd finished, Felcher squinted in disbelief and said, "Show me."

Chance glanced sideways.

Samantha spat and begrudgingly lifted the coffin lid. Madame Felcher's jaw dropped. It jiggled her bosom. "My God." For the first time, her eyes smiled at Samantha. "Don't suppose you'd be interested in reopening negotiations?"

Samantha closed the lid. "No."

"I can respect that," Madame Felcher's fan fluttered. "But I'll insist you keep it in my personal quarters."

Papa's Navy Colt between her fingers, "I don't leave my mother's side...ever."

"I can respect that too, but...you see. My quarters contain the only door with a lock in the dump. In fact, as a sign of my hospitality..." her diamond rings found her chest, then swung in a big arching gesture towards the hotel. "...I'll turn it over to you for the duration of your stay." She turned to Chance. "My two best gals will pay you a visit once you've settled in. As for my other three guests," Rosie's eyes twinkled, "welcome to the Garden Bloom. Our customers agree it's the best little whorehouse in the lone star state."

AUGUST 1867

THE WHOREHOUSE REEKED OF tobacco smoke, menstrual blood, and spilled whiskey. Crawl across the floor with the scorpions and you still wouldn't breathe fresh air. And even down there, the summer heat was thicker than a hermit's beard. Claire leaned near Samantha's sweaty face. "Cozy, ain't it."

Samantha knew it could've been if it weren't antiquated with youthful solicitors. Felcher led her guests through the parlor. Girls lounged in various stages of undress. One flexed her knees together, rapidly wafting air on her crotch. While another rubbed a cool rag over her neck and armpits. Two took turns fanning each other with a newspaper. Another pair pretended to play chess while waiting for their next customers.

In the curl of the staircase, one of Felcher's girls knelt over a standing John. The fool leaned far backwards. His head knocked against the railing. His knuckles whitened. The Madame ignored the vulgar calligraphy of the contortionists. Too busy following the coffin carriers upstairs.

Claire covered little Johnny's face and quipped, "Make you miss your captain?"

Samantha turned slowly. Vindictiveness in her words. "The exact moment your baby drops," her battered lips curled, "prepare for war."

"I was just kiddin," Claire said. "You don't gotta make idle threats."

"Consider it a promise, then."

Claire gripped Johnny's arm and slunk on in a huff. The boy trailing behind her like a rag doll.

Samantha lingered a moment longer. The drunk John moaned appreciation for the whore on her knees. Samantha wondered how many Brigadier Generals could be listed before that musty clunker popped off.

"Enjoy watching, huh?" A soft voice spoke from somewhere unseen.

Samantha spun around startled, "Pardon me?"

From a dark corner, Samantha saw a match flare. A somewhat pretty face ignited an oil lamp. "Didn't mean to scare you," said the whore as she replaced the lamp's globe. "Funny how those who watch never think someone's watching them watching others."

"I wasn't watching I..."

"No judgements here," said the whore. "Gotta fella pays me three bits a-week just to watch me tickle my backdoor." She nodded off her right shoulder. "Hides behind yonder screen—diddling himself. Call him the *Howling Dripper*. Ever met one of them afore?"

Samantha shook her head.

"Work here long enough. You'll meet all kinds of men. The dusty knucklers, the rough and readies, the marrieds. As for the Howling Drippers...most are fat and older. They moan and moan, making you think it's going to come fast and blind you, only to spill a few measly drops."

The whore stood. Fingers rubbed the sheer fabric on her chest. "Madame Felcher named me Brownie, on account of these."

Two round breasts covered almost entirely by dark areolas approached Samantha.

"Like what you see?" Brownie reached and thumbed away the dirt from Samantha's mouth and looked puzzled—then frowned with embarrassment. "Why you're not a..."

"Mrs. Gray?" Madame Felcher called down the staircase.

Samantha glanced up. "Be there in a minute."

Brownie blushed, "I'm so sorry...I thought you was a customer."

Samantha didn't say anything. Her left hand reached for Brownie's chin and gently pulled the whore's face closer. Samantha could smell the neglect over her own. Brownie's eyes closed. Her lips pouted. This bitch expected a kiss. Samantha's lips hovered close. They breathed each other's stale air. Samantha gently touched the gal's face and whispered, "Darling...don't ever speak to me without my permission ever again."

Samantha squeezed the whore's cheeks tight enough they changed color. Fear fluttered Brownie's eyes open. Samantha added, "I'll accept your apology whenever it's ready to be given." Samantha released. The whore stumbled away, rubbing her jaw. Small town hatred flashed behind her eyes. She started to say something but couldn't find the right words.

Samantha answered for her. "I know exactly how you feel right now. I promise I do."

Brownie stood panting in the dim. Her frightened eyes never veered from the myth, the legend herself. A confusing mix of sultry awe and a victim's contempt.

Samantha drawled, "I'll be upstairs if you grow the balls to do something about it," then turned and climbed the staircase. Whispering names of Confederate traitors with every step taken.

October 1867

"Ain't parleyed with a white woman since last Christmas," Sheridan said. The dusty trader, his two horses, and his traveling general store brought sundries and strange ideas about lovemaking. "Forgive me if I come across coarse." He laughed again and stoked the fire. Eying his guests over the rising flames. Sheridan added, "Tell me now gal, is ye open to a little commerce? Fancy a trade?"

Samantha didn't answer. Eyes locked on the crackling fire. Her mind was a burning hell. How could she have been so stupid? If she hadn't been so selfish, Johnny would still be alive. Claire would be too. Their wagon would still be moving Mama's coffin north. Some mistakes can't be unmade.

Sheridan cleared his throat and repeated himself.

Samantha glanced over the flames. The trader Sheridan seemed harmless enough, despite his flood of nonsense. Fool must be starved for attention. His two horses didn't talk back. Samantha's brow knitted. "Trade? Trade what?"

"Anything off my wagon," Sheridan leered. "Got dry beans, gingham cloth, a cast iron set never used. And another only gently so. I believe if ye just look around, ye find something to make a woman of your quality very hap-hap-happy. And if ye don't want none of my goods, maybe ye fella here will: got shovels, gunpowder, Ching-chong fireworks, and some old dynamite if'n ye have need of such a thing."

Samantha eyed the trader's cart. Then eyed Chance—her savior—the outlaw. His bedroom eyes fixed suspicion on Sheridan. Tension tightened around the campfire. Sheridan, seemingly unaware of this, kept smiling and waiting for her answer.

Samantha shook her head. "You ain't got nothing I need."

He laughed good-naturedly. "Ye ain't even looked yet."

Chance cleared his throat. "I guess you should know..." Samantha winced. Claire and Johnny disappeared again in the back of the nursing school wagon as Chance drawled the story to conclusion.

The trader only waited for his turn to speak. "That's some tale. Since I's a nice fella, tell ye what I'll do. Go on now," He thumbed at his wagon, "pick out another item at no charge. Two for one trade. Tis easy!"

"Wait..." Samantha asked, "what am I giving you?"

Sheridan's brow arched. "I thought I'd made it clear what I wanted."

Samantha scoffed. "You must've hidden those specifics in your vagaries?"

"Specifics? Vagaries?" Sheridan scratched his chin and looked over at Chance. "Good thing my nickel and dime words sold out back in Jeff City—ye gals already got a mouthful." He looked back at Samantha. "How 'bout this for specifics?" His index finger wiggled to and fro between his guests. "Ye ain't together, is ye?"

Chance looked down at the fire. "Business partners, only."

"That may be—but ye business ain't poking her. I can tell these things. Ye don't know each other as well as ye like me to believe. Maybe ye might've gotten close, I dunno. None of my concern."

Samantha thought about the disturbance in Chance's room and kept quiet.

"She's a free agent, sure," Chance said. "But she's under my protection."

Samantha beamed at Chance. It made her cold soul feel warmer. Almost considered giving him another opportunity to yank around her chain. She shuddered at the thought and the terrible truth behind it.

"Trades up to her," Chance added. "She don't need me to negotiate."

Why the very idea. She wasn't the one walking around with something horrid between her legs.

"Settles all accounts then," Sheridan said. "How 'bout it gal? Care to join me behind the wagon? It'll be a spot colder away from this here fire, but it'll save ye um...partner here, some modesty."

Samantha felt outside herself. An entire world full of crude men who did not understand women. But bound and determined to exploit them none-the-less. They'd been making good time since leaving Dallas in a hurry. Almost caught the lost wagon train, but now she'd lost more than she'd bargained for. What good's a coffin stuffed with gold, if your loved ones ain't there to help you say goodbye to it? Samantha glared at Sheridan. "Go behind the wagon for what?"

"Gott-dang gal. Do I gotta recite the whole alphabet for ye. I give ye any two of my top-notch goods and ye just gotta gimme a high-quality pudding clank."

Samantha didn't understand.

"A goshdanged dusty knuckler!" He blustered in disbelief, "A lingo-finger? A knuckle union? A rusty smuggler?"

Samantha looked him over queer.

"I ain't trying to split ye beard or nothing!" Sheridan shook his head, "For a gal in trousers ye sure don't know the ways of man, do ye."

Chance chuckled.

Samantha glared at him. "What's so funny?"

"I'm trying to imagine what in the hell's a dusty knuckler?"

The salesman saw his opportunity and took it. "It's the latest thing. Best guard against the scourge of syphilis, I know. Way better than those lamb skins ye get from a chemist. And it melts the north pole between strangers so they can get to know one another." His fist thumped his chest. "I'm disease free and fancy a bit of ye time gal. Best part, we don't even have to touch each other—until the end, that is. Ye see, we stand in front of each other. Ye slip into ye birthday dressings. I keep on every stitch and only produce my pecker. I rub it like a mad bastard while appreciating ye feminine mysteries. I get close but no touching. One hand to God, the other clutching my ramrod." His hands demonstrated the maneuver. "Now don't take offense—Dunno where all ye been. Most gals express increased titillation afterwards. One even told me it was more exciting than most bible studies men make ye suffer through. All ye do is tell me sweet lies while I punish meself. Don't worry. If ye dunno what ye should say. I'll be ye guide—just repeat the words I say. Me Johnson will swell like a python after dinner...then to finish things off—" He gushed with excitement, "This is the best part, mind ye. At the moment of rapturous joy, I fill my other palm with fresh seed. Squeeze it together so it lathers real thick and..." His voice rose in pitch. "...this is where ye shine the brightest. Ye sit back on ye heels and lick the hand clean of me sweet-sweet love jelly. Whaddaya say?"

Samantha sighed loud enough it silenced Sheridan's laugh. Her maw a dark hole like the barrel of Papa's Navy Colt in her face. "You ought not speak such evil in front of a lady."

Sheridan's mouth churned with confusion. Lips formed a dozen word fragments. He squinted. Gave her small frame a once over. Crossed both arms and sullenly leaned forward. "Ye ain't no lady. Ye may be one bangtail gal. But no lady I met yet, tougher 'n' ye gal."

Samantha's lips cracked a small smile at his backwards compliment. He opened his mouth again. "Injuns known to take woman folk every chance they get, and they didn't lay a red finger on ye."

Samantha's face dropped. "We didn't see no injuns. Came along afterwards."

Sheridan's mouth twitched, but he recovered swiftly. "Uh...Bloody foul savages. And I should know—a businessman must know the customer or suffer bankruptcy. But ye don't know—the Comanch! Ain't much different from us. Hell, they just as American. I say if ye can't make a deal with a Comanche brave, ye ain't worth the salt God wasted to make ye."

"Deal?" Chance asked. "You don't make deals with radishes. You eat 'em."

Sheridan's palms rubbed his trousers nervously. "Besides earlier, how many ye ever met, fancy lad?"

"None running around free and don't plan on it," Chance said. "Everyone knows Comanche drink the blood of their kills. I'm fine with letting them dry out and go thirsty."

"Thirsty for blood?" Sheridan asked and shook his head. "In my experience, they prefer whiskey. One can travel far across the Comancheria, if ye willing to part with a little corn liquor. Makes the red devils milder than fresh barnyard milk."

Samantha's chest tightened. "You work with the plains people?"

"Aye, not exclusively, but enough to know me way around."

"Would you know which tribe attacked my brother and sister?"

Sheridan scratched his stubble in thought. He walked over and snatched arrows from a dead steer. "I might. If one didn't know better...ye'd mistake these arrows for Comanch."

"Do you speak Comanche?" Samantha asked. "Could you parlay?"

"Gal," Sheridan said. "Them's ain't Comanche. They's the same breed but different. One of the last of the true savages. Ye can tell by the mud used to paint the chevrons here." He pointed at the shaft near the arrowhead. "Can ye smell it ain't like regular?"

Samantha shook her head.

His face fell. "Ye did say that sister were pregnant?"

Samantha nodded. "Due in two months."

Sheridan swallowed nervously. He spoke the words she feared most. "She's probably dead already. Baby cut from her belly. A war trophy to pass around, during their blood rituals."

Samantha stood. "Then there's no time to waste."

Sheridan cackled. "Ye gonna ride in and volunteer to take her place?"

"We can't sit here. We have to do something."

"We?" Sheridan cackled again. "Ye a pistol, ain't ye—ye and this pretty boy think you got enough stones to parlay a release from the white-clay-folk?"

"Depends..." Samantha said. "Would they'd negotiate?"

"With two strangers?" Sheridan shook his head. "Not a chance, pale face. They'd cut ye to enough ribbons, they'd turn them kaolin pits pink."

Samantha squinted. "Conduct much business with them?"

"Not when I can help it."

Samantha introduced Papa's Navy Colt. "Can you help it now?"

He glanced at the gun. "Here I am offering ye kindness and sanctuary from all evils of this land and ye going to draw iron for me troubles. I know ye lost ye family gal, but that don't concern me."

"Listen here, you old pervert," Samantha cocked the hammer back. "No one kills my sister but me. If she's dead, then I want her head and her baby's head. And the head of the one who's done it."

"That's hard jacked," Sheridan looked at Chance. "Ye goin along with this?"

"You talk to me, old man," she eyed his wagon. "What do they trade best with you?"

"Ain't got it on me no more anyhow," Sheridan scolded. "And I ain't losing me whole inventory for some urchin pair of no relation."

Samantha smiled. "We can pay you for it?"

Chance snapped to attention. "What are you talking about, Sam?"

"Money," she ignored the outlaw, "we got plenty."

Sheridan laughed hard, "Not only is ye an ugly piece of chicken—ye got a mouth clucking jokes!"

Samantha didn't dither. "We do have money. More than you've seen or ever will again, especially if the broke-shake you peddle represents the best you offer."

Sheridan scrunched his face. "Ye cracking jokes is one thing. Every trader loves a good laugh. Ain't no man expected to weather an insult. Especially from poor white trash with unlearned manners."

Samantha gripped the gun with both hands. "I can prove it, salesman."

"Don't do this Sam..." Chance said, "...a word, please."

"I'm listening."

"I meant a word away from this old coot."

"Whatever it is, spill it. If this disgusting fool don't agree to help get Johnny and Claire back. He'll keep our secrets forever."

Chance paused. "My half ain't on the offering plate."

Samantha spoke through her teeth. "I will put on offer whatever I need to offer."

"Give him all of your share if that boat floats," Chance said. "He gets none of mine."

Samantha stared him down. "You swore you'd help get us on our way."

"Our deal stands—but what's left of my half belongs to me."

"Our deal is null and void if you can't deliver all three of us." She turned back to the trader. "And until that job is completed—all of it remains mine. And I will do with it as I see fit."

"Yeah...that's what I'm worried about," Chance said. "It sounds like you're about to buy a farm with no well. What did you say to me back at Rosie's? I dunno this person. We'll neither of us can vouch for this son-of-a-bitch. You show this old cooter and you can say adios to both our halves."

Samantha thought quick, "We make sure he don't."

"Care to elaborate?"

"We make him a reasonable offer." The pistol steadied in her hand. "One so good he'd be a fool to refuse."

Sheridan showed his palms, "Uh...I don't negotiate with women outside of Knuckle Unions and mealtimes. But...uh...I especially tend to not trust one who's cocked a widow maker at me. I might be obliged to help. Now I said *MIGHT*. Put the piece away or I'll take the tribe's campsite locale to hell with me."

"Okay, salesman." Samantha eased the hammer back and lowered the gun. "Squawk."

"First," Sheridan hesitated, "show me ye got the goods for a parlay."

Buttercup whinnied as they approached. The quarter-master remained silently watching from beneath the ruined quilt. The coffin lay in the wagon beneath a sky dotted with the myths of heroes. Samantha held the lamp. Chance shoved aside the mangled quartermaster and lifted the lid. Soft yellow light spilled across their treasure.

Sheridan's eyes went wide. "My *Gawd.*"

August 1867

DARK HANDS DEPOSITED THE heavy coffin in the office. The Madame dismissed their owners and gestured at Claire. "Over yonder, you'll find the brass bed I brought from New Orleans. Before you make yourself at home, please take advantage of our hot baths. It'll separate you from the road and make my sheets last longer."

Claire nodded and rubbed her belly.

Madame Felcher asked, "When's the last time a doctor visited you?"

Claire didn't answer.

"I see." Madame Felcher nodded. "Get yourself good and clean and I'll fetch the doc."

Samantha stood in the doorway and cleared her throat. "Ain't no need."

Madame Felcher tightened her lips and fixed her eyes on the door. "All three of you are well undernourished...your sister is pregnant and not under the care of a midwife. If you're staying under my roof, I insist she receive a visit from a physician."

Samantha sneered, "We ain't paying..."

Madame Felcher cackled, "Ole Doc Schoolcraft serves the Garden Bloom on retainer. There will be no charge. You and your family are my guests...and again, I insist."

Madame Felcher moved to a wall. A pair of velvet ropes hung along wooden etchings of naked women surrounded by men exposing themselves. The Madame pulled one of the ropes. Somewhere a bell rang. A plump girl in an apron appeared behind Samantha. "Yes, Madame?"

The boss barked orders: run four hot baths, one for Chance to be administered by a couple of whores—both named Hope, somebody named Penasco needed to bring something named Tequila Oscuro, and someone else needed to send for Doc Schoolcraft.

Within a few minutes, the Madame's will was more or less done. Claire and Johnny were led out. When Samantha didn't follow, Madame Felcher eyeballed her suspiciously.

"Won't leave mama unattended," Samantha said and sat on the coffin.

"As you can see," Felcher parted her arms. "There's only the one door."

Samantha eyed it, and its friends, the four walls. Looked from brass bed to wardrobe, vanity to bureau, where a statuette sat. The polished green stone watched over everything. From a distance, one might mistake it for human. However, the face swarmed with feelers of some kind. Whatever the battle-box thing was, menaced Samantha with vague familiarity, and she looked back at her hostess.

"And this," Felcher opened a drawer and procured something metal, "be the only key."

Samantha squinted at the brass lock-breaker. "What about your *secret passages?*"

The question hung in the air for a moment, as her host considered it.

"My, what a fancy imagination you have." Felcher chuckled, "Do tell where you heard such nonsense?"

"Books," Samantha rubbed her nose on the Captain's dirty sleeve.

"Had no idea I was in the presence of a reader." Felcher's laughter was thick with mockery.

"Secret passages are from Dumb-ass," Samantha's fingers tapped aggravation on the coffin's lid. "Ever read him?"

Her chuckles petered out. "I believe the man's name is Dumas. Not Dumb-Ass."

"Ever read him?" She asked again.

"*Count of Monte Cristo,*" Felcher nodded. "Some say the printed word can be blamed for the majority of the world's ills." Felcher rummaged further in her drawer. Collected a box of matches struck one on the little green statuette. Touched the fire to a cigar. Soon smoke clouded around her and the green menace. Samantha's blood ran cold. Her hostess noticed the sudden shift in mood. "See you're admiring my totem?"

Brow wrinkled, "You're what?"

"Totem..." said the Madame and delicately caressed the statuette's bald dome. "Lucky charm of sorts—from my days in the Crescent City. Just a little something to make a strange place feel more like home."

"It's ugly as hell," Samantha said and turned away. She couldn't place the statuette's face, but she knew she'd seen it somewhere before.

"Beauty is in the eye of the beholder," Felcher smiled crookedly. "Given to me by the famous Voodoo priestess, *Canola Rapeseed.* Ever heard of her?"

Samantha hadn't.

A boulder of a man darkened the doorway.

"C'mon in, Penasco."

The man waddled over. Placed two glasses on the desk. Pulled a cork and splashed a finger of brown in each. Madame Felcher held one. "How's the house tonight?"

"Slower than a Saturday," he drawled, glancing once at Samantha, "for a Tuesday."

"Send Doc Schoolcraft in as soon as his old bones arrive."

The boulder didn't move. He and the madame shared a worried look. Some unspoken code between them. "Madame Rosie," Penasco finally said. "Them minstrels is back."

She sighed, "Business or pleasure?"

The round fella didn't know.

She scoffed, "Do they got instrumentations or is their peckers out?"

He counted each on thick fingers. "They got fiddles, banjos, squeezebox..."

She waved her hand. "Set em up in the parlor. Regular spot at the regular rate. Half a dollar or a poke a piece. If that don't satisfy, they can do their screeching elsewhere."

The man turned to exit without the bottle.

"One more thing, Penasco," Felcher said. "Have we heard from Gretchen?"

The boulder's head shook side to side.

"If we do," Felcher's tone dropped as if pregnant with worry. "If we do, send her in at once."

And just like that, he was gone.

Samantha's eyes landed on a series of wall prints. Heavy papers hung from nails. She asked about the girl named Gretchen.

"She's my..." Felcher paused. "...cousin. Been missing a few days." Downstairs, sounds of muffled laughter wafted up. "Went shopping for possibles down at Kolakowski's." A guitar tuned, followed by a fiddle, a banjo. "She's new to the area. And... well." An accordion leaked part of a melody. "Doesn't matter. She'll be along soon. I'm certain of it."

Downstairs, the evening's entertainment prepared itself.

"Admiring more of my decor?" Asked the Madame. "Don't they tie the room together?"

"They ain't fancy," Samantha sneered. "seen 'em once before."

Felcher pushed one of the glasses across her desk towards her guest. "Visit the French Quarter often?"

"No...never," Samantha ignored the drink and approached the wall instead. Stuck her forefinger in the middle one. "This'n here I saw in a book once." She traced the outlines of the women and men in various lewd embraces. "...in my husband's library."

"Husband? I saw no ring."

"Oh, he gave me a couple, alright." Samantha spoke low, "Don't show 'em off much."

Felcher exhaled a smoke ring. "Give ya them bruises, too?"

Samantha stopped, pointing. Hands covered one another. Rubbing her still purple wrists.

"Don't be ashamed, my dear," said the Madame. "*Juliette* is beyond brutal. Sexy...but brutal."

"*Justine*," said Samantha. "Book weren't called *Juliette* when my husband had it. Marcus De Said wrote it.

Couldn't tell you the story none...don't read French. Same drawings, though."

Madame Felcher lowered her voice. "Did they excite you?"

Samantha scowled. "They're stupid and cause evil."

"So..." the Madame nodded once, "shall we drink to cherished memories then?"

Samantha turned from the wall. "Some I'd like to forget."

"Well then, it's settled." Felcher held up the glass. "We drink to forget."

Samantha shook her head. "Don't drink. My husband..." she trailed off.

"He ain't here," Felcher said. Irritation rose in her voice. "Besides, one must never make *new friends* with a dry mouth."

Samantha's tongue was fat with dehydration. It swiped her gritty teeth. Tasted her bleeding gums.

Felcher's face wrinkled as she swallowed the brown liquor. Immediately, poured herself another. "How did my sweet boy Chance come to make friends with the likes of someone...well, like you?"

Why the very idea?

Samantha briefly considered the question. "We just did."

Felcher smiled tight, "Impolite to make a lady drink alone."

"A true lady don't drink at all. Whether she's alone or not."

"Then you have no excuse to refuse." Felcher cackled loud and bawdy. "Or maybe you're just afraid of having a good time."

Downstairs, someone piped a flute. Followed by the ticky-tack snaps of spoons against a washboard. A fiddle climbed up and down its scales. The band was about ready.

"Ain't afraid," Samantha grabbed the glass and knocked it back and grimaced and wished she hadn't. The Oscuro burned. Her stomach quaked. It was the first thing Samantha had consumed since the stolen chili, and that was weeks ago.

Madame leaned forward. Diamond hands criss-crossed—like a mesmerist preparing to dazzle. "It'll give a coward courage, a drunkard a lift, and hopefully it'll relax someone as tightly wound as you. Frankly, I don't care what your story is...I don't cotton to tension. Breeds monsters amongst my gals. Relaxed whores can milk a man much faster. And that's good for business."

Felcher poured another round. The glass touched Samantha's lips. A dulcet melody drifted in: *"Look away! Look Away! Look Away, Dixie-land! Oh, how I wish I was in Dixie! Hoo-ray! Hoo-ray!"*

"First hit takes your breath away. The second..." Felcher sniffed. "Lifts you into the ether. Now go wash your stinking ass. A fella catch this place downwind of you and he'll be scared plumb away. And that's bad for business."

Samantha killed the glass and refused to budge. "Like I said...Don't leave my mama unattended...ever."

AUGUST 1867

A Little Later — Washing Off the Road

The room was a mistake. Built in the Garden Bloom's corner, one of the walls angled from the headboard to the door. Once the outlaw wiggled inside, he could barely move. No need for guests to waste time in the dump not humping. Nothing more to do in here than lie horizontal. Even lacked a window. No scenic attractions to observe unless you brought them in with you, and those at the Garden Bloom charged by the quarter-hour.

Good ole Rosie, Chance thought, *still squeezing customers for every nickel and dime.*

He managed to close the door and began the arduous task ahead. Hesitation was to be expected. A damaged undercarriage slows more than your wagon. And Chance was in no hurry to examine his. Something was wrong, terribly wrong, but he didn't know exactly what. And he hated uncertainty. You would too if you spilled an inkwell every time you peed.

His guts sang that old familiar gurgle. From somewhere in the room, Lloyd spoke: *Just delaying the inevitable, you know.*

"*Ain't we all,*" Chance answered before realizing he'd done anything. "Blast it, Lloyd," he muttered under his breath. "*Why can't you go on and leave me be?*"

The door knocked. Chance paused—unsure if he'd imagined it or not. When the knock came again, he cracked it open.

"Someone in there with you already?" asked a half-dressed blonde.

"Are we too late?" Asked a matching red head.

"Naw ladies..." Chance flashed his grin, "...you come at the exact right time."

One of the Hope's made a joke about returning the favor, but the best Chance could offer was a half-hearted chuckle. The Hopes were big in all the right places. A sight much prettier than the trio he'd ridden in with. Sheer nightgowns teased their tourist attractions. The Hopes led him out the cramped room, scuttling like a crab down the hallway.

Steam rose from the claw-footed tub. The Hopes each took an arm. Worked off his nasty clothes. Each layer stank worse than an onion. He wondered if there'd be anything left inside when they'd finished peeling him.

"Sorry for the smell, ladies," Chance said and closed his eyes. The pair struggled to pull down his ruined trousers—too rigid with dried grease. He reopened his eyes and saw the promise of spring. Both Hopes disrobed. Four pale orbs stared back, wall-eyed. If Chance didn't hurt so bad—he would've enjoyed their bathhouse show. Rubbing each other—making their chaps hard. The blonde Hope noticed Chance's lack of enthusiasm. "You'll relax once you get wet."

Chance cowboy'd up and stood knee deep in the hot bathwater, unwilling to sit proper in the tub. "Ya'll two do your business from here."

"Ain't you gonna sit?" asked the redheaded Hope.

"Naw ladies," Chance said. "Afraid my craw's too chaffed from the road. Might be the cure's worse than the symptoms?"

"Whatever you say, handsome," the blonde Hope answered.

Warm water sponged over his shoulders, chest, abdomen, and points further south. He hadn't been touched like this since New Orleans, when he found Rosie's establishment under new ownership. At least his oldest friend had left a forwarding address.

The Hopes did their duty.

When it happened—his neck corded.

A groan strangled in his throat.

Every muscle cramped.

A thousand stars popped across his vision. Pain rocketed beyond nebulas, galaxies, comets, and millions upon millions of spinning infinities. At once, he saw straight through the universe. His mind reeled.

AUGUST 1867

The Garden Bloom — A Confederacy of Diseases

Downstairs the band played, *"Hurrah! Hurrah! For the Bonnie Blue Flag that bears a single star!"* Doc Schoolcraft held Claire's freshly bathed wrist and checked her pulse. His eyes, however, looked elsewhere. "What symptoms plague ye?" he asked absently. "Morning ills?"

"Not since June." Claire shook her head.

The doctor didn't notice. "Have your paps engorged?"

Claire surveyed her chest and didn't see any difference. She looked at Samantha, who sat pensively on top of Mama's coffin. Downstairs sang, *"First, gallant South Carolina nobly made the stand, then came Alabama and took her by the hand."*

Schoolcraft concluded his examination with a distracted pat on her shoulder. "Recommend elixir salts for digestion. And rest...plenty of it." He stood. Eyes fixed on Johnny. The boy slurped at a dish of ice cream, unaware of the man looming behind him. Schoolcraft observed the boy so tenderly, you might mistake it for falling in love. He leaned forward. Nostrils flared over the crusty sores spotting across Johnny's pate. "Fascinating specimen," he muttered.

Samantha cleared her throat. "That'n's my brother you're fancying."

Schoolcraft nodded, "Fascinating young man."

Samantha observed him—observing the child. Her fourth dram of firewater pumped in her blood. "Johnny don't like people staring at him."

"Quickly, followed, Mississippi, Georgia, and Florida. All raised on high, the Bonnie Blue Flag that bears a single star. Hurrah! Hurrah!"

"I'm a professional scientist, my dear. I can assure you; this is more than a casual observance."

"I don't like people staring at him either," Samantha felt for Papa's Navy Colt. "...professional or otherwise."

Doc Schoolcraft rubbed his chin. "By any chance know what caused your mother to depart?"

Samantha flinched. The memory rushed back. Mama's face blurred with sweat, discoloration and mucus. Papa pacing and agitated. Samantha didn't want to remember this—not with a head full of tequila, anyway. If she'd known it would be the last time she'd see her mother alive, she would've handled things differently.

"Ye men of valor gather round the banner of the right, Texas and fair Louisiana join us in the fight, Davis, for President, and Steven's statesman rare. Now rally round the Bonnie Blue Flag that bears a single star! Hurrah! Hurrah!"

"Worked in Baltimore—the only reason I ask," said the doctor. "—before the war. Serviced some unique clientele. Sailors, mostly, with their neck tattoos and the thin pajama clad women who love them. Those types run across some very nasty little critters—"

Samantha didn't react.

Doc pointed at Johnny. "Seen this condition before."

"Hurrah! Hurrah! For Southern rights Hurrah! Hurrah for the Bonnie Blue Flag that bears a single star!"

"What condition?" Samantha asked and poured herself another drink.

Schoolcraft scratched his face nervously. She could tell he regretted bringing the matter to attention. But his curiosity demanded satisfaction. "Did your mother happen to die from syphilis?"

"Hell no," Claire said. "Why would you even ask such an awful thing?"

Schoolcraft held his hands aloft. "Your boy here's got the congenital. It's what causes grooved teeth and square irises like he got."

Samantha spoke low, "Don't like what you're saying about our mother."

Schoolcraft showed her his palms. "I'm not saying she did. But I've never seen it on anyone else unless their mother was suffering. Did she suffer at the end?"

Mama's voice between her ears. *A happy wife is one who serves the lord and her husband.*

Claire squealed. "Our mother was a wonderful woman."

Schoolcraft re-observed the boy, "I'm certain she was a saint."

Claire shook her head in disbelief. "Is you gonna let him talk that way about mama?"

Samantha raged at her sister. "Keep yourself to yourself. Our mother..." She lost words, just like she'd lost Mama's face. The room swam around her, and she sat back on the coffin.

Schoolcraft straightened. "Do tell...what were you told was wrong with him?"

"Nothing's wrong with him," Samantha said. "He is a blessing from God."

Claire piped in, "I thought papa said mama got kicked by that horse?"

Samantha cut her eyes at Claire, then back at the doctor.

Everyone looked at Johnny, who sat alone in his little world, licking the silver saucer clean. Schoolcraft snapped his fingers at Johnny, who stared at the man's hands curiously. "I see he ain't lost his hearing or sight...yet."

"Johnny can hear and see fine without you snapping at him."

Schoolcraft stepped towards Samantha and asked quietly, "Has he ever spoken?"

"He don't talk words." Samantha clenched her teeth. "But we understand him."

"I only ask because in some cases...it's inevitable. The blindness, I mean. The eyes just stop working." Schoolcraft sighed remorsely. "To see the world through eyes that only open so much and then to be plunged into darkness. Part of the disease. Almost the cruelest thing God could've added to it."

"You know something crueler?" Samantha asked.

"Life's cruel enough for most of us without stacking the deck. Lord works in mysterious ways. Don't get me wrong. A mighty intelligent designer. Systems tightly constructed to keep life perpetuating itself on earth. Must've taken eons." The doctor paused. "Wonder how long it took him to finish creating syphilis and cancer and cholera and gangrene. Did he rest shortly after to observe the beauty of his work? Or was it all an accident like most decent things?"

Now here's to brave Virginia, the Old Dominion State,

"What's that gotta do with Johnny talking?"

"Disease may have spared him his sight since it took his voice."

With the young Confederacy, at last has sealed her fate.

A half-dressed whore burst in. "Doc Schoolcraft!" She panicked, "Come quick!"

"Whores," Schoolcraft grated with annoyance. "Never fails. I find something worth my time and one of them's pulling my attention to something else!" His face screwed up mockingly. "*Doctor Schoolcraft, Doctor Schoolcraft, check this lump. Doctor Schoolcraft, my pussy burns, Doctor Schoolcraft, what do you mean it's malignant?*" He glanced over his shoulder. "What's the trouble now, whore?"

"Gotta fella," cried the blonde anxiously, unaware a shoulder strap slid down as she spoke. "Gotta black thing growing between his balls and asshole." The other strap dipped. Her nightgown remained sweat-stuck to her bust, and clung for life as she said, "Hope and I were giving him a bath and one of us accidentally touched it. I think it were Hope that done it, but she'll say it was me."

Schoolcraft touched his forehead. "Fella's got a black spot?"

"Thought it was a big-ole dingle-berry, and that's why I...mean Hope wiped at it with a brush. Fella's foaming at the mouth now. Think he's having a seizure!"

Samantha watched the room clear. The little statue on the desk watched her knock back the rest of her drink. Clustered eyes above a beard of overgrown noodles. She couldn't take its grim visage anymore. Collected the vile thing and shoved it in a drawer. Good luck or no—she could do without its ugliness. Down the hall, Chance screamed bloody murder. The world spun when she stood. Vision elongated. She gripped her stomach, then the wall, and waited for it to pass.

She hated to make sick—the mud butt and the bubble-guts could make you wish for a swift death. The booze, the smells, the memories of Sweet Pine, all too much. Samantha doubled over a nearby spittoon and purged.

Then here's to our Confederacy,
strong we are and brave,
Up it came in hot spasms.
Like patriots of old, we'll fight,
Groaning as the bitter acid splashed out of her.
And rather than submit to shame,
to die we would prefer,
At this tiny brass altar, Samantha prayed for swift deliverance.

So cheer for the Bonnie Blue Flag that bears a single star.

August 1867

The Garden Bloom — Another Infection

Samantha stole a drunken glimpse. The outlaw writhed soapy and naked on the floor. Agonized vowels foamed at his mouth. "AAAEeeiiOOOUuu!"

Samantha found his wet leg between her hands—strangely bereft of hair—helping Schoolcraft and the Hopes in transport. Placed him on a wobbling breakfast table. The man of science took one look at the outlaw's business and hollered, "*Christ a-mighty!* How long's this been troubling you, son?"

Why the very idea?

The outlaw, her savior—the man with the beautiful face, could not answer. He'd gone blood simple with pain. A black boil below his testes gave the appearance of two dark assholes.

"Maybe an in-grown hair," Claire laughed flippantly. "But he ain't got none nowhere else. Smoother than a baby doll that boy is."

Schoolcraft ignored her and barked orders. *"Fetch my bag!"*

The blonde Hope obeyed. Straps appeared in Samantha's hand. She stared at them drunkenly. When she didn't do anything else, someone shoved her aside and took the belts themselves. A tiny knife glinted in the gloom. "Ye gals better hold him down. If'n he jerks a smidge, he'll lose more than that infected cyst."

The whores threw their bodies across the outlaw. Schoolcraft lowered the blade. Sweat poured off his nose. His wrist twitched as he cut. Blood spurted between the outlaw's legs. Everyone flinched. Catch a whiff of infection souring the air and you'd flinch too. Samantha caught Johnny looking.

His ruined face contorted with ugly worry.

He knew—she knew—he shouldn't be here.

AUGUST 1867

THE BAND SANG ON, *O ole Zip Coon he is a learned skoler, O ole Zip Coon he is a learned skoler, O ole Zip Coon he is a learned skoler.* All the way down the hall to the office, Samantha's forehead burned. Sweat formed at her temples. The world elongated around her. Her feet felt a million years away. Johnny's wrapped arms—an anchor that kept her body from floating away free.

Sings posum up a gum tree an coony in a holler.
Possum up a gum tree, coony on a stump.

Samantha managed to turn down the bed. Johnny clamored in. With no change of clothes to his name, one of the whores had dressed Johnny best she could. The sheer night shirt revealed his worm's wood skin, amongst other things. At least the thing was long enough to cover the boy's bare behind.

Possum up a gum tree, coony on a stump.

Samantha wiped her wet mouth and pulled the quilt up. Johnny flopped side to side. His arms pushed against it. Samantha asked, "Too hot for a quilt?"

Johnny clicked his jagged sawtooth teeth twice.

Possum up a gum tree, coony on a stump.

It used to make Samantha wretch, but she'd grown to love his uniquely unpleasant face. Love corrects all transgressions. She started to stand and go back for the bottle. Johnny whimpered. His hand caught Samantha's elbow.

Den over dubble trubble, Zip coon will jump.

Samantha closed her eyes. *"What is it?"* She asked, as if he could answer. Without re-opening her drunken eyes, she said, "Time for night-night, Johnny. We're all tired."

O Zip a duden duden duden zip a duden day.

Johnny insistently pulled on her arm. His breath was a high-pitched whistle in his malformed throat. Tonight, he would not go gentle. Tonight, he wanted something else. A shock of disgust swirled around her belly. Of all the nights to need something extra.

O Zip a duden duden duden zip a duden day. Johnny's whimper sounded so pathetic Samantha gazed down blearily. *O Zip a duden duden duden zip a duden day.* She stared at his nose to keep from looking at the leaking scabs everywhere else.

Zip a duden duden duden zip a duden day.

"Tonight? Of all nights?"

Johnny nodded.

O ist old Suky blue skin, she is in lub wid me

Samantha squinted. His hideous features blurred.

O ist old Suky blue skin, she is in lub wid me

For a second, Samantha thought she saw their mother's face on Johnny's head. A kind of forever death on the face of her brother, the family's only male heir.

O ist old Suky blue skin, she is in lub wid me

It couldn't be helped for whatever reason.

I went the udder arter noon to take a dish ob tea.

Folks all shared the same expression whenever they saw the boy. A form of pity reserved mainly for church on Sundays.

What do you tink now, Suky hab for supper,

He'd never be confused with the sharpest tool in the workshop, but he wasn't stupid. If anything, he knew how to get along better than any of them. As long as he got fed and watched over some, Samantha knew Johnny was as good, if not better, than a regular boy. He deserved better than he'd ever gotten from Papa, and definitely not from the Captain. Even when people are spitting on him, Johnny never got upset. Even when people are shooting at him, Johnny never panicked. Johnny's features blurred back into focus. All the faults and flaws of genetics were written large across her brother's face. Samantha knew the hand of God when she saw it. On the day Johnny was born, a moment forever burned into her memory.

"We've had a rough night," Samantha said. "So, I'll only tell you a short bedtime story."

Tequila Oscuro maintained its grip on most of her mind. She did the best she could. Slurring out something about pigs and wolves and those eternal rivals masons and carpenters. The boy listened to her nonsense and stroked her hand until his strange flat eyes closed. When she finished her story, she blew out the candle. The room darkened. She could still hear the noise from the operating room. Shouts and screams and panic and fear. One can either close their eyes or cover their ears. You can't do both without a little help.

Downstairs, the band sang:

*O ist old Suky blue skin, she is in lub wid me
I went the udder arter noon to take a dish ob tea;*

Samantha wanted the madame's help. Or at least more of her liquid courage.

August 1867

Sounds of a good time drifted upstairs. Curious of the commotion, Samantha went exploring. Fingers gripped tight on the handrail to steady her wobble. The Garden Bloom buzzed with the flowering of the hour. Minstrels led the room in a singalong. *Camptown ladies sing this song do-dah, do-dah...*

Samantha wasn't sure how she managed, but she found the bar. A dim corner of the dump lit with candles flickering in the mirror behind Penasco. He stood behind a plank across two barrels, polishing mason jars. Samantha found an open spot. Two dusty cowpokes nursed whiskies on either side as she wedged between them.

"Want no trouble," Penasco laughed.

"Don't want none neither," Samantha said and braced her elbows on the plank. She wasn't going anywhere and waited for the puke to stop his laughing. Her mind swirled.

Camptown racetrack five miles long, oh da doo dah day!

"If not trouble," Penasco frowned. "Have drink. Trouble soon follow. What you like?"

"Dunno..." she motioned with her thumb, "Upstairs? What darkness was I drinking with frilly fat-chap O'puddin'?"

Penasco mimed holding a pair of melons. "You mean Madame." Shook his head. "Especial tequila. Only pour for Rosie. Upstairs drink and drink her drink. Down here—only whiskey."

"Why'd ya even ask then?"

"Don't want trouble," Penasco's face fell.

The cowpoke to her right hiccuped and inserted himself into the conversation. Voice high and slurring with drink. "Red eye here ain't the best in Texas, but it'll sure make the ugliest whore here worth the ticket to ride. Buhahaha"

Samantha laughed defensively. "Ain't interested in no whores."

"Why else would you visit this dump," asked the man, "if not to dandify the Yankee?"

Gwine to run all night! Gwine to run all day! I'll bet my money on de bob-tail nag, somebody bet on de bay.

Samantha didn't comprehend.

Cowpoke then asked, "Ratify the constitution?"

Penasco sat a glass on the plank and poured. Whiskey spilled into it, and the stranger beside her cupped his mouth—thinking she was hard of hearing—and shouted, "Get your pecker wet!"

Samantha waved him off. "Ain't no concern of mine."

This caught the cowpoke's attention. His voice cracked. "Lost it in the war, did ya?"

Samantha turned real slow. Her vision sparkled in the dim. The man's face was wet with drink and sweat matted down his beard. His eyes—two red marbles.

She thought of Mama and grated, "I'm a gal, you jack-ass."

The cowpoke reeled in for closer inspection.

Samantha stiffened his hands and slung her elbows. "You want trouble, skimmy?"

Camptown ladies sing this song do-dah, do-dah...

He hiccuped. "What kinda woman drinks in da whorehouse? Is you working me? Cause if'n you is—I just wanna say..." Hat doffed and clutched chest high. The gallantry in his gesture caught Samantha off guard. Made her blush. Then he opened his mouth. "...I'm flattered, but you'd have to pay me for the privilege."

Samantha's face fell.

Why the very idea.

Camptown races five miles long oh dah-do-dah day!

Quick as lightning in a storm, Papa's Navy Colt appeared. *SWAAP!* Charged joy burned between her legs in a small frenzy. She moaned and bit her lip. The Colt swung across the drunk's nose. Spinning the fool on his heels and crumpling him limp-kneed. Catching the corner of the plank and keeping himself somewhat upright. Blood seeped between the fingers holding onto his face.

"What in the sam hell did ya do that fer?!" He whined.

Samantha's neck hair prickled. Panting as if she'd just climbed a mountain. Pleasure surged through her veins. Made her light-headed—mind completely blown from the eruption in her loins. She realized the violence had caused it, had been causing it. The booze helped, sure, but what about all them other times she was sober? Then she saw what she had done and felt a twinge of guilt. The man bowed up.

She leveled the pistol.

Too late to take it back. "Considered yourself paid unless you can cash out hot lead."

The drunk spoke through his nose at the gun, "I beg
your pardon, ma'am—meant no offense." Both hands
held aloft in surrender. Bloody nose broken and already
swelling purple. She told herself, the moment you put
away Papa's gun—he'll get the upper hand—just like in
Shakespeare.

*Gwine to run all night! Gwine to run all day! I'll bet my
money on de bob-tail nag, Somebody bet on de bay.*

He doffed his hat and bowed. "I ain't ever drank no
whiskey with a woman afore. Be happy to buy your first
round."

"I can afford my own whiskey."

He bowed again. "Let me buy your second and third
while we're at it. Who knows—maybe you'll grow bigger
tiddies in the meantime."

Penasco was no help, he just stood there smiling that
stupid smile. Did he not see the gun in her hand? Or
was he like all the others? Taking one look and misjudg-
ing her for another woman, they'd be forced to contain
the hysterics of. She was not hysterical. She practiced the
Tao—she knew the way of the great silence. She'd once
taken seventeen lashes and not uttered a peep. She'd once
allowed a lost Yankee to steal her virtue in order to keep
her younger siblings safe. She contained multitudes and
by god she'd make this fool suffer like she'd suffered. That
would show them all who was hysterical.

She heard herself and winced.

Blood dripped from the gun. She stowed it into her coat
pocket, but didn't let it go.

Another cowpoke came over. "Randy, what the hell
happened here?"

The bleeding man waved him off. His voice was high and nasally, "I'm alright...I'm alright...it was my mistake."

"You're bleeding out, ya damn fool," said the friend. "Barkeep! What in the hell happened to my cousin?"

Penasco pointed a thick sausage finger at the culprit.

She turned her back to the pair. Eyes locked on them over Penasco's round head. In the mirror, Mr. Friendly pulled his jacket back to go for his peacemaker. Penasco saw this and shook his head quickly side-to-side. Samantha readied to return fire. Time slowed—sound quieted. Just the breath sawing in her lungs to the quickening beat of her heart. This was it, she thought. She didn't mind one bit. Knowing flat well that as soon as she killed the son-of-a-bitch, she'd come harder than an overdue bill.

Papa's words between her ears, but she couldn't hear them.

Faces in the crowd stretched in silent screams. She knew—they knew—she knew what came next. In the coat pocket, Samantha thumbed the hammer back. One click—two clicks—then paused. Suddenly, she squeezed the trigger, easing the action back down to safety. No need to draw and fire after all. Instead, she watched the cousins slink away in the bar's mirror. Disappearing into the growing flotsam and jetsam of the whorehouse. Finally, she thought, cooler heads had prevailed.

She also saw she was being watched.

Camptown ladies sing this song doo-dah! Doo-dah!

Samantha lifted the whisky to Brownie's reflection before awkwardly downing it. An agonized grimace followed. She feared she'd wretch again. And wanted no more of Penasco's fire water. Brownie's eyes tracked each step Samantha took across the parlor. One hand touched the banister. One boot toed the first step. She looked over her shoulder—dirty lashes batted for the whore to follow her upstairs.

Going to run all night, going to run all day, bet my money on a bobtail nag, somebody bet on the bey!

The whiskey and tequila fought for control as Brownie poured hot water into a claw-foot tub. Samantha commanded her to disrobe. The whore obeyed. "Now take my clothes off," Samantha said. Brownie hesitated, but complied. The Captain's words coming out of Samantha's mouth, "Look into my eyes while you do it, bitch."

The myth, the legend herself, was mighty hammered, but even she saw the vacancy in the girl's eyes as she stared into Samantha's drunken face. Samantha knew—She knew—she wouldn't refuse.

Not this poor gal's first rodeo, Samantha thought. Just another job that doesn't pay very well. She pictured the handsome outlaw as the naked whore covered her in suds. When Brownie discovered Samantha's hidden hardware, she gasped.

"Enjoy what you see?" Samantha asked.

Eyes flashed with genuine concern. "Does it hurt?"

Samantha's hands looped her silver chain around the whore's neck, pulling her close. Breath hot on Brownie's lips, "Wash me."

Tingles vibrated quickly. Hot breath rushed. The spirits lifted Mrs. Jakes higher and higher until the world spun her comfortably down to sleep.

For the first time—since forever—no nerves, butterflies, or worry. She slept and dreamt again about the Yankee she'd buried in the backyard three years ago. The first man she ever killed.

AUGUST 1867

A RUDE AWAKENING — THE KITTEN'S CLAWS

SAMANTHA AWOKE WITH A start. She didn't recognize the room, or the naked girl sweating beside her. Between her ears, a military parade marched in tight formation. Blocking all memories of the night before. The drummers pounded in syncopation as she sat up. Didn't see Johnny, or the Outlaw, or...she jumped from the bed. Frantically searched for her clothes—found none—not even the Captain's coat. She whirled around and snatched linens from the bed. The girl never noticed—sawing logs, unaware she was now alone.

Claire and the Madame sat together at the bureau. Startled when the myth, the legend herself, flung open the office door clad only in a sweaty bedsheet. Felcher laughed, "Did ya have fun last night Mrs. Jakes?"

The coffin still sat in the middle of the room. Lid squealed open. Samantha stared at the treasure. Trying to recall yet unsure of the count from yesterday. Had some grown legs in the night and walked off? She couldn't be sure.

"It's all there," said the Madame. "Feel free to count if you don't trust me. In fact, bring it over here and I'll get a couple of my gals to help."

Samantha slammed it shut. Another mistake, since the noise boomed between her ears. Eyes closed. She touched her temples and croaked: "I've got two questions: Where the hell are my clothes?" She stabbed the air at her sister. "And why the hell are you talking to this diabolical bitch?"

"The clothes are being washed. A courtesy I'm extending free of charge." Madame Felcher fluttered her eyes. "And your sister here was just chatting about the weather. Seems your plan to go west might be ill conceived. Should've left Texas back in the spring if'n you wanted to make the Oregon trail before winter come."

"So..." Samantha sat the coffin lid. Johnny bounded over and crawled into her lap—frenzied with excitement and puppy love.

Claire smirked, "Calendar says May 1st is the last day to leave Independence."

"Independence?" Samantha asked. "That near here?"

"Independence, Missouri." Claire laughed haughtily, as if she'd known all along.

Samantha wanted to shoot her and patted her side searching for Papa's Navy Colt.

"Relax, my dear," said the Madam, opening a desk drawer and placing the revolver between them. "It's right here waiting for you..." Felcher leaned forward, her neckline plunged, "...but first...listen to my offer."

Johnny, the lapdog, wallered. Samantha ignored him. Easier and easier to do lately.

"Stay on here at the Garden Bloom until spring comes. Your sister here is due this December. I personally wouldn't wanna give birth while snowbound in the mountains. I mean, I wouldn't wanna go to California to begin with—too many Mexicans. Now Kansas City's a town I hear's up and coming."

Samantha knew—Felcher knew—she would refuse.

The Madame sighed at Claire. "You'd think after a night of tequila and whores your sister would be at least a little happier."

Claire nodded. "Guess some folks are just born to be miserable."

Johnny rolled off. Samantha advanced for the desk. Claire avoided eye contact. Samantha collected the gun and started to exit.

"Ain't ya even gonna ask about your business partner?" Madame Felcher's voice stopped her at the door. "Your sister and I been up with him all night. Making sure he was comfortable."

Apparently, Dr. Schoolcraft's operation succeeded. Seven stitches meant the outlaw couldn't be moved for at least a week to recover. The suture needed cleaning three times a day to stave off infection.

Samantha spoke over her shoulder, "Think we'll be moving on without him?"

"The hell you will," Madame Felcher slapped her desk. "Mr. Glass's interests are under my protection while he recuperates."

"Don't worry sister," Claire added, "I've been doing the same for ours."

Samantha turned around slow. "Excuse me." Pure small-town hatred passed between them. "Need a private conference with my sweet sister."

The Madame hesitated, but pushed back from her desk and closed the door behind her.

Samantha clenched her teeth. "I forbid you from speaking to that woman or Chance."

All the air vacuumed between them. Two alley cats squaring off. Claire hissed first, "Jealousy don't look good on you, sister." She laughed, "But of course, nothing does."

Samantha leapt forward—blinded by rage—thumb and index squeezed Claire's broken nose. Good tingles came fast. Claire wailed and raked her fingernails. Samantha moaned. Waves of pleasure turned painful. And the sisters spilled off the furniture. Bedsheet unfurled. Cleared off the desk. The little ugly statuette plummeted into a mass of flailing limbs and curses. Claire yanked hair between fingers. Samantha held firm. "Think I ain't ever had my hair pulled? You'll have to do better than..."

Claire tent-poled her knee. Cracked against Samantha's wedding rings. Her violent orgasm ruined. She winced and folded into a naked ball. Silver chain spilled from its coil. Thighs clamped hands between, rocking away the pain. The little bitch rested on her knees and elbows. Panted and sweated and spat on her naked sister. "You disgust me."

Samantha writhed in agony.

"The Captain was right. You're just a dumb cu..."

Samantha found the ugly statuette and swung and caught her sister's ear. But swung too hard—losing her grip. And lost where the statuette landed. They fell on each other again. Grunting vowels—all gnashing teeth and hair.

"Get off me, you carpet chewing succubus!" Claire choked on her words.

Samantha throttled her. "You evil slut-ditch! I'll kill you!"

Claire's fingers found silver chain. Jerked sideways. Trying to rip out the rings. Samantha howled. Claire wrapped Samantha's neck with the chain, choking her. The vicious world began to dim. In desperation, Samantha slammed her forehead on Claire's broken nose. Again and again and again. Claire dropped the chain. Air rushed into her lungs. Both rolled away, exhausted. Both scrambled to stand again.

"Stay away from me!" Claire's left hand clutched her bleeding nose. The right held the green statuette like a cudgel. "When my king finds me—he's gonna cut off your flat teets and...and..." her voice nasally with impotent rage, *"make ya eat 'em!"*

"If that bastard shows his face," Samantha panted. "I put one in your baby's head—so I hope for your sake it happens soon. Solve two problems with one bullet."

Claire seethed. "Don't you threaten my baby again."

Samantha sneered, "Ain't a threat—but a fair shake promise."

"In that case," tears spilled down Claire's face, "Your shack job whore better sleep lite—for your sake."

Samantha stared her sister down. "Threatening me, sweet sister?"

"No..." Claire wiped away the tears, "...it's a fair shake promise, too." She never took her eyes off Samantha. Nor dropped her weapon as she knelt and collected a medicine bottle. "Clean Mr. Goodface's balls with this." Placed it on the desk. "If I can't talk to him—I ain't helping him either."

Claire slammed the door behind her. Samantha didn't watch her go. Instead, found the Madame's mirror. Fresh scratches around her eyes blended in with everything else.

She looked a frightful mess—a supreme disappointment. Behind her, Johnny wheezed and slapped the coffin lid twice. The boy's emotions were like blots of spilled ink. You needed to stare a minute to recognize the pattern. Familiar pangs of guilt crept into Samantha's soul. She knew exactly what upset him. Arms outstretched for the boy, but her brother wouldn't come. She called him and he still didn't budge. "No one is killing anyone while they sleep," Samantha cooed. "Them's just angry words, Johnny. Nothing to worry about." He must've believed her because he bounded over, nearly knocking her back with the force of his hug. She rubbed his ruined back. The boy slapped his thigh once. Samantha didn't have the energy to try to interpret the boy's nonsense. Not with the hangover whistling dixie in her head.

She loved him. But this was no place for a boy. Especially one as troubled as Johnny.

Papa's words between her ears, *The Goddess of Fortune favors the bold.*

Mama's words between her ears, *Children are blessings sent from Heaven.*

Felcher stood in the doorway. Holding her lucky charm. And surveyed the damage.

Samantha wiped the blood off her mouth. "I'll pay for the mess."

Felcher silently crossed to her desk and restored the ugly green thing to its place of honor. "When my sweet Chance awakens," said the Madame. "I'm..." Her voice trailed off. Eyes dropped. Her face fell.

Samantha trembled with self-realization. Her secret exposed. All pretense—all her required toughness—collected her offending shame. Madam Felcher looked away as

Samantha rewrapped the silver chain in silence. Samantha's eyes over Johnny's blistered head locked on the wall prints, at the dirty pictures of naked ladies suspended above burning coals, held aloft by hooks gouging their voluminous breasts through stretched nipples, pretty faces of strained agony somewhere between misery and joy, while heavy men pulled on ropes, wide smiles more than pleased with their torture, and exposing large erect phalluses tethered to metal gags in the mouths of prone women, with wrists bound to ankles, nightmarish images pregnant with evil and stupidity and as dangerous as her Papa's decision to marry his oldest daughter to a bad man of good breeding.

Johnny lifted the bedsheet, so Samantha didn't need to bend over. His hideous face filled with the trauma of their parents' marriage. Of the hard times and the failed businesses. Of the visitors who called on Mama and required the Gray sisters to take long walks. These visitors were never there when the girls returned to the cabin to find Mama half-dressed and counting new money. Johnny's wet oblong pupils overflowed with some kind of empathy.

Felcher spoke to Samantha's spine, "I don't allow gals to fight in my estab..."

"There won't be anymore..." White sheet covered Samantha's nakedness, and she added, "Could I borrow some clothes...my errands today won't run themselves without me."

SEPTEMBER 1867

NARY TEN P.M. — THE SPIRIT OF CAPITALISM

THE PROPRIETOR OF KOLAKOWSKI'S Mercantile sat at the back of the store, keeping books. Unsure exactly of what to do with his sudden good fortune. The figure at the bottom of the ledger was so big, Mr. Kolakowski rendered the figures out three more times. Finally, satisfied with the result, he closed the accounting book. After months and months of struggle, could the poor man dare to dream about future possibilities? He'd rolled the dice two years ago and now his gamble looked to have finally paid off.

The boon's euphoria was short-lived.

A knock came on the locked front door. Kolakowski kept perfectly still, hoping the visitor would give up and go away. No such luck. The knock came again, louder and more persistent.

Kolakowski slapped his desk. "Come back tomorr-y! Closed for the night!"

Glass shattered. A dark hand snaked through the hole and unlatched the lock.

He stood. "Now see here...I done told ya I was closed for the..." When he saw the intruders, he swallowed his words. Five in total. One of them shoved another forward. He came stumbling towards the proprietor. The wounded man caught himself on a cracker barrel to keep from sprawling.

"Can I help you?" Asked the proprietor.

Cracker barrel man straightened. "I do beg your pardon, sir. My associates believe you have something that belongs to them."

The proprietor shook his head. "Don't believe I've ever traded with them afore.

"You ain't traded none," said the man. "Regardless, they believe you have their property. And if I was you—I'd not tarry."

"Umbridge! Umbridge, I say!" *Kolakowski* folded his arms. "Run a legitimate business, sir. I will not be intimidated by ruffians. Besides, I've already paid my tithe to the Sheriff...which makes my license to conduct my affairs good till next Sund-y."

Pause.

The wounded man spoke low, "There's no changing their minds on the matter."

"What...um...property am I supposed to have?"

The man limped into the light. Bloody rags wrapped around the left hand. A photograph clutched in the other. "Has this little plain gal paid you a visit?"

The proprietor slipped on his glasses for a better look. "Yeah, I couldn't forget a face as sad as hers. One of the surliest young women I've ever had the displeasure to conduct trade with."

He looked up from the photograph, startled.

Four of the intruders had closed in. Kolakowski saw his frightened reflection in their black eyes. The one who wore a red beard growled, "When did you last trade with this woman?"

Kolakowski swallowed the lump in his throat. "Yester-dy. She took a shine to my haberdasher's wares. Bought four complete wardrobes, all black for some reason. And a brace of new pistols. Forty-four caliber Whitneyville's if'n I remember correctly. As well as a third of all my possibles."

A dark man stepped forward. Black hair, black eyes, black obelisk dangled below his scruffy Adam's apple. He touched both lovingly and asked with a voice like striking a match, "Where's the gold?"

"What gold do you mean?"

The dark man didn't flinch—waited for Kolakowski's answer.

The proprietor's eyes went to the back of the store.

It didn't take long for the Lovecock Gang to lay hands upon the money. Each taking a coin in hand and moaning loudly in a strange language he'd never heard before. Then their black eyes became human again.

"Jesus Christ!" Kolakowski shook with fear. "What in the sam-hell are you folks?"

The dark one whistled. Hands seized the trembling merchant. Steel flashed its razor's edge. Kolakowski's bald head bounced twice on the rough-hewn boards and rolled to the side. Before all lights dimmed, it saw the intruders gorging on the blood from his headless neck.

LATE AUGUST 1867

NEAR THE WITCHING HOUR — A STRANGE PENTECOST

THE SERPENTINE CONGREGATION MARCHED single file from the wilderness. Fire and brimstone erupted as the Pastor spoke. And the crowd praised *Amen*. His flock skewed heavily female. A scatter of men stood like birthday candles amongst the frosting of petticoats. Lit torches revealed craggy faces and sunken eyes. Warbling unhappy noises, loud and off-key and sans accompaniment—no way to keep time. A small improvement over the band inside the Garden Bloom, who, like so many others in attendance, flocked to the windows to gawk at the sudden visitors.

Already vendors erected oilcloth stalls on the outskirts of the mob. Whatever wares they peddled, the Garden Bloom's front porch held no vantage. It struck Samantha as the funniest thing she'd seen in a month of Sundays. Like the almighty dollar says, wherever thy join in my name—there shall I be also.

"What's all the noise?" Samantha asked the madame.

"I assume they're like most customers," Madame shook her head, "horny as hell...cept these fools dunno what to do about it."

The choir settled and quieted.

"This house hath brought hell to God's little acre." His index finger saluted the sign above Samantha. "They present themselves as common Jezebels but be not fooled by their lewd enticements. Their flesh may be for sale, but their souls are already owned outright by Satan he-self!"

And the crowd said, *Amen!*

Samantha Jakes snickered at their hollow gasping. It seemed a little too well rehearsed. Too well built through hours of repetition. And yet something remained chaotic about it. At any moment, Samantha reasoned, this uninvited prayer meeting could collapse like saloon songs on a spring afternoon. Blossoming with ejaculations in a steady call/response. The sheer bizarro tone edged Samantha's frazzled nerves.

Felcher sensed it too and called over her shoulder, "Boston Mark!"

A burly fellow answered slowly, "Yessum?"

"Load my elephant gun with buckshot. These zealots seem more riled than normal."

"Happen a lot?" Samantha asked, never taking her eyes off the impromtu country revival.

"Infrequently," Felcher said. "Pastor stops by once a week for a bishop's roundtable."

Samantha didn't understand.

"Ain't heard tell of it neither until I moved from the Big Easy to God's country." Felcher chuckled, "Requests three of my gals for a private visit. Talks Jesus and the gal's ears off for an hour, before nerving up to ask them to stroke one out for him. The whores complain more about the sheer boredom than anything else, but the dusty knuckler pays, so I have no beef."

Samantha wiped her nose across the Captain's freshly cleaned sleeve. Butterflies swarmed her belly. A strange threat hung in the air. She spoke flatly. "Seems he has beef with you."

Madame Felcher scoffed. "He's putting on a show for his customers." Her head was tight on a swivel. "This is just a fan-fan dance," her mind raced. "his rent must be due. It's simple economics." And the crowd sang, *Amen!* "The church collects money to rid the world of sin. And he pays me to ensure he knows it when he sees it."

Amens like cannon fire! Felcher jumped slightly at the *noisy burst.* The Madame's *tough veneer chipped* away as more hallelujahs erupted with frothy ecstasy. "Guess tonight he wants everyone to see it, too."

Pastor preached, "They use the blessed act of sexual congress to scoff at the laws of Moses. Eager to turn away from the good book and turn on the charm whenever it un-suits them."

A section of insidious looking grannies heckled, "Jezebel, Ruth, Delilah, *Eve!*"

"Temptation sold with one hand and evil practiced with the other. Right hand knows the left and revels at its witchcraft." The pastor searched the crowd. "*Brock Alexander!* Confess your sins before God and your fellow man. We are with the Lord, and he is with you now. Confess to ye brothers and sisters."

Brock stood shoulder high-a-jackrabbit in the middle of the worshipers. His reedy voice cracked, "Lord knows I am a sinner! I visited this wicked place last payday." Salt tears welled in the fool's eyes. "And two more paydays before that'n. I knew it be a sin but couldn't turn from the temptation."

The crowd boomed, "Preach brother! Preach!"

"Weren't but two days later I felt the curse cast by these she-devils. Felt hell fire each time I...I..." Brock looked at the ladies around him. A weirdness twitched in his face. The joy of mischief in his voice. "Painful red orbs stacked along my nethers. I seen em with my own two eyes. There, in my darkest hour, I prayed for guidance. *Jaysuss! Won't you come and help me!*"

"Praise the name! Praise the name!"

Crowd firmly behind Brock now. He brought it all back home, "The lord spoke unto me. Do what thou wilt to the whole of my law! And I knew then the worth of my willpower. May you all know it too! And if not now...as soon as we're done punishing these wicked whores. Their evil rituals must stop before they spellbind the whole country."

Felcher's fists met her hips. "I don't recall your ugly face ever stepping into my establishment. Whatever whore shares your crotch rot ain't one of my gals. Mine are certified clean each week or the flea-bitten bitch is sent packing! We offer only quality merchandise at the Garden Bloom."

The Pastor smiled, a devil in his teeth. "There she stands, brothers and sisters. The wickedest woman in Texas!"

The congregation barked. Or something close to it—so sudden and throaty Samantha could compare it with nothing else. They barked again and froze with eerie stillness. Samantha heard one of the whores ask the silence, "What in the blue hell is they a-doing?"

Now the congregation shifted and twitched. Stepping jerkily in unison. Shoulders swayed tightly side to side. Skulls straight ahead and unshaken by staggered movements below, dancing sloppy yet regimented box steps.

Murmurs chattered inside the whorehouse, "Some kind of Shakers dance?"

Felcher shouted over the spectacle. "If I'm so wicked, how come I ain't spread the word on your whoremongering pastor, yet?"

"Lies! Do ya hear em? When the devil confronts righteousness—falsehoods spew forth."

And the crowd screamed, *Amen!*

Felcher called aloud the dancer's names she knew on sight as customers. "Clyde Baggis! Alton Summers! Templeton Peters!" But her loud scolding got lost amongst the strange menace of these good, kind, country folk magic Quakers. Blurring the thin line between cognitive dissonance and free will. These folks had all been baptized in the blood. These folks all shared the same mind—right or wrong. All here on the exact same mission.

"There's only one way to cleanse this den of inequity and restore God's grace."

And the frenzied crowd shouted, *Amen!*

Felcher turned—searching for Boston Mark and her shotgun. When she didn't find either, she disappeared inside the bordello. By the time Felcher returned, the choreography had split, creating two nearly equal halves. Torch light flickered insidious shadows across angry faces. Someone wheeled a cart in the furrowed lane between them. On the cart sat a crate pocked with air holes. The kind used to frame chicken coops. Two men dumped it over and a girl spilled out, filthy, and barely clad in rags. The sobbing girl reminded Samantha of someone she knew too well. Especially when the gal attempted to run. An unseen hand yanked on the tethered collar, ensuring she didn't get far. Eyes went wide as the cord tightened around her throat. Her face disappeared behind her as she was pulled, sending dirty feet skyward. She fell hard. Panting in the dirt. A male congregant sat on her. A neck cord wound around her arms behind her back. The crowd sang, clipping hymnals as he worked. When finished, another church elder entered, singing and holding a bucket. The girl wept helplessly as the brackish liquid covered her hair and face. It reeked of varnish and coal tar. The girl choked and screamed, "My eyes, my eyes are burning!" Her cries blended with the fervent singing!

"Gretchen?" Madame Felcher said, returning to the porch.

"That the gal?" Samantha asked.

"She's my..." Felcher gritted her teeth, "my cousin." The Madame stepped forward, shotgun loose in hand. She approached, but somewhat half-heartedly. Her tough demeanor rattled good by the mob's sudden revelation. Fear glinted in the Madame's eyeballs. Only way to explain what happened next. In a moment of second guessing, she hesitated. In the brief pause, someone snatched the shotgun from her uncommitted hands. Madame Felcher gripped the empty air. Someone stood over Gretchen with a fresh torch and dropped it.

Whoosh! Flames erupted. And the crowd over-shouted immolation, amen and hallelujah!

Papa's words between her ears, *when trouble comes...*

Papa's gun appeared in her hand. As if it had always been there. As if it were just an extension of her arm. Hammer thumbed back as if on its own accord. All she needed to do was stabilize her hips and defy the tornado.

Felcher screamed as another bucket was brought out to dose her next.

Papa's gun aimed with both hands—electric surges of anticipation. She sighted the target, then let it float sideways. Just like she'd been taught. Physics be damned.

The Navy Colt bucked. Samantha's breath hitched. Pleasure spasmed as the fella holding another bucket dropped to his knees. Fluid spilled. The bulk splashed onto the already burning Gretchen. A bright fireball roared. Heat dried sweating faces. Those on the front line—zealously standing too close to getaway—erupted with flaming spillage.

The cult snapped out of their synchronized shaking.

Samantha didn't waste another second. She aimed for the pastor, but the son-of-a-bitch had seen the light and vanished a step ahead. One of the burning choir fought to escape through the crowd. Everything he touched—burned without limit. Incendiary fools stumbled through the confused fanatics. In the corner of her eye, Samantha saw something move. She twisted just in time to see Madame's stolen shotgun. The fella, who snatched it, lifted its business end, ready to blow Samantha a kiss goodbye.

Electric current jolted from her hips to her fingers.

Samantha moaned—fired again.

Darkness bloomed from his chest. The shotgun wilted—then fired. Gretchen rocked backwards with the blast. Her arms no longer flailed—too limp to put out the yellow flames engulfing her. Samantha moved straight for the Madame. Crooked an arm under her and pulled.

Felcher struggled to stand.

Samantha levelled the pistol at the nearest stranger and felt another thunderbolt strike inside her. Samantha triggered the Navy Colt into the manic scramble. Frightened followers, some on fire and some stomping over elderly women too slow to avoid the rush, scattered in all directions. One of the oilcloth merchants beat furiously at his burning goods. No matter what he did, nothing could dim the night.

His business flamed over, nearly taking out two neighbors.

Samantha blasted again into the thinning crowd. A gush of warmth spread all over. Each bullet triggered felt better than the last. Papa's Navy Colt bucked again and again with ecstatic release. Those unlucky few who'd caught on fire were left behind to burn themselves out. None of Felcher's people attempted to extinguish them. Nor should they. Focused solely on keeping the damage away from their place of business. Air thickened with the scent of burning hair and coppery rust.

The kinda stink that clings to your nostrils forever.

Somewhere in the distance, a bell rang. Summoning volunteer fire fighters— a rag-tag crew of ex-Confederate soldiers — hell-bent on looting as much as they could before losing everything to the fire. Samantha reloaded Papa's Navy Colt in preparation to defend Mama's coffin, and her savior—the outlaw, the man with the beautiful face.

Fire brigands would arrive an hour later and find this archipelago of little ruins still burning. When they went to sack the whorehouse, Samantha breathlessly came with the speed of thirty horses, and drove the bastards back into the wilderness. Two hours later, an official-looking fella in a beige suit arrived. Took one look around the smoldering bodies. Covered his nose and mouth and asked, "Was Heather Kate burnt alive?"

Felcher answered no.

"Alright Rosie." He nodded once. "Be at the courthouse tomorrow at noon to make your statement and pay your fine."

"Fine?" Felcher balked. "What in the hell are you talking about?"

"Burning rubbish without a permit is a five-dollar offense." He nodded again. "And I count close to twenty code infractions. So if'n my math's right, then you're looking at a hefty enumeration. Expensive enough, you might wanna handle this matter off the book," he chuckled and winked. "if'n you catch my meaning?"

Felcher rolled her eyes, "How many off books you talking about?"

"At five a throw..." The official looked at the rafters and did his figuring. "and it goes without saying that number does include a hot bath and a banjo tuning,"

Just as he was about to answer twelve, the Madame said, "You get two pokes in Heather Kate. One can include a friend of your choosing."

The official protested. Quick as a flash, Samantha stuck her gun in his chest. Her voice was dead serious. "Take her deal or I take your life."

The official in the wrinkled beige suit stiffened at the meanness in her face. He nodded once. "It's settled."

Samantha stepped aside without lowering her weapon.

The officer of the public good entered the house of ill repute—unmolested further, by Samantha at least.

Madame Felcher's brow darted. She produced a square case and stuck a brown cigarillo between her teeth. It bounced on her lips anxiously. "I believe you deserve a thank you, for saving me."

Samantha slid Papa's Navy Colt into her pocket. Ran the tip of her tongue over teeth. Papa's words between her ears.

"If you really wanna thank me," Samantha struck a match and lit the Madame's smoke. "I have an idea."

LATE AUGUST 1867

"WHAT THE HELL'S A Sister of Nightingale anyhow?" Claire barked from the back of the covered wagon—the bandage on her nose yellowing with nasal discharge. The busted thing would just not heal. Her new dress, bought off the madame, fit poorly but looked clean. Samantha pushed back her new white sombrero. She'd fancied the cap enough to pay the merchant's asking price.

"Sisters of Nightingale. Dr. Schoolcraft vouched for their integrity," Samantha said, not taking her eyes off Johnny. Who didn't look nearly as awful in his short-pantsuit. "Something about starting a nursing school in Kansas City."

"Nursing school?" Claire frowned. "Why would a woman wanna waste the time?"

"Told them about Johnny and you...and your confinement. They nearly paid me to take you two off my hands." Samantha lied. The Sisters of Nightingale wanted no part of a pregnant woman going across the country on a wagon train. Convincing them otherwise cost Samantha ten gold coins. The Sisters took her offer but were quick to clarify conditions.

Samantha tightened the red bandana around Johnny's nose and mouth and tossed the other one at Claire. "What the hell's this for?"

"The Sisters ain't sure what ills Johnny...so ya'll wear these masks as safe precautions."

"Don't make me do this, Sam," Claire pleaded. "I'll run away...I swear, first chance I get."

"Hope you do scratch that itch," Samantha didn't blink. "I'd love to hear you wandered off lost—only to be found by some Comanche brave—wonder what he'd do to that worm growing inside you. Would he eat its heart and leave the rest for buzzards or make you do it?"

Claire folded her arms over her belly. "Maybe I'll meet me some handsome cowboy on this cattle drive—who offers protection until I see my Elrod again."

"Any man willing to burn himself touching your oven is either a desperate fool or outright trash. Whichever he is, you're welcome to have him all to yourself."

"That's your reason, ain't it?" Claire scoffed. "You want no competition for Captain Goodface." Her brow darted. "As if someone like him would want someone like you. Every whorehouse gal would throw him a free poke and pay him the privilege."

Samantha lowered her voice. "I got the one thing that you or them other bitches ain't."

Claire shook her head, baffled. What on God's Earth could her ugly sister have more...Claire's face fell. "I'll tell everyone where you got the gold."

Samantha scratched her wedding bands. "I've entrusted the Sister's leader with a purse. Sworn her to secrecy—even from you. Once you've reached Missouri, she'll hand it over."

"A purse?" Claire changed her tune. "How much did you put—"

"Probably more than you're worth. There's another for Johnny. Now don't be a fool and put on the mask." Samantha hoisted Johnny into the covered wagon beside her. Samantha spoke a half-truth. "If everything goes as planned. The outlaw and me will catch up before you reach Kansas City...be a couple of weeks."

Samantha turned and walked away.

A puff of photographer's smoke plumed.

Early September 1867

A Late Harbinger — Bayou Hoodoo

Nothing surprised Chance anymore. Eyes fluttered open. Lloyd stood above him on the bed. Silent as the grave. Chance groaned at the phantasm. "What do you want now?"

Lloyd's ghost did not speak. Still, archaic words echoed in Chance's ears. Blood leaked from Lloyd's eyes. Dripping off his soft round chin and painting the bedsheets. One blackened finger pointed at the bloody spot between Chance's legs. The site of Schoolcraft's operation. Lloyd smiled, a mouth of glistening red. Then clinched his fist. Something squeezed Chance's guts in a vise. The outlaw moaned and writhed. "Call off your dog Lloyd…leave me be!"

Pleas went unanswered. Chance clutched his cramping abdomen. Bowels clogged with searing constipation. As if the very limits of the exit organ had maxed out. The need to push came. Pain burned throughout his torso. His pelvic cavity bulged. He howled, "What are you doing to me, Lloyd?"

Chance's legs spread unnaturally. Knees buckled with the split. Bedsheet rose by itself. Horror seized his good senses. Some proboscis—like a newborn fern—unfurled, tasting dank air. This writhing and undulating monstrosity, a bona fide nightmare, coiled on Chance's hairless stomach.

Chance recovered the sheet. It rose and fell independently. He closed his eyes. Out of sight—out of mind. Was he losing his?

"Something bothering you, Chance?" Rosie asked.

Reality swam back to him. He lifted the sheet. And saw nothing. The top sheet dropped with aching relief. "Nightmare...must've been a...Rosie what happened?"

A cool rag touched his forehead. "You had an accident; you'll be fine soon." She smelled of lavender and pouch tobacco. "You've slept for two whole days."

It hurt to move, and Chance told her so.

"Don't bother," Rosie said. "You're in good hands—for now."

An eyebrow arched. "Kicking us out, Rosie?"

"Just that gal," Rosie said. "Worn out her welcome. But you can stay on as long as you need to heal, and maybe even longer. Could always use a trusted friend."

Chance patted her knee. "I'm heading north too, then."

"You're still going on with that ugly piece of trouble?"

Chance closed his eyes and nodded once. A hurt like he'd never felt before.

Rosie shook her head. "What's she got on you anyhow?"

"Nothing," Chance snorted weakly. "I know of worse folks than her."

Rosie spoke under her breath, "She's screwier than a two-story jakes."

"Ain't all women?"

"Watch it, Mr. Glass," Rosie said. "Just about to give you something for the pain."

"Don't threaten me with a good time," Chance tried to laugh, but couldn't.

"Speaking of threats," Rosie relayed the harrowing events from the night before.

Chance quieted, then asked, "How much time before the law comes a-looking?"

"Not much. Forty-eight hours maybe. Stick around much longer and you'll have a front-row seat at a necktie party on the front porch." Rosie twisted open the laudanum bottle. Pulled out the glass dipper. Three drops hit his mouth. He gagged on the bitter taste.

"Don't usually keep this stuff on hand," Rosie said, putting it away. "Gals tend to hoard it or sneak nips and forget what they're here for." She touched his chest. "What are you here for, Chance?"

"Me?" Chance closed his eyes. "Half a fortune's better than none. Wouldn't you agree?"

"You know it's hard to make a living. Especially on easy street. No amount is ever near enough. So..." Rosie spat a line of brown tobacco juice into a brass spittoon. She wiped her chin. "Escort this gal and her mama north. Then what? Divy up?" She scoffed. "I thought I taught you better n-that."

"Dunno what you mean, Rosie?"

"You really think she'll keep a bargain?" Rosie squinted. "More gold than any person could spend in ten lifetimes. You'll see. Mark my words. Come time to divide, you'll see just what kinda gal she really is."

"I saved her life," Chance confessed. "She don't strike me as the kind with no lack of memory."

"You can't trust someone holding a grudge." Rosie clucked her tongue. "Couldn't get the whole story before she packed off her kin."

The news raised an eyebrow. Chance pictured the two urchins. "Sure as shootin' trust her better than Frank."

"Frank?" Rosie asked.

"Yeah, Frank," he licked his dry lips. "Frank Lovecock."

Rosie gasped.

Chance looked her over queer. "Know of him. Rosie?"

"Canola Rapeseed."

Chance didn't follow.

"Crescent City's famous voodoo queen. Frank was her...what's the word I'm looking for? Prodigy? Familiar? Hatchetman? If her magic couldn't fix the problem, she'd send Frank."

"You don't say..."

"I sure as hell do." Rosie wiped her chin. "Steeped in so much evil, he reeks of sulfur."

Images of the first slaughter sprang to mind. That night in Nacogdoches, the one that got him on the wanted posters. Brutality that made his name and the rest of Lovecock gang worth two hundred Yankee dollars a-piece. "Sure as shooting never met a man with such a taste for murder."

"He ain't no man...at least not anymore." Rosie scoffed, "Some kind of djinn, I think."

"The drink?"

"No," Fear crept into her voice. "My dear sweet boy, how did you step on that devil's tail?"

Chance tried to smile. "Me and Lloyd left Andersonville before the war ended. We'd seen enough. Headed home. Seems you'd picked up stakes and headed here. At least, that's what we heard. No place else to go. Found a saloon and overheard a fella recruiting a protection squad. Something political. Guard work for some freedmen trying to vote. Called it a convention, but it was more like a riot. Us, the paid guards, didn't lift a finger as the locals lined em up, lynching everyone that foolishly stood still long enough to get caught. Next thing I know, Frank's talking about gold. More gold than any man would ever need. Sounded good enough for me. And Lloyd..." Chance paused. Half expecting to see the bastard appear again. "He made a terrible mistake and let his guilt get the better of him."

He remembered Doc Buie and the shot of blood he'd forced Chance to knock back neat.

"Where's Frank now?"

Chance shook his head. "Ain't his keeper."

"It would be wise to know," Rosie said flatly. "Never turn your back on a snake."

The door to the tiny room opened.

Early September 1867

SAMANTHA STOOD IN THE doorway. The outlaw—her savior. The man with the beautiful face awkwardly changed conversations upon seeing her. "Rosie says you killed six men."

Samantha silently scuffed the floor with her boot.

"Sheriff stopped by while you was out running more errands," said the Madame. "Seems he got upset kin wanting to know why he didn't arrest the sum'bitch who killed their relations."

Samantha stilled. "Did the Sheriff tell 'em it was self-defense?"

Madame Felcher declined, "Good clean country folk don't care one way or the other. All they know is murder at a whorehouse. And no one's hanged for it yet. As a favor to me, Sheriff Winniford gonna wait forty-eight hours before doing anything about it. But the clock's ticking."

Samantha couldn't believe it. "I kept them loonies from burning your place down with you in it. This is the thanks I get?"

"I bought you forty-eight hours to get away. Not to mention making arrangements for your sister and that boy."

"We've no time to waste then," the outlaw groaned and pulled back the blanket. Samantha kept her eyes on the Madame, who kept her eyes on the outlaw. Chance asked, "Is mama still with us?"

"She'd better be," Samantha grated.

Felcher stole a glance at the outlaw's naked body. Dabbed her bosom, causing it to ripple, and spoke to Samantha. "Hope you don't mind, but I went ahead and had them dirty rags cleaned Chance. I'll have one of the Hope's come help you dress."

The outlaw realized he was naked and covered himself. "Think I can manage from here."

"Suit yourself, handsome," the Madame smiled. "Wish I could say it was good seeing you again. But at least I got to see you at all. Guess that's what it's worth."

Chance nodded. "It is what it is."

Rosie frowned at Samantha. "Forty-eight hours." She exited.

Chance squinted at Samantha. As if looking her over, "Something different about you."

Samantha pushed back the hat and blushed. "Done some shopping."

She collected the package from the hall and tossed it on the bed. The outlaw looked at the brown paper and asked, "Paid from my half, I suppose."

Samantha blushed, "No. It's a gift. Now get dressed."

Samantha folded her arms and waited for him to comply. She wasn't going anywhere. Not without getting what those new clothes had bought her.

The outlaw just laughed, then hesitated to pull back the bloodied sheet.

Samantha couldn't wait for her present to wrap itself. She grabbed an edge and flung it off.

Her rings clinked.

EARLY SEPTEMBER 1867

TWO ALONE — UNDERSTANDING CARNAL KNOWLEDGE

SAMANTHA PEELED DOWN HER onion gook. Her pubic chain cascaded on top of the pile. She stood naked before him. Her savior—the outlaw. The man with the beautiful face sat on the bed, naked and dumbfounded. He didn't take his eyes off it. Finally, he asked, "Don't that hurt?"

Samantha shook her head. Bent and collected the leash. She started re-wrapping her waist. The outlaw stopped her. "Hand it over."

Samantha halted. Butterflies fluttered. Her rings tingled as she handed him her tether. Moisture bloomed between her legs. She bit her lip. Slowly, he reeled her in. "Not hurting ya none, am I?"

Samantha shook her head. Heart raced *bump-bump-bump*. All around them, stars twinkled and popped as if falling under a spell. Her head was lighter than air. Now they stood dangerously close. Samantha looked into his dreamy eyes and spoke huskily, "I'm not gonna have sex with you."

The outlaw's head tilted. As if looking between her lying words. His forefinger curled for her to come closer. Again, she complied and leaned forward. Anticipation swelled. He was the most beautiful thing she'd ever seen in her entire life. And now nothing stood in her way. She would let him have all of her.

Silver flashed between his hands. Chance looped the chain over the back of her neck. Pulled her closer. Whispering hot breath on her earlobe. "You're right, we probably shouldn't do this." His mouth found hers. "Especially if it's personal."

"No..." Samantha said. "This is strictly business."

They kissed. The deepest one she'd ever had. Electric current vibrated through her lips to her hips. Memories of the Captain disintegrated. Samantha felt born again, right here in the whorehouse. Finally, they pulled apart, gasping with the thrill of first contact.

She reached for his manhood.

Chance closed his eyes. Head lulled. He moaned. Hand rapidly stroking him. Their heartbeats raced. Something unseen reached for her wrist and coiled itself like a snake.

Samantha looked down, completely baffled by the dark tube wrapping her forearm.

In the Gospel according to the medical book, it's called the perineum. Some folks refer to this lonely strip of anatomy as the taint, since it t'aint the balls or the asshole. Thirty-seven percent of the entire animal kingdom sports one of various lengths. With the smallest being found on the female of the species. On some men, the gooch comes with a demarcation line showing where stem cells once divided—unlocking genetic passwords to run set-up operations, unleashing biomechanical energy, creating little miracles that will one day become some son-of-a-bitch of average build and height, who leaves the toilet seat up.

"What's wrong?" Chance asked, unaware of the slimy tentacle's return.

Samantha didn't respond and couldn't look away. Another slimy tube emerged from the wound between his legs. Which didn't resemble a wound at all. More like a dark and craggy vulva.

The outlaw saw it now and freaked.

Black oil oozed dread from the gash. Twin tentacles undulated in the evil menstruation. Coating the bed beneath his nethers.

Chance clenched his teeth. "What's happening to me?"

Dead fish stink wafted from his strange wound. Samantha feared she'd go insane. Then they heard it. His bowels rumbled as if hungry. An ancient roar, deep and watery.

Samantha slapped the thing hard. But it did no good. Both tubes sucked back into the outlaw, bringing her with them. Chance climbed the wall. No way to create distance. Samantha was pulled along for the ride. She shuddered as dark dew leaked out, blacker than a preacher's deepest secret. Her fingers felt the strange watery coldness. A cough of dead marine air escaped the void.

Chance grated, "Get it out of me!"

Samantha looked quickly around the room. Saw the only thing not nailed down. With her one good hand, she lifted the spittoon. Smashed it at the suckered arms. Ink black spurted from the gash, but still it refused to let go, coating the room in the color of death. Samantha didn't relent and kept bashing the thing with the brass bucket. Mercifully, the tentacle released—immediately sucked back into the dark and jagged wound of this strange, irregular vagina.

Samantha fell back.

Mama's words between her ears: *Ignorance is bliss.*

The need to flee came suddenly. She dressed in silence. Her nerves hummed. Her mind raced. She entered the office and quickly gathered her things. Put her coat back on. Checked Papa's Navy Colt and stuck it in the Captain's pocket. She was out the door and half-way down the stairs before she remembered. She wouldn't get very far without Mama's coffin.

She turned around and Brownie's voice stopped her. "Have you seen Madame Felcher?"

Samantha hadn't since before the...

"Cuz there's a fella down here asking about his wife."

Chills covered her skin. Samantha turned around slower than a glacier's birth. And knew the cold truth before Brownie asked, "You don't happen to know a Mrs. Elrod Jakes, do you?"

EARLY SEPTEMBER 1867

DENIAL, ACCEPTANCE, AND OTHER STAGES OF GRIEF — THE GARDEN BLOOM

IT DIDN'T *HAPPEN*. IT never ever happened. It *couldn't* happen. Chance dressed in a daze. Head stuffed with fear and loathing. Completed a crude inventory: Guts bubbled, check. Nethers ached, check. Shock and awe pumped through his veins. Double check. Sutures ripped open, blood and terrible ooze dried along his inner thighs. A strange survivor haunted by a great notion he'd looked beyond the veil and seen his own doom. Chance had seen POW's scat worms in Andersonville. But those wriggling critters didn't compare with what he'd just seen. But he didn't see anything, his psyche pleaded. It didn't *happen*. It never ever happened. But something had. Blame the laudanum for the hallucination at your own peril, he thought. Lose two days outright and you'd go blood simple too.

Could he ignore the ten-ton elephant? Had Rosie been right about Mrs. Jakes? Was the gal crooking the wheel in her favor? Securing some kind of control over their partnership? And if so, could Chance really blame her? Hard to make a living the legitimate way. Do what you gotta do to stay in the black. At least the incident that didn't happen—that never ever happened, would make her think twice about throwing him another "free" poke.

Could've. Would've. Should've.

When Mrs. Jakes come for him, he was dressed in black. "Chance, we got a problem."

Damn right we do, he thought. "I swear...that ain't ever happened to me afore."

"Not that!" Mrs. Jakes tossed him a brand-new belted set of pearl handles.

Chance looked her over queer. "Another gift?"

She ignored him. "The Captain's downstairs!"

Chance didn't understand. Everything coated in an opium malaise. His hat shook.

Hysterics quaked her voice, "MY *Captain!*"

Her words finally landed. Chance cinched the gun belt around his aching waist. He'd never owned two pistols before. Could he be as quick with two as he was with one? Chance's mind moved like a stick in mud.

Mrs. Jakes helped Chance limp down the hall. A familiar voice murmured up the stairs. Although the outlaw couldn't quite place it. Whatever it said, Chance didn't learn. Once inside, with the door firmly closed, he whispered, "How'd'ya know your old man was here?"

Mrs. Jakes didn't respond.

Chance asked again.

Stones made more noise.

"What gives, woman?" Anger rose in his voice, "Now ain't the time to gimme the silent treatment."

Could've. Would've. Should've.

Her jaw hanged. He followed her eyes to the floor and joined her confusion. Time stretched into infinity. Realization dawning like the Eastern sun. Then the moment passed.

"Maybe Rosie moved it for us," Chance defended his lifelong friend, "since she knew we was leaving soon."

He limped to the office window and peered down. Didn't know what he expected to see, but he knew he didn't see it. His belly gurgled and sank with unease.

The lady simmered with quiet rage. "She moved mama's coffin, that's for certain. But..." Mrs. Jakes checked her pistol's drum and snapped it closed. "She ain't done it none for us."

"Ain't like Rosie at all."

"Would you guarantee with your life?"

Chance protested, "Rosie ain't no thief, Sam."

She turned to leave the office.

Chance hollered after her, "What are you gonna do?"

The gal toed the threshold. A grim-faced reaper beneath a white straw hat. This bringer of doom—this agent of chaos—this slight frame of only nineteen years glanced over her shoulder. "Whatever a girl's gotta do."

And out she stepped to go kill the Captain.

EARLY SEPTEMBER 1867

WARM REGARDS — TO PLUCK A BLOOM

FRANK DIDN'T KNOW ABOUT the missing gold. Only Samantha and Chance. And she refused to speak. Had done so ever since the bastards appeared behind her husband in the parlor. Chance hadn't expected Mrs. Jakes to greet what was left of the Lovecock gang. It happened so fast. He understood the danger—did she? Might've had a good idea after the room cleared. Everyone else, whores and patrons alike, took one look at the pungent rustlers and up and skedaddled.

The outlaw stood on the landing above. Unable to stumble down the stairs without drawing unwanted attention. Even without nibbling on the cheese, Chance could sense the trap snapping around them. He paused briefly and considered his options. None looked good enough to write home about. He leaned over the banister. A grandfather clock kept time halfway down the drop.

His chest tightened. His fingers gripped the rail. He was up and over in one agonized hop. Boots struck the top of the clock. For a split-second, it threatened to topple. Chance stuck his weight to the wall, and the thing stilled. From here, he hopped onto the velvet of a soft chair. It creaked under his weight. He played possum.

The element of surprise—worth a month of birthdays. To get the drop on them, Chance knew he needed to find a way around. Get outside—maybe a window—come through the front door blazing.

The Lovecock gang still hadn't noticed.

Lloyd floated in an adjacent room. Beckoning the outlaw to follow.

Chance gritted his teeth. Knees bent slowly for the floor. Calm determination settled his nerves. One hand followed the other as he crept after his dead cousin.

———————

Frank whistled loudly. His goons, Kid Nobody and Angel Ojete, seized Captain Jakes by both arms. Dragged him over to a table and restrained him. Doc Buie lifted his medicine bag for an impromptu operation. Frank introduced himself to the lady and added, "Mrs. Jakes. You know why we're here. Give us what we come for now. And you'll get what's left of your husband back—somewhat in one piece."

Samantha's nerves pushed their limits. This dark fellow scared the bejesus out of her. A darkness like she'd never seen before lurked behind shiny black eyes. "What makes you think I want him back?"

"Did ya hear that, quartermaster? Don't nobody want your sorry self for nothing—except me and mine." Frank squinted at Samantha. "Guess you won't mind if Doc Buie cuts out our pound of flesh, do ya?"

Samantha's voice quaked. "Take two pounds while you're at it for all I care."

Frank whistled low.

A barber's straight razor flashed. It caught the light and glinted with menace.

Samantha felt outside herself. They cut away the Captain's trousers. He struggled, of course. But she knew—he knew—it wouldn't do any good. A curious acceptance in the man's desperate thrashing.

Samantha couldn't shake a queer notion. Like she'd been here before. Except she was tied to a post, and the Captain held the whip in hand. Her déjà vu melted quick. Strange, what the mind finds worthy of time when there's none to spare.

Frank touched the black talisman below his throat and nodded at Doc Buie. The bald fella with thin glasses asked, "You ever hear tell of the fruitful marriage of the black widow and the blue wasp?"

Samantha never took her eyes off her husband.

"The poisonous spider keeps time in a red hourglass. Waiting on a suitor to come a-calling. Only the cleverest bridegrooms will survive pitching woo at this femme fatale. Whether she devours her lover or not, she will spin a silk egg sack and grow her progeny. On the other hand, the blue wasp practices a more sadistic form of lovemaking. Ladies idle away their time, making home, while their lovers prowl for the gal who keeps time in a red hourglass. The blue wasp inflicts its will on the black widow and carries her home to meet the missus. Don't weep for the widow. She's still very much alive as the lady of the house walls in her new guest. The spider's paralysis will soon wear off. Awakening in a dark and cramped dungeon, confused and exhausted. Imagine her surprise when she learns she's not in there all alone. The gal's red hourglass is now running out of sand. She must escape her muddy tomb before the blue wasp larvae begin to feed. That's where we find ourselves now."

Samantha swallowed the lump in her throat. Papa's Navy Colt heavy between her fingers in the Captain's coat pocket.

Doc Buie laughed and addressed the Captain without looking. "The Quartermaster here served Bankhead Magruder. And we served his supply routes. So, it was only natural our Quartermaster and Captain Lovecock would go into business together." He slid the blade back and forth over a razor strap. "For six months we ran the blockade between Galveston and New Orleans. Yankee dollars lined our pockets. Damn near close to amassing a fortune." Thumb checked the razor's sharpness. "And wouldn't you know it? Some misguided fool went and leaked our scheme. And Bankhead Magruder locked us up and threw away the key. All except for the Quartermaster."

A bead of blood sprouted, and the Doc sucked his thumb. "Imagine our surprise when we learned our friend here had gotten off scot-free with our money. While we wasted away," the razor pointed at her husband. "Governor Murrah himself had promoted him up the ranks to commissioned officer."

Doc Buie gripped Elrod's wrist in one gnarled hand.

"And wouldn't you know it? The Quartermaster was still running a blockcade of sorts. Imagine his surprise when we found him in Austin and refused to shake hands."

The Captain's neck corded. The table darkened under the now three fingered left hand. Doc Buie lifted the severed finger. And stuck it into his opened maw, slurping the color from it.

Frank cleared his throat, stroked the talisman, His voice metal across your eardrum. "Tell us where you're hiding that gold, and we won't cut off anything else."

Samantha spoke smoke, "Would you believe it's not here?"

Frank's lizard tongue touched his teeth. He whistled for the Doc to continue.

Papa's words between her ears: *Be careful of what you wish for, Sammie Jane. Small blessings turn into big curses.*

Samantha stood frozen in place. Once upon a time, she'd prayed to see this man suffer. She wanted a trauma that could rattle your bones awake at night. But she hadn't expected such a gruesome horror show. The Doc went to work. Examining the Captain's testicles and penis. Vile sickness settled in the pit of her stomach. She knew—Frank knew—she knew what was coming next. She needed a distraction. Familiar names of Confederate heroes sprang to mind.

Jubal Early.

The Captain writhed in agony.

Nathan Bedford Forest.

Doc Buie's blade penetrated the Captain's soft foreskin.

Joseph Johnston.

Encircling the tip of his manhood.

James Longstreet.

Blood spilled from the paper-thin slit.

John Bell Hood.

Doc's razor sliced tip to root.

George Pickett.

The Lovecock gang laughed manically as Doc Buie de-gloved the Captain's penis.

John Breckinridge.

A weeping flower. Blood gushed from the flayed and peeled appendage.

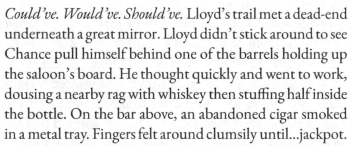

Could've. Would've. Should've. Lloyd's trail met a dead-end underneath a great mirror. Lloyd didn't stick around to see Chance pull himself behind one of the barrels holding up the saloon's board. He thought quickly and went to work, dousing a nearby rag with whiskey then stuffing half inside the bottle. On the bar above, an abandoned cigar smoked in a metal tray. Fingers felt around clumsily until...jackpot.

Kid Nobody and Angel Ojete never saw the firebomb hit them. The flames rushed up their legs like a sinner's punishment. Their brimstone eyes witnessed their doom. All discussion ended as every head snapped around at the dirty mirror over the bar.

Chance stood. Both pearl handles aimed waist high. "Hey Frank!" He crowed, "Feel cheated yet?"

OCTOBER 1ST 1867

DALLAS DAILY REPUBLICAN — VOL. 02 NO. 10.
2ND EDITION

FRONT PAGE OF THE upstart tabloid had three-inch bold letters: TRAGEDY IN HELL'S HALF-ACRE!!

In the gospel, according to this newspaper: The notorious house of ill repute, which shall remain nameless to spare our reader's modesty, has officially been condemned by Sheriff Norval Winniford, who engaged the militia to hunt down the culprits of the recent massacre of the Peaceful Fellowship of Christian Congregants. This week alone saw the body count rise to twenty-three lost souls over a period of five days. Sheriff Winniford has identified the Franklin Lovecroft Gang as responsible, after having escaped justice for the fourth time in as many months. These murderous outlaws must be considered dangerous, and no attempt should be made at a citizen's arrest. Rumor has it that Sheriff Winniford plans on demolishing the building as a memorial for the Union soldiers who died in the battle of Sabine Pass.

In the gospel according to this newspaper: The Garden Bloom welcomes all visitors to Dallas County, with spirits and fellowship, and good times for all weary travelers. Now with clean beds. Stop by and speak with M. Rose Fletcher, proprietor.

NOVEMBER/OCTOBER 1867

GIVE THANKS — THE TAO OF MUD

SWEAT BROKE ACROSS CLAIRE'S brow. Huffing and squeezing Aunt Clara's hand so tight, the knuckles paled. The myth, the legend herself, gnawed on an ear of sweet corn with cold detachment. This wasn't Samantha's first rodeo. While present for Claire's entrance, Samantha owned no memory of it. Too young for it to make an impression. However, Johnny's egg hatching remained vivid. Now eleven years and nine months later, she saw no reason to stop thanksgiving dinner over something as common as having a baby. Jane Clara Falkirk *nee* Samson claimed she'd been a midwife. Samantha had her doubts after Mama's sister saw amniotic fluid paint the floor and Johnny fell out.

Uncle Joe's rocking chair bucked as Claire thrashed. Aunt Clara's husband did not protest its use, since a cliff fall broke his neck the month before. Leaving a modest, mouse like woman behind to run his Colorado claim all alone. Aunt Clara bore more than a faint resemblance to Claire. And both favored Mama—or best Samantha could recall. Any attempt to solve the puzzle using surrogates only conjured Johnny's pitiful face—crusty scabs, oozing warts, et al. Of all the memories a head can store, why had this most important one been permanently erased?

Papa's words between her ears. *Blood, Sammie Jane, is always thicker than water.*

Aunt Clara had thrown open her home. A quaint little cottage on the edge of the sky. Weeks of search finally told them to look for a little path snaking up the flatirons.

"Gimme something for the *pain!*" Claire whined.

"Tis a blessing from the lord," Said Aunt Clara, as if that would suffice. "To remember our original sin."

"I've some Laudnum," Sweet corn spewed from Samantha's mouth. Ignoring Papa's Navy Colt, she fished it from her pocket. "Think there may be a swallow left. Found I'm mighty partial to the taste." Samantha shook the little brown bottle at Mama's dopplegangers. Aunt Clara reached for it one second too late. It shattered.

"Jinx on you, Sam!" Claire screamed, then whined, "You dropped it on purpose."

"Nonsense." Samantha bit into the sweet corn and chewed. "Guess you're gonna have'ta make do with thoughts and prayers alone."

To think only weeks ago the Gray sisters had acted happy to see each other for the first time in forever.

Bonfire glowed over the white kaolinite. Samantha and the outlaw approached the ridge unseen. Fifteen sticks of dynamite split between them. Trader Sheridan lay somewhere else alone in the dark. Enough firecrackers to forget the words to Auld Lang Syne. The old pervert waited for her signal. Promising to light up the sky.

The heathens wildly crowded around the fire.

"Do ya see 'em, Chance?"

"No—not with all of them sum-bitches slathered in white clay. We'll have to get closer. Go teepee to teepee."

"We take them alive," Samantha said. "Or we take all of them with us." She snatched up the rucksack. "I mean it...Chance. If Johnny and Claire are dead. Don't leave a dog alive if you can help it."

Should old aquaintences be forgot? And never brought to mind?

Finally relieved of its yellow treasure. Samantha belched weakly, tossing the husk at the legless quartermaster. The mangled man sat adjacent and didn't notice. Too busy keeping watch over the miracle interrupting their dinner. His lone eye wet with anticipation for the birth of his child. The only one he'd ever be able to sire.

Doggone shame the cherub would not live long afterwards.

Claire clenched her teeth. Fingernails chipped on wooden armrests. She screamed over the cramping spasm. Samantha spooned stew into a clay bowl. Blew gently over the steaming liquid. It smelled real special. Must've been Aunt Clara's secret recipe for prairie coal—made from whatever she could find. From the looks of it, Aunt Clara hadn't done much of a search.

Chance and Mrs. Jakes raced between dozens of hide covered huts. Not a soul inside. The entire tribe was summoned to gather around the bonfire.

On the outskirts, Chance trundled over a patch of wet clay and went sprawling. Mouth first. Stars popped. Next thing he knew, Mrs. Jakes stood over him. "You're a ballywise genius."

Chance didn't feel too smart as he spat out wads of white clay.

She knelt. Scooped a handful. And smeared her own face with a lick and a promise.

It dawned on Chance, "Sure you need camouflage? Awful dark out here."

"Throwing my dynamite in that fire." Mrs. Jakes dropped trow—not a stitch but her curious silver chain—and wallered head to toe. She stood. "This should help get me there."

Chance spat out another cheekful of clay. "Maybe wiser to keep some distance."

Mrs. Jakes ignored his sound advice and moved on without him.

"Hell," Chance spat again. "You always wanted to die standing up."

Both his hands shoveled on the cold kaolin.

Samantha slathered rancid butter over a hunk of moldy bread. Then dunked the abomination to soak up the stinking stew. After a pause to summon courage, Samantha choked it down.

"*Aaaaah!*" Claire screeched bloody murder. "It's coming out! It's coming out!"

Aunt Clara panicked and sagged against the rocking chair. "Help! I think this bitch fainted!"

Samantha only carved meat onto her plate. Buttercup tasted as he lived, tough and hard to stomach in large doses. Samantha wiped her mouth and tried to swallow, then kept on chewing. Eyeballs tilted with a frog's effort. Finally, spitting the greasy mule back onto her plate.

Claire hollered, "Help me, Sam! *Pleeeaaassseee!*"

The myth, the legend herself, patted dry her mouth and pocketed the carving knife. Pushed back from the board, and plodded languidly to Claire and the crowning child.

Top of the baby's head gorier than one of Johnny's open sores.

Drums of dried skin joined flutes of human bone. Foreign noises to Chance's ignorant ears. A riot of rhythm—Mrs. Jakes was there inside the hypnotic chaos—then she went plumb native. Lost in the frenzy of the dancing circle. Any second now, Chance just knew she'd cause some rude disruption. Force him to come blazing in again to save her.

Do something once, it's kindness, but do it twice—unjust expectation. He couldn't wait to be shed the responsibility. But until then—dynamite rattled his saddlebags.

But the fierce ritual never ceased. He knew it meant only one thing. Chance saw his and took it. Dashing unseen through the camp on borrowed time.

As sudden as a late winter snap, the fete stopped. An eerie quiet, so still only the bonfire's crackling settled over everything. Chance surveyed the crowd. Everyone stared into the fire. Whatever fortune they saw, just like Mrs. Jakes, was lost to Chance.

Someone howled.

Other savage throats joined in. Somewhere sonically between a funeral rite and a war whoop. This discordant chanting shivered chills all over.

Guts bubbled.

He clutched his belly.

No, he muttered. "Not now—not here—not again!"

The gift kept on giving.

Warriors carried their captives slung from spears. Parading the unlucky few through the hungry crowd. Johnny and Claire counted among the number of Americans. Sixteen limbs bound. Four spines bowed. Plowing divots, en route to some frightening altar of smoke and skulls.

Chance noticed none of these facts.

Already his eyes glassed over blacker than a cephalopod's inky defense. Behind these windows you saw only frenzied auras. A kaleidoscope of corporal forms morphing in-out of aurora fog like sinister ghouls, constantly temporary.

The timbre and meter of their primitive music shook the outlaw to his core. Summoning hell from ancient depths with every descending note. Intestines swelled and kicked. Black water broke between his legs. The quickening had begun. He knew...He knew not why or how the cosmic portal opened. He knew...He knew he needed to flee, but it was too late. He knew...He knew there's nothing worse than too late.

You'd have thought Claire was a dying rabbit the way she squealed. Of all the Gray children, she seemed the most incapable of suffering pain. She should've been ashamed for carrying on so. *Me-Me-Me*—facts never change. Claire gave it all she got. Bowels evacuated. Fresh muck oozed beneath her, dripping brown stink down her legs and out the back of the rocking chair. Each labored howl like the one before. *Me-Me-Me*—the princess of Sweet Pine and her never-ending cry for attention.

Frankly, Samantha wasn't impressed.

Fingers tightened around the carving knife. Her sweet sister lifted her knees. Feces and birthing fluid clumped down her calves to ankles. Both heels planted on the befouled seat. Toes gripped the roughhewn edge. The little bitch grunted and dug in. Cheeks reddened. Breath held. Tears leaked. A moment passed, then another...and another.

And the quarter-master's bastard spawn still refused to drop.

The tribe's alpha male sported a wild boar headdress. High razorback pelt flowed. Spears tilted vertically. Johnny and Claire sagged upside down. Hands and feet still tied tight. Mr. Razorback unsheathed a stone blade—yodels fluttered and hooted. He held it aloft for all to see. Then his eyes found Claire. He spoke in snorts and howls. His community ebbed and swayed in unison. All mesmerized by the blade snicker-snacking in deliberate martial arcs. Now he took a look at Johnny, writhing weakly against the pole. Still not satisfied, he examined another. Samantha felt outside herself—and didn't fully recognize the danger they were in.

Mr. Razorback hacked through the first sacrifice. Viscera spilled. Exultant crows and catcalls erupted. A lieutenant snatched a length of offal, and now it uncoiled through the maddening crowd. Hands outstretched to smear gore through fingertips. Samantha watched the disemboweling encircle the radius of the fire. Already the executioner moved on. Claire flinched as he caressed her swollen belly. Tip of the bloody machete hovering uncomfortably close to her business.

Samantha's fingers moved for the dynamite.

Papa's words between ears, *When trouble comes...*

Claire's rabbit squealed, "Whaddaya gonna do with that thing?!"

Samantha gripped the greasy knife with both hands. Sharp edge angled. Lips smacked. Tongue and teeth sucked at a piece of stuck corn.

Again, Claire demanded an answer.

"Shut up! I'm trying to remember," Samantha said. Unable to tear eyes away from the wiggling thing trapped in Claire's tar pit. Eleven years and nine months ago, Samantha Jakes *nee* Gray was eight years old. And mama labored by the hovel's stove. And the midwife. And the fire. And the obstruction they would christen Johnathan Samson Gray refused to evacuate, just like this bastard now.

"The baby's shoulders are stuck," Samantha said. "I seen it before."

Claire hyperventilated with misguided hope. "Okay...! You know how to fix it?"

"You ain't gonna like what I gotta do." Samantha lowered the blade. Passing wet fur, and the baby's crown, to that thin piece of real estate known globally as the perineum.

"Do it, Sam!" Claire cried. "Get it out of me!"

Samantha remembered Mama's midwife, an old fat bitch everyone called Aggie. She aimed shears—the kind shepherds used to cut wool—and counted to three.

Sweet Pine's princess painted her downstairs in smeary excrement. Samantha doused it, best she could, from the quarter-master's drinking glass. Then stuck the pointy end below the portal and breeching head.

"Alright..." Samantha drawled. "Three count. You ready?"

"*AAAEEEEIIIIOOOOUUU!*

"One..."

On two she cut.

...you can't waste time on fear. Claire writhed in hysterics. The executioner readied. Goaded on by his sect. Samantha's dynamite in both hands.

And all hell followed.

The ultimate apex predator—awoke from eons of sleep—roared with the angry throats of every newly minted mother losing a child. Savages spun in place. Seeking out the sound in all directions. Mr. Razorback paused and lifted a chalky hand to calm his people.

The watery call of annihilation rumbled again. The earth shook.

Outside the kaolinite pits, Trader Sheridan mistook the sudden noise for the go signal.

The sky boomed.

Variegated sparks exploded. Red glaring rockets whizzed and whirred. The Milky-Way shattered like innumerable psychedelic suns. Much of the bat population over the Comancheria disappeared. The spectacle was seen miles away and mistaken for the prophecy of the Seven Fires by Pottawatomi and Ojibwe elders. The spectacle burned down to ashy legend for many spontaneous beings of the First Nation's thunderbird—the people made from nothing. Frightened and confused, a wagon party of fundamentalist Mormons stripped down to their magic underwear and sang hymnals while awaiting Moroni's new demands of their privacy. And yet still, the noise reverberated as far away as the WASP nursery of John Pierpont Morgan's infant son Jack, who would inherit the family fortune in forty-six years, and go on to broker deals for his father's company to be the sole supplier of munitions for Anglo-Franc efforts in the Great War, earning a commission of thirty million Yankee dollars. While another house in the hardscrabble Penn-Dutch farmland welcomed the birth of Harry Alonzo Longabaugh, soon to be known as the Sundance Kid, noted scofflaw and skilled robber of trains, and romanticized to legend for best embodying the American spirit of capitalism and the protestant ethic during the terrors of the Gilded Years. And directly below these sulfurous clouds of black formed a freak storm system over much of the Midwest.

Samantha Jakes gulped for air. It tasted of moldering aquatic death. She didn't want to look. Didn't want to see two dozen nautilus tendrils and one clawed forearm poking from the outlaw's business end and propelling his body forward like a puppet on a hand.

Somethings can never be unseen.

Everyone scattered. Dynamite sailed through the air. Samantha dove for cover.

The eruption was enormous.

Seconds counted down slower than hours on a sundial. Debris of white clay and flaming limbs snowed in downy sheets. Samantha righted herself and charged through the blizzard.

The monster inside the outlaw wanted free of its cosmic vulva. But the heathen warriors had other ways of dealing with outsiders. They dug-in and attacked the odd intruder. Only to be lifted by the ankle and bashed hard against the bloody ground. Their courage before the demon faltered, and some backed down, while others retreated entirely. Those that failed at either never saw another day.

Safely distanced from the destroyer of worlds, Samantha's shadow found Johnny and Claire. Hands and feet tied tight enough to cut off circulation. The headless torso of a warrior flopped near, still clutching a rattle of arrows. Samantha snatched the bolt—snapping it over her knee and sawing away her sibling's ropes.

It was too thick, and Samantha told Claire so.

"Do what you gotta do and get me out of this!"

Samantha pulled her thirty-six and felt an uncannily familiar sensation.

She squeezed twice. The Colt and Samantha bucked each time. Claire dropped free. Samantha turned to Johnny. The little boy writhed and wheezed.

She lifted the gun—it dipped—arms went stiff to her sides. "Thank God you came!" Claire had wrapped her arms around her sister and held her from behind. Head buried on her shoulder. She cried, "Didn't think I'd ever see you again!"

For a brief moment, the Gray sisters owned no history but the love of family. Christmas mornings before the onset of puberty and their first bleed. Laughter before, during, and after mama's home cooked dinners. And of course, late nights in Papa's cabin, huddled under quilts, trying to ignore the strangers visiting mama's bed, and her tears after they had left.

"Help me free, Johnny!" Samantha said, breaking the curse of family.

Kablam! Kablam!

The boy collapsed like a sack of taters. Immediately sprang back. Wrapping his unfortunate arms around both his sisters. Bounding with a puppy's energy. Slobbering and drooling and excited to be set free. For a brief moment, his face seemed clear of biological tragedy. When the errant tentacle snatched him by the ankle, Johnny didn't have time to react. It was this face Samantha would remember forever. It was a look that said goodbye.

The thing birthing its way out of the outlaw's cosmic vagina loomed over them. Johnny's feet kicked air, as the thing snatched him away.

Claire screamed.

Samantha didn't miss a beat. Turned to fire. Another tentacle knocked the gun from her hand. It vanished in chaos. Everything happened so fast. Next thing Samantha knew, she clawed through the soft kaolinite, narrowly avoiding swinging limbs overhead. Until finally, her fingers found the stone sword. She didn't notice its heft as she lifted it and stood. The myth, the legend herself, went slashing once more into the fray.

Blood sprayed from the cut. Samantha dropped the knife. Stuck both hands in her sister's nethers and instructed her to "push! Push like a mad bastard! Push!". The chair rocked. Claire screamed so loud, a little further down the mountain, Frank Lovecock heard the noise and whistled at the only friend he had left. And then together, they continued climbing up the rocky path.

Gore and birth oozed between fingers as Samantha dug the child out. Reached down for the carving knife with zero ceremony. Nothing but meanness in her face. She knew what needed to be done. The baby's mama too weak from labor to protest more than a feeble, "Don't..."

Samantha ignored her. Eyes locked on the little pink thing still attached to its mother's placenta. The coiling umbilical cord, like a tentacle, stretched and...

...wrapped around Samantha's throat, choking her. Johnny, seeing this, sprang to action. Sank his jagged teeth into the slimy appendages. It bucked and roiled but did not release. Claire watched from a safe distance. When her bare foot stepped on something hard and metal. Papa's Navy Colt gleamed up at her from the white clay. Other than practicing with Mr. Goodface, Samantha's little sister hadn't much experience. She pointed it more than aimed. Samantha and Johnny were somewhere in the mass of limbs. One click, two click, three click, primed. She squeezed. The shot rang out. Recoil sent Claire sprawling backwards across the pale clay.

Samantha fell free just in time to see Chance's satchel come loose and fall into the bonfire. "Get down!" Her words were lost in the compression of the second explosion. Just managing to cover Johnny as warmth rushed over...

...her. Sentiment came in strange waves. As sudden as spring rain, tears wet her eyes. She felt immense confusion. A ramble of emotions whipsawed her between two different poles. Samantha no longer wanted to cut the cord and use it to strangle the Quarter-Master's bastard son.

She glided with an easy and determined air towards her husband. The charred and crooked creature she'd hated for months, and nursed back to health, only so she could allow it to see the birth and death of a child, that had thankfully not been birthed by her.

Samantha held the baby up so his one good eye could see, "It's a boy, Captain Jakes."

A solitary tear spilled down his blackened and burned face. He whimpered wordlessly as she placed it on the table between them. Slashing down with the carving knife and severing the baby from its mama. Cord blood spurted. Quickly Samantha wound it around itself to stop the bleeding. The baby cried and cried in the cold of this new cruel world. Her crippled husband could not contain his feelings, nor express them beyond his own present limitations.

"I think we should name you Johnny," said Samantha, unable to keep her own eyes from watering. She held the baby close, and at once knew a sacred truth. Forgiveness can never be earned. It must be learned. And like the best lessons in life, forgiveness must be learned the hard way. When she looked at Claire. All of their history, all the hurts, miraculously vanished. "Think you should name him after his uncle. Whaddaya think, Claire?" Samantha beamed. "Don't ya think Johnny would've liked it?"

Her sister never answered. Already the new mother sagged and wilted in the birthing chair. Unable to keep her head from lulling forward. The difficult birth was complicated by a transverse rupture of her womb. The hidden seat of all life. No matter what Samantha tried, blood leaked and pooled, just like Johnny. The baby held tightly to her chest, wiggling and rattling, just like Johnny did the night Claire's errant bullet landed in the middle of his chest.

Mama hung on. Papa hung on. Claire hung on. But Johnny's heart stopped on impact. Such accidental mercy had set him free. It took an hour for Samantha to regain composure enough to search out the outlaw—her savior, who lay writhing and bleeding, yet somehow still alive.

The thing inside him chased back into its hiding place.

For how long they did not know.

Trader Sheridan helped bury the baby's uncle in a place that even today has no name.

October 1867

The Boggy Depot Gazette Vol. 1 No. 10 5th edition

In the gospel, according to this newspaper: Monday Afternoon found an Atoka scribe on the Texas Road bound for Ft. Wayne. The day was cold and raw, and the appearance of things was not particularly inviting to a stranger, but he determined to make the place and thereby fulfill the mission. Having spent the night before visiting with Rev. Christopher Roy of Shermanberg, Texas who'd journeyed through the territory to visit the very sick. Our scribe started out the morning north bound and by lunch rode upon a most terrible scene. The Texas Road can be a harrowing stretch for any lonesome travel, made all the more difficult by meeting a pair of murderers clad all in black. One should never ease drop on the tail end of any pitched conversation between two women, but our man from Atoka admits it could not be helped. The dispute seemed centered on ownership of a coffin in the possession of a lady best described as a peacock of the evening variety. One of the murderers, a feisty gal in a white hat, demanded the return of her mother. One must assume for proper burial. She had already killed the peacock's associate, who on first glance resembled an overfed Cherokee. No way to discern a face as it had been splattered across this Land of Lincoln. The Peacock went for a hidden Derringer and was unceremoniously disarmed with a shot to the middle by the other outlaw, who fell to pieces with a parade of sincere apologies. The peacock begged to be finished off. The outlaw's nerve failed. Unable to pull the trigger a second time. But the other one, our scribe would learn to be named Samantha Jakes of Texas, owed no such qualms. The most frightening woman, he would later confess, ever seen this side of the Mississippi. Firing her pistol point blank into the victim's head. Seeing a woman executed so inhumanely caused our man in Atoka to give himself away. The murderers fell upon him post haste, but after learning he was an unarmed newspaperman, he was shown no uncertain mercy. Mrs. Jakes claimed to have killed twenty men. Her associate spoke not a word. The gal took our man's horse and saddle with strict instructions to return to Boggy Depot by foot and report the story of the meanest woman in the Southwest. A posse formed by the U.S. Marshall, Jershua Dixon, was refused entry by the Choctaw, and the search party was begrudgingly called off. All travelers be advised to proceed with caution if coming across the company of Mrs. Jakes or her associate, the Quiet Kid.

In the gospel according to this newspaper, D. Rassmussen, ATOKA, L.T. Watchmaker and Jeweler and dealer in Gold, Silver, and Nickel watches, a fine line of cuff and collar button vest chains, ladies breast fins, bracelets, neck and guard chains and fine solid gold rings. Including spectacles and spy glasses, announces repair services for all fine metal instruments with especial attention paid to clocks and other heirlooms. Free consultation. Will pay cash for gold.

December 1867

Samantha's clock ticked. Under the shadow of the barn, Doc Buie swaddled Claire's baby. They waited thirty yards away. Her rings clinked. She pulled Papa's Navy Colt and fired. She didn't see the baby fall or Doc Buie's head explode.

Frank leveled his gun. Eyes darkened. He fired. Bullet zipped past her ear as Samantha triggered her last round. Frank fell back. Her view of the baby cleared. No time to lose. Boots crunched over gravel. She ran, running down the names of famous traitors.

Jefferson Davis!

Breath fogged over her shoulder.

The baby wailed.

P.T. Beauregard!

Samantha closed the gap.

Robert E. Lee!

Hands out in front as if chasing chickens.

John Wilkes Boo...!

She never saw the hand that tripped her. Gravel sprayed. She sprawled. Papa's Navy Colt bounced away amongst the pebbles. Unseen hands gripped her ankles—spun her onto her back. The shape blurred into focus and the blade flashed. It happened so fast she could not fight him off.

Frank plunged the dagger into Samantha's chest. Unspeakable pain. Agony reflected in his obsidian eyes. The black totem dangling from his neck glowed hot purple. He twisted the blade. Left arm howled then went limp. Right hand clutched his wrist to fight back weakly.

"Shh..." Frank hissed. "Dunno when to quit, do ya, gal?" He whispered hot death. A maniac's joy in his voice. "You've lost. It's over."

Samantha struggled for air.

Frank twisted harder. "Givin ya a great gift gal," Spittle flew. "Longer you hold on—the more it'll hurt."

Breath fouled. Teeth rotted. Samantha felt the pop before she heard it.

Frank cackled, "Quit lingerin' and le'go. Don't embarrass yourself in front o'Death, gal."

Blood pooled at the back of her throat.

"Slip along the void with some dignity..." Her lung collapsed. "You dumb cunt."

Gurgle. Cough. Gurgle.

Why the very idea?

She'd successfully fought off savages of all walks of life, including a tornado. And after everything, here she lay dying in the Rocky Mountains from a snake's bite.

The end arrived rather suddenly.

In the darkening sky above, a powerful white light blinded her. *Gurgle. Cough. Gurgle.* She released his wrist—fingers like tendrils—hooked around his necklace and yanked it free. The fist searched a scruffy cactus face past the narrow nose. Gurgle. Cough. *Cough. COUGH.*

Samantha's vision tunneled.

Gurgle. Cough. Gurgle.

The Tao rushed through her veins. Every last ounce of strength surged. She drove her fist forward. The glowing obelisk, like a knitting needle in her hand, plunged into Frank's eyeball and stuck. The devil hollered. The outlaw's socket leaked black eye-jelly. The totem piercing it smoked. *Gurgle. Cough. Gurgle.* Rack-focus cleared. A blur of bright light beamed from the evil socket, then dimmed with no daylight behind the overhead clouds. The other eye cleared. A spell had been broken.

"AAAEEEIIIIOOOUUU!" Frank screamed only vowels. Clutched his wounded hole and backed off, ready to retreat for the hills.

Samantha fingered her silver chain and swung it hard. It caught Frank's boot. She fell back and pulled. The outlaw's face met slag.

Gurgle. Cough. Gurgle. Her fingers gripped his knife handle. Breath ragged and wet with blood. The soggy accordion pumped and hacked.

Papa's words between her ears, *Anything worth doing, Sammie Jane is worth doing right.*

With great effort, she gritted her teeth and pulled herself more or less upright. Red stuff gushed from the rupture. She'd done her best to cover, but failure oozed between the whitening fingers.

Frank cried like a stuck pig. Revealing the universal truth about bullies. They may be able to dish it out, but none seem too keen on taking it themselves. Pathetic fools all of them.

Samantha labored to move. Down on all threes, one hand dragged the rest of her forward. Frank's lost dagger held close to the hole in her chest. She crossed the devil's bloody trail and now her nineteen-year-old shadow loomed over the demon. Head lighted from blood loss. She tried to think of something smart to say, but her brain—too woozy to be clever.

She knelt on Frank's chest. Felt the sand running low in both their hour glasses. No need to wait. Elbow jerked. She swung the knife, slit across; his throat leaked.

Frank Lovecock flopped and flicked. And don't you know it, the perfect thing sprang to mind as the dusty knuckler bled out, "Slip the void with some dignity, ya dumb cunt!"

Gurgle. Cough. Gurgle.

Samantha pictured herself outside herself. Clad in black and red from head to toe, like a widow in this chaotic web. Tongue paradoxically swelling with dehydration, it protruded from her mouth. Stuck out like an overheated bitch in the town square. All around, stars popped across the Rockies. Silent fireworks glimmered. She reached unsuccessfully for them with many outstretched and vaporous arms.

This warrior princess topped her foe.

A goddess sculpted of clay and blood.

Skin paled to ghostly white. Almost blue. The color of death.

The myth, the legend herself.

Claire's baby cried and cried and cried. One more problem to solve. Then it would be over. Samantha moved. Her iron will unaware all strength had finally escaped. She collapsed. No longer sensed the Colorado cold. No longer fully inside her own body.

"I'm sorry baby..." Her words were as thin as the mountain air, "...Auntie Sam ain't gonna...ain't gonna...ain't making it this time." Her cheek met the bloody slag. "Cry baby..." Her voice croaked, "...cry and don't ever stop. Maybe...maybe someone'll find you—tell...tell you your story."

Somewhere nearby, a wolf's ears caught the high-pitched sound.

Gurgle. Cough. Gurgle.

Samantha Jane Jakes sensed her death—just another Ozymandias—just another destroyer of worlds. Aunt Clara's house imploded on itself. Everyone left inside was already dead. Shards of house and debris rained over the mountain as the thing hiding inside Chance finally freed itself.

Up from the trestle ruins arose a giant; clad allover in green scales and bearded with hundreds of enormous snaking feelers and tentacles. All coiling and reaching for purchase through the air. Slithering over a honeycomb cluster of yellow cat-like eyes. Razor-sharp claws extended from all six hands, dripping with muck and reeking of salt-water and blood and rotten flora, some ancient foulness conjured into existence from eons of sleep beneath the Earth, this unspeakable brute, now awake and ten-thousand hands high.

A dark cosmic lord, hungry for destruction and fully unleashed.

Samantha recognized the colossus at once. She'd seen him before. Carved into the dirt walls of the Jake's family crypt. Then again, on Madame's desk. Instant despair for her savior—the outlaw. The man with the beautiful face. She hoped he'd crossed Big River before birthing this monstrous demon into existence.

The sky above Aunt Clara's claim dimmed to vanta-black. Absorbing all light into the ether. Ultraviolet electricity, like veins of lightning, cracked overhead. Another struck the strange beast in quick staccato bursts. The dark lord bellowed cosmic static louder than the Big Bang. Hundreds of tornadoes spun funnels, storming and twisting over the territory, and skirted this side of the mountain. Samantha's wits said fare-the-well.

The photographer's camera ploofed that familiar smoke.

His familiar white head emerged from under the black cloth. Unconcerned with the angry elder god towering above and growing in strength. He said it before Samantha could ask, "You're probably curious as to why I'm here...now of all times..."

He removed the plate from the back of the camera and tossed it aside without examination and said, "You prayed often for deliverance. Like other mortals do. While I am always everywhere, I only interfere in the rarest of moments. Found a long time ago that my presence often did more harm than good. But today, just so happens, well..." The photographer laughed grandfatherly.

Samantha gurgled, "My wedding photographer?"

"Had my eye on you Sammie Jane a while now," he grinned over his shoulder at the hulking beast destroying the earth and reigning a thousand years of gloom and doom. "Gal..." he shook his head, "...done got yourself in all kinda mess, haven't ya? To think all ya wanted was to get humped by someone who truly loved ya and now..." His eyes sparkled, "...Space and time are being ripped apart before our very eyes. I should've made you in more of my image than the others."

Samantha coughed, "What. *Are. You?*"

"Don't you know by now?" The Photographer smiled and unbuttoned his trousers. "We contain multitudes."

Samantha watched in curious horror as the white-haired man reached inside the opened fly. What he exposed wasn't human. Girthy and colored greenish brown and bigger than any she'd ever seen and spangled past its owner's knees and kept on dropping and uncoiling.

Nameless and endless.

The photographer's eyes rolled. Only the whites now. Bones cracked like celery. He bent backwards. Hips split as the first tusk emerged. In an instant, the photographer broke apart—his nozzle morphed into an elephant's trunk. This giant kaiju sprouting from the Photographer shimmered. It was everything, all the time—clocks oozing seconds, and minutes, and hours, and days of calendars marked with x's. All things—your birth, a puppy's smell, the bright blue of a sunny day, cold air on a Texas spring morning, your favorite song, your hated rival, your father's father's father, and beyond your mother's genealogy, this prose and book remarkably still in your hands—all at once. Four additional heads sprouted behind its flappy ears. Together, they wore the universe as a beard. This Lord of Infinity, this mistaken juggernaut, this gosh-darn ten-ton gorilla of a problem trumpeted—an eternal arrival. All six arms prepared for battle and squared off with the giant demon.

Oh, how the world shook as these twin titans clashed.

Sparks found the hidden dynamite. Energy split atoms. Gold hot—an instant liquidity. *Kaboom!*

Samantha felt warm all over.

One of the monstrous hands of the god pulled her into its terrible flesh and lifted her past infinity.

She felt safe.

No butterflies or worries.

Anticipation swelled—No more delay to their union.

She knew—he knew—she wouldn't complain.

Acknowledgements

PC3 *for the initial opportunity*, Steve *for the second chance,* Max Sheridan *for the beta,* my family *for the support,* my mom and dad *for the conception,* Ang *for the humor,* Chaka *for the soul,* Gigi *for the fun,* Eric and Lance *for the boost,* Liamtek *for the salvation,* Kissel and Henry and Parks *for the flavor,* Leone *for the scope,* Morricone for the *noise,* Stephen Foster for the *lies,* John Brown's body for the *truth,* Abe for the *union,* Crockett for *the myth,* Pee-Wee *for the Alamo,* Mercer *for the gig,* Gloria *for the dream,* Jenkins *for the cool,* Dante *for the heat,* Ashberg *for the smoke,* Hilltop *for the beta,* Didi *for the confidence,* Dixon *for the guilt,* Red *for the failure,* Jordy *for the pardon,* Little Bill *for the hope,* Zomaddie *for the fireworks,* Moxie *for the boops,* and JJ *for the love.* You know who you are, and I thank you. For good or nought, no one holds this book now without the help of these people. Except for Moxie, who is a dog. I enjoyed feeding these angry words into this hungry machine. And always remember if you read it—*REVIEW IT.*

ABOUT THE AUTHOR

J.D. Graves is an award winning film producer, author/playwright from East Texas. J.D.'s stage-work has appeared at the New York International Fringe Festival, Manhattan Rep Theatre, Hollins Playwright's Lab, and Austin's own FronteraFest, to name a few. His short fiction can be read in: *Black Mask, Mystery Weekly, Mickey Finn Vol. 2, Tough, Rock and a Hard Place, Switchblade, Santa Cruz Weird, Pulp Modern: Tech Noir*, and others. His cheap thrills shorts: *The Sweetheart Sour, Just Another Job That Doesn't Pay Very Well*, and *Her Coffin's Colder Than The Mink Glove*, are out now. He has served as the founder and Editor-in-Chief of neo-pulp rag EconoClash Review, an imprint of *Down and Out Books*. J.D.'s short film productions have received laurels from numerous film festivals across the country. J.D. currently lives deep in the woods with his wife and kids.